Mind Out

What do you do when your scientist husband, having disappeared on a visit to the States, returns home with his own mind, memory, personality, even voice, but a different body? Belinda Watson soon found the change lent a certain piquancy to marriage. After all, she and Charles had been getting a tiny bit bored . . .

As for Andrew Taggart, the journalist who had been investigating her husband's disappearance (and incidentally consoling her), she didn't mind kissing him goodbye.

Then the new 'Charles Watson' is murdered and the innocent Taggart is arrested and charged. Taggart had learnt too much about the way in which the original Charles Watson had been lured to the States to feel easy about it, and a visit to the Prospect Psychodynamics Clinic in New York, where Watson was last seen, had added to his anxiety. Nor was he the only one to suspect those activities at the Clinic which appeared to involve a senior British civil servant and a distinguished academic . . .

by the same author

LEFT, RIGHT AND CENTRE

RUTH BRANDON

Mind Out

COLLINS, LONDON

William Collins Sons & Co. Ltd
London · Glasgow · Sydney · Auckland
Toronto · Johannesburg

for CARADOC

The Author asserts the moral right to be identified
as the author of this work.

First published 1991
© Ruth Brandon 1991

British Library Cataloguing in Publication Data

Brandon, Ruth
  Mind out.—(Crime Club)
  I. Title
  823.914[F]

ISBN 0 00 232328 1

Photoset in Linotron Baskerville by
Rowland Phototypesetting Ltd
Bury St Edmunds, Suffolk
Printed in Great Britain by
William Collins Sons & Co. Ltd, Glasgow

PART 1

CHAPTER 1

Reluctantly, Charles Watson tore himself away from the familiar, dusty depths of the London Library. He always felt slightly guilty if he spent a morning here, just as one does if one spends the morning reading novels—unless one is reviewing them, of course, in which case it's work and all the pleasure is lost. But Charles, Reader in Mind Sciences at East Midlands University, did not review novels, though that, or something like it, presumably was the job of those mysterious persons who spent their lives snoozing in the deep leather chairs of the reading room. At any rate they were mysterious to Charles; he didn't know them, except by sight because the same people seemed to be sleeping in the same armchairs every time he visited the place, say four or five times a year. Then there were severe young men and women who occupied the tables, surrounding themselves with castles of books and mountains of industry. He didn't know them either. In fact the whole charm of the place was that he never met anybody he did know, on account of being both non-metropolitan and a scientist—the Science section of the London Library being, as everyone knows, a joke, academically speaking. But Charles, on these escapades, was not after Science or academe. He had abandoned his scientific persona and resumed that of the truant-playing schoolboy. Nobody could contact him, nobody knew where he was. Research assistants could not worry him about grant applications, people could not bully him into chairing committees, he could step for a moment off the razor-edge of university politics and plunge into long-forgotten recesses of Edwardian speculation and never-opened biography. But no longer. It was time to go. He took out his diary and reconfirmed the appointment. Peter Fischer, 12.45, Reform Club. He glanced at his watch. Two minutes to get there: it was 12.43. Well, it was his prerogative to be late. This lunch was nothing to do with him: he was merely a neutral participant. If Peter Fischer wanted to see him again after however many years—twenty-two? twenty-three?—then that was his affair. It wasn't as if they'd been friends particularly—or at all: Charles had vague memories of having punched Peter Fischer—he *thought* it was Peter Fischer—on the nose over some point of principle whose details he could not now recall. A weedy fellow, with a high forehead towering over a somewhat morose face. 12.45. He'd better get going.

He'd never been to the Reform Club. London gentlemen's clubs were not his scene. It was by now 12.50, and he made a conscious effort to slow down. No point in arriving out of breath and apologetic. He climbed the steps at a leisurely pace and entered a double-height atrium plentifully sprinkled with marble columns, trying to look as if he'd been there hundreds of times before. He had just given the porter Peter Fischer's name when he saw the man himself, materializing from behind a column like some sort of leprechaun.

'Charles,' said Peter. 'Good to see you after all these years.' He hadn't changed to speak of: still that dark slick of greasy hair above the high forehead, the spectacles, the rosebud mouth, the rather fleshy cheeks. Charles wondered if he remembered the occasion of their last exchange. He smiled guardedly and held out his hand. Peter shook it rather limply, an odd continental habit in which he did not normally indulge. 'Sherry?' he said, and led the way towards a leather sofa stationed strategically behind a pillar. Elsewhere in the atrium, respectable-looking gentlemen were slumbering peacefully in leather armchairs. These, presumably, were the ones who had not been able to find a seat at the London Library. They sat down. A Turkish-looking waiter bearing a tray with two glasses of sherry appeared as if by magic. They each took one and Peter signed a piece of paper. Charles sipped his. It was very dry. He didn't much like it, but this was Peter's show, he was a mere spectator. He wondered how long he would be able to go without saying anything.

'I expect you wondered why you suddenly heard from me.'

'Mm.'

'Well, by the end of this lunch I hope that will be clear.' Peter sipped his own sherry with satisfaction. Pompous ass he was. Charles hoped he had punched his nose. He would have done it again, for two pins. He tried to remember what it was Peter Fischer did. He seemed to remember having heard he had entered the Civil Service, though in what capacity he had no idea. As far as Charles was concerned, the Civil Service was a machine for churning out memos and inventing committees, both of which he took to be substitutes for ever actually doing anything. Charles finished his sherry and realized that his host had been waiting for him to do so for some time. He smiled vaguely. Peter stood up, briskly efficient. 'Shall we go and have some lunch, then?' he said. Charles nodded. He had not yet spoken. He wondered if Peter had noticed this. Perhaps he thought he was dumb or had a speech affliction.

Peter led the way to a long dining-room which stretched along the back of the building. They sat down at a secluded table and studied the menu, which seemed full of complex dishes and contained neither the steak and kidney pudding nor the rich nursery sweets which Charles had been expecting, and to which he had been rather looking forward. They ordered (Charles now breaking his silence) and Peter poured them both a glass of wine, a Sancerre which he had selected with great attention. 'Mm,' he said, sniffing appreciatively. In fact the wine tasted rather odd to Charles, but since it was evidently very expensive and he was not paying for it, he said nothing. 'Well, then,' Peter went on, putting the glass down and looking directly at Charles almost for the first time. 'To our muttons.'

'Whatever they may be.'

'You were surprised, then.'

'Well—after our last meeting,' said Charles lamely. It

seemed rather bad manners to revive the memory of a twenty-year-old humiliation. 'And all these years.'

'Ah yes.' Peter's tone was one of unexpected relish. A masochist, perhaps? 'I suppose I ought to apologize, really.'

'Apologize?'

'Well, you know—for flooring you like that. Didn't realize my own strength, I expect. I seem to recall I was pretty surprised.'

'But—' With an effort Charles bit back his next words. Now was not the moment to enter upon an argument as to who had knocked down whom in a stupid fight half a lifetime earlier. He contented himself with saying, 'I haven't any memory of that at all.'

'I suppose one blots out unpleasant memories,' said Peter. 'Here comes our soup, I believe.' He took a few spoonfuls and then said, 'It may surprise you to hear that I've been taking quite an interest in your career, actually.'

'It certainly does surprise me,' said Charles. 'I can't say—' Once again he bit down the rest of his sentence. There was something about Peter Fischer which made it impossible to hold a conversation without being abominably rude. Something about his attitude to the rest of the world, or at any rate to Charles Watson. The wholly unjustified assumption of superiority. By the same token, he very probably wouldn't take in the fact if you *were* rude to him. He probably didn't even envisage the possibility.

'You perhaps don't know about my career since we met.'

'Haven't given it a thought.'

'Oh. Well. Well, I've been around the houses a bit to begin with, they like to move you around, but for the last several years I've been at the MOD.'

'Overseas development, is that?' Charles was surprised. He somehow couldn't see Peter Fischer doling out help to the developing countries, not even in the most patronizing and paternalistic of spirits. Nor could he see what that could have to do with him. Curiouser and curiouser.

'That's the ODM. The MOD's the Ministry of Defence.'

'Ah.' Defence? The mystery was no nearer clarification. Charles could think of no aspect of his work which could be of any interest to the Ministry of Defence. But before things could proceed any further they were interrupted by the removal of the soup plates and the arrival of some poached salmon. Peter had recommended the salmon and Charles had felt no compunction about acquiescing. Why shouldn't he enjoy some of the fruits of his own taxes?

'What made you choose the Civil Service?' Charles inquired over a sip of Sancerre. It certainly did taste odd, but maybe that was just what Sancerre was like.

'Not sure this wine isn't a bit over the top, perhaps it's a bit too old.' Peter sipped gingerly, peering into his glass over his spectacles.

'Maybe.' Charles was noncommittal.

'I liked the idea of governing people. Running the country. It's interesting.'

'I suppose so.'

'You sound doubtful. Believe me, I'm right. Of course, it involves a certain degree of cooperation. You can't just run off on any mad tangent you fancy.'

'Is that what I do?'

'Isn't it? You're a Reader. All you need do is research. You haven't even bothered to apply for a chair, have you?'

Charles wondered how Peter could possibly know this. 'I'm not sure I like the feeling of being spied on. Is that what the taxpayer's money goes on?'

'Don't you want to be a Professor?' Peter was not deterred by niceties. 'After all, you're an academic. That's the top of the academic tree.'

'Since you ask, no one but a masochist would want a chair these days. Have to spend your entire life fighting for funds and doing administration. Not my cup of tea.'

'Exactly what I was saying . . . Suffering from the cuts, are you?'

'Isn't everyone?'

'Some more than others.' Peter leaned forward confidentially. 'Aren't I right in thinking there's something rather nasty in the pipeline for EMU in general and your department in particular?'

'We're hoping to battle through. We have before.'

'But will you this time? I understand there's quite a lot of pressure. The government doesn't like East Midlands University. No blue blood. Wasn't it going to be downgraded into teaching only? Perfectly good research in your field going on at Cambridge. Perfectly good research in every field, come to that. What's the use of churning out research psychologists when all anybody wants these days is computer scientists?'

'I believe that was something they were floating, but it's not on the agenda any more.'

'Don't you believe it. They couldn't do it that way, but they'll try other ways. And then what happens to you? No research, no Readers.'

'We'll face that when we come to it. If.'

'Take my word,' said Peter. 'Not if. When.'

'What makes you so well-informed about these things? I thought you were in Defence, not Education.'

'I told you. I've made it my business to keep informed about you. Within a very short time, believe me, your research funds will suddenly start to dry up.'

'Among the many things I can't understand about this peculiar lunch,' said Charles, 'is why the hell you take this great interest in me that you keep on about. What have I ever done that could be of the slightest interest to you? My work doesn't have any military applications. If I thought it did I should probably have stopped doing it. If I have any interest whatever in your department it's to see it shut down as soon as possible. Take the taxpayer's money out of guns and tanks and put it back into education where it could do some good.'

'All right,' said Peter, 'now you've said your piece and I expect you feel a lot better for it. Perhaps I should try and answer some of your questions. Would you like some coffee?'

'I'd like the answers more.'

'I'm sure the two can be combined.' Peter stood up and led the way out of the dining-room into some back recess containing two armchairs. He sat down in one; Charles, after some hesitation, in the other. His dislike for the other man was undiminished. Twenty-odd years had not improved Peter Fischer. He felt more than half inclined to repeat the performance which had severed their acquaintance before and punch him on the nose in the hopes that this would make for another twenty years' freedom from his company. At this point a waiter appeared with a tray containing a pot of coffee and two glasses of brandy. The moment passed. Charles found himself holding a cup of coffee.

'You mustn't take anything I've said to imply that you're anything but in the forefront of your field,' Peter said now.

'Really? You're too kind.'

'You know it as well as I do. And a very interesting field it is, too.'

'Interesting to me. I can't imagine that it is to you.'

'Neurobiology—isn't that the technical term? Location of brain function.'

'That's roughly it.'

'What I am offering you,' said Peter, 'is the opportunity to ensure that whatever happens you will be able to go on with your research.'

'Oh yes? That's most kind of you. I'm glad to say that at the moment I think I see my way clear to doing that anyway.'

'We've already discussed that,' said Peter, unperturbed. His large forehead gleamed above his spectacles; his rosy cheeks shone with the reflection of the brandy glass. 'You don't have to believe me, but I can assure you that I'm right.'

'And what's the quid pro quo for this kind offer? I assume there is a quid pro quo.'

'Yes, of course. But you shouldn't find it too onerous. We're interested in a particular aspect of your field.'

'Which is?'

'The location of memory.'

Charles burst out laughing.

'I really can't see what you find so funny,' said Peter, apparently for the first time somewhat nettled.

'There is no one particular location. In my opinion. It's everywhere. All over the brain.'

'Others don't necessarily agree with you.'

'Go and talk to them, then.'

'They aren't as good as you. We're only interested in the best.'

'Look,' said Charles. 'Quite apart from any personal feelings I may have about you or your employers—'

'You,' returned Peter, with exaggerated courtesy, 'are one of my employers—'

'—And even if it were possible, I wouldn't want to work for the military. Not just because I disapprove, which of course I do. But because of the conditions you set. It's the antithesis of the way science ought to work. I've seen it again and again. Everything secret, embargoes on publication—'

'Well, of course. I'm afraid one must be realistic.'

'Sorry,' said Charles. 'I'm afraid I'm not interested.'

'At the moment, maybe. But don't forget. The offer stands.' Peter stood up. 'I see you've finished your coffee. I'm afraid I've got to get back to the office. Which way are you going?'

Andrew Taggart was walking down Pall Mall just as the two of them left the Reform. Peter turned towards Whitehall, Charles in the opposite direction, towards Piccadilly tube station: he was feeling so unsettled that for the moment he could contemplate nothing more demanding than the train ride back to EMU. Taggart, as it happened, knew them both, in the way that any journalist gets to know people, running across them from time to time in the course of business. Now, seeing them together, he stopped dead and stared. They were about the two last people he would have expected to see in that particular situation—i.e. having apparently finished a cordial lunch together at the Reform Club. It wasn't just that this wasn't Charles Watson's habitat: what was he doing having cordial lunches with Peter Fischer *anywhere*? He was—as Taggart knew, because he had reported Charles's activities on more than one occasion—an active agitator against virtually everything that Peter Fischer represented. Not that anyone was precisely sure exactly what Fischer did represent: he didn't cultivate a high profile or proclaim his activities from the rooftop. But Taggart, like everyone in his line, was aware of Fischer and deeply interested in him: an interest Fischer himself returned with profound suspicion. But Charles Watson? What would *he* know about Fischer? And what was he doing hobnobbing with him? Perhaps old Charles was a more complicated figure than one would have expected, Taggart reflected. Perhaps underneath that model of a liberal intellectual there lurked—what? Secret ambitions, a lust for power that the academic life *tout pur* couldn't satisfy?

Almost without thinking, because one has to go one way or another, Taggart began to walk down Pall Mall in the same direction as Fischer. He wasn't really thinking of following him. But he had heard Fischer's name recently—where? As the round head bobbed along in front of him, Taggart racked his brain to remember who had been saying what, when.

After a while Peter Fischer, instead of continuing on into Whitehall, crossed the road in the direction of Piccadilly. Walking purposefully now, he glanced at his watch, and, with Taggart still following on behind, made his way towards Mayfair. Down Charles Street he marched, across Shepherd Market and stopped at a tall house which had once been very grand indeed. Now, however, the front door, though smartly painted and flanked by bay trees in pots, bore the phalanx of doorbells which marked its decline into flats. Fischer pressed one of these, spoke into the entryphone and was admitted.

After the door had closed safely behind him, Taggart strolled across to have a look at the names in the slots beside the bells. At the same time he remembered what it was he'd heard about Fischer. Someone had said he was one of the many lovers of Juliette Correa, that gorgeous Goan who'd been hitting the headlines recently because it emerged that everybody, but everybody—everybody who was anybody, that is— was sleeping with her, or hoping to do so in the near future. Similar rumours were in circulation about a great many people, of course, but Taggart had been struck by this one because it seemed, on the face of it, so unlikely.

Peter Fischer? That greasy doughnut? What could he possibly have to offer a stunning creature like Juliette? But then, the long string of her other imputed lovers was not exactly distinguished for physical beauty, either. Power and money, that was what they had: that, and inside information. Well, Fischer certainly had *that*. And information is power, or can be. What Taggart found hard to credit was the thought that Fischer would ever have been so indiscreet as to let himself be drawn into the circle of someone like Juliette Correa. After all, she must have her price, and what could Fischer have to offer except what he knew? Which, if what Taggart had heard about him was right, was plenty. About everybody. But not, strictly not, for publication. Of course, she, too, would have her own attractions in that direction. What she must know about some people . . . Taggart could quite imagine that a self-righteous type like Fischer might very well justify his little visits as strictly in the way of business, information retrieval. Purely for medicinal purposes, like the five-star cognac in the bathroom cupboard.

So was this where she lived? The panel of bells was sadly uninformative. Just numbers, no names. Taggart strolled thoughtfully back in the direction of Berkeley Square. It shouldn't be too hard to find out where Juliette Correa lived, if he really wanted to know. Which he probably did. Information is power, and he was in the information business.

It turned out that his guess had been correct. The Correa hideaway was indeed located just behind Shepherd Market. And as it happens, a paragraph appeared the very next week in the *Eye* hinting that the lady's attentions had not been limited to luminaries of politics and the press, but that senior civil servants whose activities were intended to remain strictly veiled from the public gaze had also been noticed enjoying her company in a variety of venues . . .

Taggart read the paragraph with interest. He wondered if Fischer had seen it. In case he hadn't, Taggart kindly cut it out and sent it to him at the office. He didn't bother to enclose a covering letter. It was a despicable thing to do, but why should despicableness be confined only to the one side? And a person in Peter Fischer's position ought to know what rumours were circulating about him. Rumours were his business.

After he'd dropped the letter into the box, Taggart felt the glow of a job well done. Then he turned his attention to other things and forgot all about it.

CHAPTER 2

As soon as he was back in his office at EMU, Charles found that the strange lunch with Peter Fischer receded from reality. The whole episode seemed more and more dreamlike, especially by contrast with the day-to-day absorption he felt in his work. Charles had a chimpanzee called Bertha with whom he had been working for a long time. She was blind; Charles was trying to find out if new nerve pathways could be established by which Bertha might be trained to see again, and if so, in how limited a way. Would she respond to movement? To light and shadow? It was becoming clear that some aspects of Bertha's sight were returning, that new brain pathways were being activated. Now an interesting sequel was in prospect. A surgeon in Derby who had read his papers had written to Charles about a patient of his, a young girl who at the age of six months had suffered a brain lesion very similar to Bertha's. Charles's work seemed to offer her the possibility of some sort of sight. Would it be possible for him to work with her? Charles was immensely excited at the prospect.

It was in fact just after his return from a visit to Derby that he found the note on his desk from his professor, Harold Hawkins. He was so absorbed in the day's experiences that for some time he didn't even notice Harold's piece of paper until his secretary drew his attention to it.

'Harold seemed rather anxious to talk to you,' she said, pointing to the note. 'He came and left this himself first thing this morning.' It was now five o'clock, and the note lay in solitary splendour in a pool of space in the middle of his desk. Other clutter of infinitely more interest had been shifted pell-mell to the periphery to make way for it, Charles noted with irritation.

'Is he still here?' he asked crossly. Harold was not one to hang around the office, especially on a Friday, which this was.

'I'm afraid so.'

'Can't you tell him I'm not back? I never came back this afternoon. I'll be in on Monday.' Charles's mind was wholly engaged with his blind girl and the kind of work he hoped to do with her, the design of the exercises he was going to give her, what he hoped they might achieve. A talk with Harold about some tedious matter of routine or office politics—which was what it would inevitably be: Harold was wholly immersed in administration and politics—was the very last thing he wanted just at the moment. He was on a high; Harold would puncture it; had very nearly done so already. The very thought of Harold and his concerns destroyed intellectual excitement.

'I'm afraid not. Maureen just telephoned to ask, and I said you were here.' Maureen was Harold's secretary. Charles's, shared with three other colleagues, was called Olive, a rather timid woman who was the sole support of her semi-invalid mother. Charles sometimes idly wondered which quarter of Olive it was that worked for him. Not her head, he had concluded.

Reluctantly he opened the note. It said, 'Dear Charles, would you come to see me as soon as possible about a matter of great urgency. Yours, Harold.' He stared at this for some seconds and said, 'Oh, Olive, I really don't think I can bear to see Harold about urgent matters just now. Tell Maureen I left again before you'd been able to catch me, how about that?'

'I could,' she said doubtfully. Olive was not a person who entered joyfully upon other people's deceptions. She was a member of a sect of Exclusive Brethren (Charles could see the attraction: her life was intolerable, and a sect which taught that the more awful life upon earth, the likelier the eventuality of eternal bliss, would naturally have its appeal under those circumstances) which frowned upon deception of even the mildest variety. This made for difficulty more often than might have been thought: it is surprising how many of life's small transactions are faintly immoral. On this occasion, however, the difficulty with Olive was avoided by the arrival of Harold himself, which pre-empted Charles's evasive manœuvres.

'Oh, hallo, Charles,' he said comfortably. 'I hoped you might be back by now.' Harold was a plump, pipe-smoking Yorkshireman, incapable of neurosis and openly scornful of less equable temperaments. These included most of his colleagues, and he treated them, whenever disagreements arose, either with that studied tolerance which one tries to apply to three-year-olds in the midst of a temper tantrum, or else as prima donnas, to be humoured until the limits of even Harold's tolerance were overstepped, when he simply squashed them flat. He was only a year or two older than Charles, but the difference might have been a century. It was clear that he had adopted his present persona at the age of twenty and sustained it unvaryingly ever since.

'I was just rushing off again, actually.' Harold always made Charles feel brittle, even physically. There were no corners on Harold, while Charles, tall, thin and angular, consisted (at least in Harold's presence) of little else. He felt that his physique always stood him in bad stead with the professor. It indicated a nervous temperament, and Harold distrusted him instinctively because of it. Charles had had his readership longer than Harold had held the chair; he would never have stood a chance of it had things been the other way about. Harold liked men about him who were fat.

'Well, don't rush off just yet. There's something I need to have a word with you about.'

'Have it, then.'

'Shall we go to my office?' Harold turned and led the way out of the door. His office was identical in almost every way to Charles's, two doors away down the corridor. But Harold liked to work on his home territory. It was part of the political game to which his life was dedicated. When they were both safely inside the room he shut the door, with rather more emphasis than was necessary, and sat down behind his desk, the implication being that Charles should seat himself on the other side, in the subordinate's, student's, interviewee's position. Charles declined this invitation and strolled over to the window. Harold lit his pipe.

'Come on, then, Harold. Out with it. I've got a lot on at the moment.'

Harold, unperturbed, went on tamping and puffing until the pipe was lit to his satisfaction. Then, choosing the moment before Charles was about to turn on his heel and leave, he said, 'It's about the future, Charles.'

'What about it?'

'Yours, in particular.'

'My future is fully occupied as far as the eye can see.'

'You're going to have to do more teaching.'

'That is not in my contract. I'm a reader—it's a research job, remember? I already do some teaching, and there's no time for any more.'

'I'm afraid you're going to have to make time. We're being pressed, and things aren't going to get easier. We're going to have to take more students and there aren't going to be any more appointments. Everyone's going to have to pull their weight.'

'That's your problem, not mine, isn't it?' Charles was aware that Harold resented him for a variety of reasons to do with the facts that Charles enjoyed his work, maintained an independent fiefdom within the department that was not under Harold's control, and avoided boring chores such as committees and most undergraduate teaching.

'No,' rejoined Harold with satisfaction. 'From now on it's yours as well. There will be no more purely research posts at this university. You will find that your contract is going to be changed. You'll have to make time. Universities can't afford luxuries like you any more.'

'I'll go to the vice-chancellor.'

'Do. As a matter of fact, it was he who came to me. It's university policy.'

'Whose side are you on, Harold? We ought to be fighting

these creeping gauleiters, not giving in to them without a whimper.'

'I'm on the university's side.' Harold began the emptying, tamping and lighting routine again. The room stank of pipe smoke. He said no more. The unspoken words hung in the thick air: You've had things your way all these years. Now I'm going to have things my way. Up the gauleiters and sod you.

Charles left the room, went down to his car and drove home. The pleasure and excitement of the day had evaporated. Harold would have been delighted to know it, no doubt. A dead spirit who couldn't bear signs of life in others.

At home, there were no signs of life either. Belinda down in the bloody garden no doubt. As usual.

The telephone rang.

CHAPTER 3

'Charles Watson,' Charles snapped into the machine as he lifted it up. He was feeling thoroughly unsettled. Just as he had managed to forget the slimy Peter Fischer with his disguised threats and hints of coercion and lose himself in an exciting new project, along came that damned pipe-puffer Harold with more threats, hardly disguised this time. It was as if the whole world wanted to stop him doing his present work. What would happen to that poor little girl if he suddenly abandoned her on account of some bloody ridiculous *force majeure*? To teach cack-handed first-years the elements of dissection and the layout of the brain. Nothing could bore him more ferociously and nothing, he suspected, would afford Harold more pleasure than the sight of his boredom. Harold thought everybody ought to endure a modicum of boredom in their job, or it couldn't be called a job. Charles snorted, then remembered he was on the phone. 'Sorry,' he said. 'Who is this?'

He realized now that the machine had made no response to his name. Was anybody there? A faint whistling was audible; then an American voice said, 'Hello? Is this Charles Watson's home?'

'This is he speaking.' He? Him? Charles had never been able to work out the grammar of this rejoinder. 'Who is this?' he said again.

'Oh, hi, Chuck, this is Wesley.'

'Wesley Mitchell?'

'Who else?'

'Where are you?'

'At Jones, where else?'

Charles had never been able to accustom himself to the fact that these days it was perfectly normal to talk to people on the other side of the world. When his phone rang he assumed, quite irrationally, that the call was probably from England, or Scotland at the furthest, and most likely London or Leamingworth, the small market town he inhabited close to the EMU campus. In this he was usually right, as these days hardly anyone telephoned him on his home number: almost all the calls were for Belinda, his wife, or, during the vacations, for their son, Stuart. Their daughter now had a job in London: since she had left home the volume of telephone calls had decreased by about eighty per cent. 'Wesley,' said Charles uncertainly. 'Well, hi.' Transatlantic phonecalls always paralysed him. It was the thought of all that distance.

'How're you doing?' Wesley had no such inhibitions. Americans didn't: they were altogether more at ease with expensive technology.

'I'm fine.' That, of course, was strictly a lie, but Wesley, it could safely be assumed, had no more wish to hear about Charles's local difficulties than Charles had to recount them to him. Wesley was one of those people who put Charles on the defensive. They were much of an age, and, in Charles's opinion, of roughly equal abilities—Charles if anything (modesty could not change facts) the more original of the two. But this was not reflected in their professional status. Here was Charles, Reader at EMU: a delightful job (when and if he was allowed to do it), an intellectually satisfying job, but wholly lacking in glamour, very largely because it was almost entirely lacking in funds. Charles's department, Mind Sciences, had little obvious market value. If enough funds were removed (such appeared to be current thinking) these useless departments would wither on the vine, the students would drift away, the remaining staff would perish of starvation or overwork, and new, *now* departments of Business Administration could be built up to replace them. Harold's assault simply heralded the final battle in what had been a long war of attrition.

Wesley, by contrast, headed a flourishing empire. His interests were similar to Charles's; but his laboratory at Jones resembled a gleaming factory wherein countless minions laboured to identify the whereabouts of brain functions. Not, indeeed, that they saw themselves as minions; doubtless each of them considered him or herself a potentially better brain than Wesley (in which they might well have been right, Charles thought) and as eventually ruling just such empires in their own right. Meanwhile, there was no doubt who was in charge. Every paper emanating from Jones bore Wesley Mitchell's name at the head of the list of authors, even though Wesley himself was rarely present in Southampton, spending his time mainly upon circling the world in search of funds and fame. Not a conference but Wesley was a speaker, not an Institute but he was an honorary fellow. His aim was a Nobel prize; it was an open secret; cynics assumed that the sheer volume of work going through his lab was his way of ensuring that, by the law of averages, he would be sure, sooner or later, to hit upon at least one world-shaking discovery.

'Are you thinking of coming over?' Charles now asked. He could think of no other reason why Wesley would be phoning him. Their relations were, for a variety of reasons, ambivalent.

'Hell, no!' Charles winced at the raucous chortle which traversed thousands of miles to assault his eardrum.

'It's not such an extraordinary suggestion. You've done it before,' he pointed out. Two summers ago, in fact: his thoughts went back to that time, when the Mitchell family had stayed at Leamingworth for two weeks, astonished to find that a family such as the Watsons could exist with only one bathroom to a house.

'Yeah, but that's why I'm calling. A little bird tells me you're having a hard time.'

'Who told you that?' The little bird must fly faster than the speed of light. Charles felt, if possible, even more outraged than before. How and why was it possible that Wesley Mitchell should know so much more about his departmental politics than he knew himself?

'Oh, you know what the grapevine's like. I forget just who it was. Wasn't anything that definite, I guess. But given the way your government feels about universities, I figured that if something interesting came up, you might be interested.'

'Has something interesting come up?'

'Sure has.'

'So what am I supposed to do about it?'

'Come over and see.'

'What's the something?'

'Come over and see.'

'You must be joking. I'm just at the beginning of something really interesting myself.'

'Well, the offer's open. Things get hard, bear it in mind. Always a space for you here, you know that, Charles.'

'And that's what you rang to say?'

'That's it.'

Charles was still staring at the phone when his wife Belinda came in from the garden.

'Seen a ghost?'

'Oh, sorry . . .' Charles averted his gaze from the phone, but his mind was not so easily brought to the present time and place.

'Someone just phone?' Belinda had removed her heavy gardening gloves outside, and was now studying her fingernails. Lined with black as usual. Nothing but a bath or doing the washing-up would dislodge that.

'Wesley Mitchell.'

'Goodness. Where's he?'

'Jones.'

'So what was so important?'

'He wants me to go over there.'

'So tell me something new. Any particular reason?'

'He thinks things are in a bad way here.'

'They're not particularly, are they? I thought you were just on to something interesting?'

'So did I, but I don't know if I'll be able to go ahead with it. Harold's poised for the kill.' He told her about the afternoon's encounter at EMU.

'But how could Wesley possibly know about that?'

'No idea. Maybe he doesn't. It's no secret that things are bad for universities here now.'

'So are you going?' Belinda was still fiddling with her nails.

'What for?'

'Didn't he say? He must have had some reason for suddenly phoning. Not just generalized philanthropy. That wouldn't be like Wesley.'

'He wasn't saying.'

She shrugged. 'Curiouser and curiouser.' Her gaze drifted out of the window and a withdrawn look came over her face. Clearly she was thinking about some horticultural problem.

'I suppose if Harold gets any more obstreperous I may go,' Charles said eventually.

'What—just on Wesley's say-so?'

'No—just to have a look. See what's up. What's so vital that he can't say anything over the phone.'

'Will EMU pay?'

'Perhaps Wesley will. It's all his idea.'

Belinda looked at him, her eyebrows lifted. 'An unexpected treat.'

'What d'you mean?'

She shrugged. 'A jolly jaunt to the States, all expenses paid. Sounds delightful. Perhaps I'll come too.'

'Well—if you really want to, of course. I expect I'll be in the lab most of the time.'

'Oh, I expect you will,' Belinda said. 'Terribly boring really.' And she drifted outside again.

CHAPTER 4

Charles, on his return to the university next day, found himself in a dilemma. What he wanted more than anything else was to start work with his blind girl. But that was now out of the question. The poor child had enough to contend with without being the subject of a course of treatment begun with high hopes and hastily terminated before anything had been achieved, or, even worse, when it seemed that something might be achieved. There was no question of doing the work in his spare time. The treatment would have to be intensive, and it would be exhausting and demanding for everyone concerned. Either it had to be done properly or not at all. There were no half-measures. That, presumably, was why Harold had been so anxious to speak to him at once. Charles had made no secret of his new project—had on the contrary talked about it fairly freely—and Harold must have realized that, once he was fairly started in on it, he could have insisted upon following it through for the girl's sake, if not his own. So it had had to be nipped in the bud before it was too late, which meant before anything had been begun. Charles debated with himself whether this point had not already been reached—whether it hadn't been reached as soon as he met the girl; or earlier, as soon as the possibility had been mooted to her. But he had to admit to himself that this was probably not so. She was not particularly eager to try out what Charles proposed—something which, if it succeeded, would totally overturn her life, would mean beginning everything again and learning to see. This project belonged to Charles and the surgeon, not to her. But there was no time to be lost. If the project was to be abandoned it would have to be abandoned at once. He felt a deep hatred for the shortsighted philistines in government and for Harold, who was so happy to go along with them. Any doubts he had had on this count were removed, and his loathing intensified, by the arrival on his desk of a memo brought by Harold's secretary and deposited with great deliberation before him. It requested him to present himself in the professor's room at two o'clock to discuss his teaching and lecturing schedules and proposals. Staring with distaste at this missive, he left the office, making a mental note of the arranging he had to do on his own account before then.

Harold looked up briefly when Charles entered his room. He was, as usual, tamping his pipe. 'Nice to see you, Charles,' he said. 'Had any further thoughts?'

'Lots.'

'Glad to hear it. Shall we start with the lectures, then? I was wondering if you could manage a course for next term. I know it's a tall order, but there's rather a gap just at the moment in the Introduction to Microbiology, and that'd mean it was ready for the new academic year, so you could perhaps even find time to work another set up in the vacation.'

'No, I don't think so, Harold.'

'Then what do you propose?'

'I'm taking a sabbatical next term. I'm owed a year, as you know, but I shall just be taking that term. I shall be going to work with Wesley Mitchell at Jones. Just fixed it up.' He had debated with himself for some time over what he should do. He could have used the sabbatical for his work with the blind girl. On the other hand, that would take more than a term, and he knew there was no way in which he could possibly get away with a whole year, however much it might be owed to him.

'I didn't know anything about this.' Harold was staring at him furiously.

'It was something I'd been meaning to speak to you about. But you rather pre-empted me last night.' So now I'm pre-empting you.

'There's nothing I can say, is there? This is all highly inconvenient. But of course you know that.'

'Well, there we are,' Charles said cheerfully. There was nothing he wanted from Harold. None of the things that might be in Harold's gift, such as promotion, held any interest for Charles. So why should he put himself out for Harold?

'When are you off?'

'What's it now—end of March—well, a couple of weeks. When term ends.' Charles got up to leave the room. 'See you in September. Drop me a note to keep abreast of developments. I'll leave my address with Olive.' Saying which, he left the room, collected together some papers from his own office, informed the startled Olive that he was off to America and wouldn't be back until the end of September, got into his car and drove home.

Leamingworth was a quiet Midlands market town set in the middle of rolling countryside of no particular interest but great fertility. It sat in the Leam valley, nestled round its old stone bridge. Its terraced streets of rambling stone houses had, until the arrival of EMU in the 'sixties, been inhabited mainly by the shopkeepers who catered to the green-wellied, flak-jacketed, purple-faced farmers from the solid farmhouses dotted round about. These houses had of course proved very attractive to the incoming staff of the new university, and in the fifteen years the Watsons had been there prices had risen so that what they had bought for £18,000 (with considerable heart-searching about the size of the mortgage) was now worth a good deal more than ten times that. It was a substantial house on three storeys, double-fronted, with an imposing Georgian front door that led to a surprisingly cottagey interior: in the usual provincial manner, details in the prevailing mode had been superimposed upon less than elegant proportions. The house, behind its flat front, was a more or less chaotic accretion of the random additions, opening at the back on to a long garden which led down to the river. At the river end there was a high wall surmounting a steep bank. The Watsons, like all the houses in their row, had access to the river down a flight of steep brick steps, at the bottom of which bobbed a small rowing-boat. Belinda, who spent much of her life thinking about and working in her garden, could never make up her mind whether or not she regretted the water-garden she might have made in the absence of the river wall, but had consoled herself by building a small pavilion which incorporated part of the wall, and where she could read and sit and enjoy the river view. On the opposite bank, water meadows stretched back to a line of low hills. This was land that flooded every winter, and so had never been built upon. The river marked the edge of Leamingworth. Originally Belinda had had visions of delectable summer lunches in the pavilion, but of course it was too far from the house for that to be really practicable. Left to herself (as she increasingly was these days), she in fact took her lunch there often, with all the pleasure she had anticipated.

Charles parked outside the front door (it was still usually possible to park outside the door) and let himself in. The house was silent. On his left was his study, a small room with white-painted half-panelling; on his right, the sitting-room, which was also half-panelled, a long, low-ceilinged room running from front to back of the house. The panelling had been put there to conceal the damp, but was now a desirable period feature. Behind the study was a staircase, and behind that a door led into the kitchen at the back of the house. A French window, directly opposite the front door, led into the garden. This, on this mild spring afternoon, was ajar. Belinda was gardening, as usual.

In fact she was standing staring at an untidily sprouting herbaceous bed running along the south side of the part of the garden farthest from the house. She turned when she saw Charles and said, 'I've decided to pull it all out and start again. It's a hopeless mess. Grey leaves and old roses and lots of little blue flowers, that's what it needs. Flax. What would you say to a drift of flax? That blue linum?' Belinda was wearing her filthy white and brown wasp-striped gardening sweater, looped and holed from too many encounters with roses. Her cheeks and nose were a matching shade of healthy pink. When Charles had first met Belinda she had just passed the Civil Service examination. She had been a slightly severe-looking young woman with short brown hair framing rosy, high-boned cheeks, a wide, clever mouth (she had taken a first) and the best legs Charles had ever seen. She was, at that time, bursting with life and vitality. She was sharing a flat in Notting Hill with a girl Charles knew from Cambridge and who had invited him to dinner with the vague intention, in which he as vaguely concurred, of starting an affair. He was then a research student at University College, London. But things had not turned out quite as the friend had intended. Charles and Belinda had taken one look at each other and had barely paused to swallow a few mouthfuls before repairing to bed where, it seemed to Charles in retrospect, they had remained with a few breaks for food and work for about the next six months. Then Charles had got an assistant lectureship, Belinda had got pregnant (whether by mistake or on purpose she would never say, and had probably never known), and on the strength of these two events they had got married. Almost uniquely among their acquaintance they were still married. Perhaps this was because excess of emotion had never been allowed to interfere with the even tenor of their lives. They had got married simply because that had seemed more convenient than remaining obstinately unwed; the same inertia kept them married because they knew each other so well and, even now when the children were grown up, there seemed no particular reason to divorce. But it had been some time since there had been any closeness between them. The baby had meant the end of Belinda's job, and a second baby had precluded any possibility of its resumption; so that instead of the high-flying potential Under-Secretary Charles had married (well, potential Assistant Secretary perhaps, prospects for women in the Civil Service being what they actually were), the middle-aged Belinda, her children now grown, was always naggingly conscious of never having used her abilities to their full extent. Meanwhile, more and more of her considerable energies now went into gardening; she was even toying with the idea of taking up horticulture professionally in some capacity. Her brown hair was streaked with grey now, and the roses in her cheeks tended to meld into a uniformly rather pink face. But the fine bones were still there, and so was the intelligence behind those rather unnerving grey eyes.

'Belinda, I've got to talk to you.'

'That sounds ominous. I thought we were talking.'

'Not about flax.'

'Well, go on then. Talk.'

Charles looked around. Clouds scudded across a blue sky and a keen breeze crept uncomfortably beneath the edges of his jacket. 'Can we go inside?'

'If we must.' Belinda cast a regretful look at the herbaceous bed, stuck her fork in the earth and made for the house. 'What's it all about, then?'

'I'm going to America.'

'Really? When?'

'Soon as possible. What I was telling you about. To work with Wesley Mitchell at Jones.'

'But I thought you'd decided you didn't want to do that. What about your work here? Isn't this all rather sudden?'

'It is, rather. It's on account of bloody Harold Hawkins.' He gave Belinda a brief account of what had just transpired between Harold and himself. She listened with her usual mixture of concentration and impatience.

'Doesn't sound to me as if Harold had much choice.'

'Maybe not, but there's no escaping the fact that he's thoroughly enjoying himself.'

Belinda shrugged. Twenty-five years of living with Charles had inured her to the slings and arrows of academic politics. She could never forget what an American academic turned politician had once observed—that academic politics are so bitter because the stakes are so low. Every month, every week, every day, brought its new crop of life-and-death struggles against venomous foes. At first Belinda had worried terribly about this hydra-headed monster of treachery. She had lost sleep on Charles's behalf (he himself was an excellent sleeper; indeeed, the more he worried, the deeper and longer he slept and the more unwilling he was to awake). She refused to speak to the enemy of the moment. Then, gradually, she began to realize that although the battles were incessant, no one of them ever lasted very long or brought about the total destruction which had been foretold. So she stopped worrying and assumed instead that her husband was slightly paranoid. Later still she realized that this was not the case, that the incessant state of siege was not just a figment of Charles's imagination, but that it was an inevitable consequence of herding large numbers of clever, self-obsessed men and women together in a competitive environment where all advancement depended upon the recognition of personal achievement. That is to say, it was just part of the job. After that she stopped thinking about it.

'You seem to be taking it all very seriously. It seems to me we've had this kind of conversation every six months since I've known you. What's so different about this time? You know Harold hates you. Why make him hate you more? Anyway, I thought you were so keen to work with this blind girl. You won't be able to do that if you go off to Jones.'

'I won't be able to do it anyway. That's the point.' That, at least, was part of the point. Charles had been wondering whether Peter Fischer was not in some way involved in this sudden attack on him. If he was, there seemed little Charles could do, and he might as well accept the inevitable and get out on his own terms rather than Fischer's. But he decided not to voice these suspicions. Belinda was always so scornful and dismissive of what she called his academic paranoia. Which no doubt this was. One heard stories like this on all sides these days. 'I'm not sure I can be bothered to keep on swimming against the current. Life's short, it takes up too much energy. I shall adopt the ethos of this government and gather my rosebuds where I may. I thought we could perhaps let the house while we're over there and then see what happens. If you want to come, that is.'

'Yes, I'd been thinking about that. I don't think I will come, thanks. Not for the moment. It isn't as if you'd resigned, is it? And I don't much like America.'

They looked at each other for a moment. Neither of them said what was really in their minds: twenty-five years had taught them the value of the thought unspoken. Charles said, 'I know what it is. You can't bear the thought of leaving your beloved garden. All that flax.'

'Perhaps that's part of it,' said Belinda.

CHAPTER 5

Southampton, Mass., the seat of Jones University, was the epitome of an Ivy League university town. Along the main street classy clothes shops jostled cheap wholefood restaurants. There was also a large number of shops selling expensive objects for the embellishment of student rooms. Behind this consumer paradise lurked a hinterland of large old frame houses, put up at about the same time as the monumental stone fortresses of the campus itself. The very biggest of these houses were student dormitories, and many of the others now contained a number of apartments. The Mitchells, however, owned an entire house. Charles had stayed there before. He had visited Jones on a number of occasions in order to work with Wesley Mitchell. The visiting was almost always in that direction because, while Wesley had no difficulty in finding funds in the recesses of the Jones coffers to finance Charles, it was as much as Charles could do, even when times were better than now, to keep his own work going at EMU, let alone pay expensive Americans for more than the most fleeting of visits. Now, as he got off the bus and made his way across State Street to the part of town where the Mitchells lived, he felt almost at home. Down past the grocery store, right, left, left again, and there it was, 704 Wyoming, the classic American house, large, white, porched, bracketed, irregular and pleasing. He barely had time to set down his bag and ring the bell before Essie Mitchell had opened the front door with that almost excessive display of welcome which Charles always found it so hard to credit, yet which appeared, even on the closest scrutiny, to be unassailably genuine.

'Why, Charles,' she cried, as she always did, 'how wonderful to see you again.'

To which he replied, as he always did, 'Great to be here, Essie,' and felt, again as always, incapable of equalling displays of American emotion. Whenever he came here he marvelled at the unbelievable pleasure manifested by everyone whenever they met anyone else. Could they really be that pleased? He, Charles, was rarely very pleased to meet anyone, and this pleasure, even when felt, was hard to detect. Was he unusually misanthropic? He never thought so except when he visited America.

'Wesley's at the department. He said to call when you arrived and he'll be right round. Let me show you your room. When did you arrive? You came by bus? Wasn't there a limo at the airport? Lulu said to tell you she'll be here for dinner.' Lulu was the Mitchell's student daughter. Professors' children got free tuition at the university, which, given the cost of tuition fees, meant that the pressure on them to take advantage of this perk was considerable. 'She can't wait to see you,' Essie added.

Overwhelmed by all this, Charles could only smile weakly. Essie took this for exhaustion and said, 'Why don't you go take a shower and a nap. You're in your usual room.'

'If I go to bed I'll never wake up again till two tomorrow morning. I'd better keep going.'

'Well, let me help you with your bags.'

The long, long day wore on. Meals were eaten, drinks were drunk. Charles spoke, but was more or less unconscious of what he said. Other people spoke: their words buzzed like flies around his head, never penetrating the skull. He renewed old acquaintance and drank yet more. Finally, at last, a time arrived when he could decently take himself off. He slipped gratefully between the covers of one of Essie's twin guest beds and had barely time to wonder how things were going to turn out before he sank into sleep.

About five seocnds later (by his internal reckoning) he awoke with a start to find a figure standing by his bed. 'Hi,' whispered this apparition. 'I guessed you'd be awake. That's the way the jet-lag goes in this direction, right? Move over.' And Lulu Mitchell wriggled into the narrow space between Charles and the side of the bed.

'Lulu! Are you crazy? They'll hear you.'

'No, they won't. Don't be silly. They're right the other side of the house.' This was true: the guest bedroom and bathroom were located in a kind of spur sticking out of the house at the back, above Wesley's study, a room he used comparatively rarely, since he was almost always either away or at the department.

'I thought you'd gone back to your dorm.'

'Yeah, and now here I am back. I have a key to the front door, remember? Hey, Charles, what is this? Aren't you glad to see me?'

'Of course I am. It's just—I feel disoriented. And we must be careful,' he hissed. Lulu's voice in his ear sounded distressingly loud. He peered at his watch, which told him it was 4.10 a.m., ten past nine by his body-clock. He felt, now he had been disturbed, wide awake; and now, for once, an ideal situation presented itself for the painless whiling away of the early morning hours which were otherwise apt to pass so distressingly slowly. Why, then, did he not feel more of the unmixed pleasure which Lulu had so obviously anticipated? The truth was, he had to admit, that he didn't feel unmixed anything. The situation was too complicated for that.

Charles had known Lulu, whose real name was Louise A. Mitchell, for as long as he had known her father, which was to say for the past twenty years—all her life. When they first met, Charles and Wesley both held research fellowships in London. Charles, Belinda and the infant Caroline (Stuart was not yet born) were living in three spacious but cold rooms in Fitzjohn's Avenue. At that time Belinda, not yet pregnant with Stuart, had not given up the idea of returning to her job, so that she viewed her child-bound life as an interruption rather than a fixture. Wesley, who disposed of much more income by virtue of being American, was renting the top half of a house in Belsize Park, not far away, where he, Essie and baby Lulu, who was then about six months old, lived a comparatively luxurious, or at least adequately-heated, life. Belinda and Essie were not natural soul-mates—Essie was too happy with domesticity, Belinda still too unwilling to accept it, for that. But they got on well enough, their husbands were colleagues and also friends, and contiguity together with the shared necessity of passing the day in the company of a small child and without taking leave of their sanity, had thrown them together. The Mitchells had only spent a year in London, but that had laid the foundation for a lasting friendship. Charles and Wesley were in frequent contact because of their work, and Belinda, Essie and the children met from time to time. As the years passed and the Mitchells returned to the States while the Watsons moved to Leamingworth, the friendship became if anything stronger. It was not so much that the reservations disappeared as that they were overlaid by the advantage of not meeting too often. Charles and Wesley made their way up the career ladder, Belinda retired into her garden and Essie mourned her apparent inability to have any more babies—for none had materialized after Lulu. She put her energies into good works: she prison visited, and ran the local chapter of NOW. Meanwhile the children, over that span of years which is at once so endless and so vanishingly short, grew up. At one meeting they were pudgy toddlers, then toothless seven-year-olds, gangling ten-year-olds, obstreperous teenagers—and then they were there no more: they had grown up, they had their own lives to lead.

On the Mitchells' last visit to England Lulu had been eighteen, in her first year at college, a self-possessed young woman, at one with herself as Caroline had never been, with a shock of frizzy yellow hair—the same texture as Essie's, the same colour as Wesley's—a lithe, slender body and a wide, triangular smile. Charles thought she was gorgeous, and told her so in what he took to be his best avuncular mode. They had been on a country walk at the time, and for some reason nobody else was with them. Essie and Belinda had gone shopping in London, Stuart was playing cricket, Caroline was spending a weekend with college friends, Wesley was occupied with some academic business. So there they were, sitting on some grassy bank on a beautiful summer's day, Lulu stretching out long brown legs and confiding her ambitions, which were theatrical: she would major in poetry and drama, and then who knew?

'You shouldn't find it too difficult,' said Charles, 'someone as gorgeous as you.'

'The trouble is,' she said, turning to him with wide brown eyes, that striking colouring of hers beside which the conventional blue-eyed blonde looked so banal—'I find it so hard to concentrate. You see, I'm in love.'

'Of course you are,' Charles replied. 'Everyone is at your age. Who with, or is it a secret?'

'You,' she said astonishingly. 'I have been for years. Don't tell me you never guessed!' Saying which, she threw herself into his not unexcited arms. He never had guessed—such a thing had never crossed his mind, it would have seemed altogether too incestuous. Did that tinge add to his excitement? That particular aspect of his relations with young girls had for so long been firmly shut off by walls of taboo and inhibition which interposed themselves sturdily between himself and the most obvious young girl of his acquaintance—namely, his daughter Caroline. Caroline so strongly recalled Belinda at her age—Belinda, that is, when he had first met her and fallen hopelessly in love with her. She had the same daunting self-assurance, the same brilliant grey eyes, the same spectacular legs. She was a knock-out, just as Belinda had been a knock-out, and Charles was dazzled by her, just as he had been dazzled by her mother—though not in the same way, of course. Of course. But he and Caroline were very close, as indeed were Stuart and Belinda, the children gravitating, as so often happens, to the parent of the opposite sex. In the seconds following Lulu's declaration, these thoughts flashed through his mind, to be returned at once firmly to his subconscious, where they belonged.

At any rate, he succumbed after the merest token of resistance, and for the rest of that stay the two of them had shared an obsessive conspiracy. It was agreed, for obvious reasons, that nobody must know or even suspect: a state of affairs which maintained their excitement at fever pitch. That had been two summers ago. Since then they had corresponded on and off and met a couple of times, once when Charles had attended a conference in New York and they had spent a rapturous night together in his hotel, once when Lulu had been on a college trip to London and had come to Leamingworth when Belinda was out for the day. Separation, they found, only whetted their appetite.

After all this, Lulu could be forgiven for assuming that among Charles's motives for coming to Jones her own presence on campus was a not insignificant factor. Was it? Charles, who had had plenty of time to consider the question in the past few days, found himself quite unable to say. The thought of Lulu undoubtedly weakened his knees. He desired her enormously; her effect upon him had been something he had not experienced for years—more than twenty-five years—and this had left him shaken. But just at present he had other worries. He had hoped, in a way, to find that she had lost interest, that she had a boyfriend of her own age, that her life at Jones would be absorbing enough to keep her from the boring parental roof. He knew that if he saw her her effect upon him would be as shattering as ever; and, quite apart from anything else, how could their affair possibly be kept from her parents in these circumstances? The vibrations between them were enough to set the furniture shaking. Despite all their discretion, he had been amazed that no one had seemed to suspect what was going on before, if only because of this almost tangible tension between them. At the time he had been pretty sure that no one *had* suspected. Now he was not so sure. Belinda's reaction when he had told her he was coming here had seemed to indicate that she, for one, had her suspicions. At any rate, he had hoped to have a small breathing-space to work things out, see how the land lay. This, however, was not to be. Here was Lulu, outdoing even herself in indiscretion, and here was he, quite unable to stem the onrush of excitement he almost—almost?—wished he didn't feel.

'Of course I'm pleased to see you. But we must be careful,' he groaned.

'We are being careful. It's four in the morning, for God's sake. I'll be gone before anybody even thinks about getting up. Oh, Charles, when I heard you were coming, I just couldn't believe it.'

Charles, who had avoided meeting Lulu's eye all evening, felt like a heel. But it wouldn't do. It simply wouldn't do.

He and Lulu were going to have to have a talk. Not here and not now. But sometime. Soon.

Studying Lulu as she lay beside him, Charles was filled, as always, with astonishment. He could see why he was attracted to Lulu—nothing very mysterious about that—but what, for God's sake, was there in it for her? Surely she must know lots of beautiful young men? Why didn't she prefer them? Here he was, ageing—well, past his best physically at any rate, there was no denying that—and married. Couldn't even offer her that...

As if she had read his thoughts, Lulu now turned to him sleepily and murmured, 'Don't you sometimes wish Belinda was dead?'

'What?' Charles was appalled—an indication, perhaps, that this was a direction not altogether unknown to his own thoughts.

'Well, not dead necessarily,' Lulu allowed. 'But wouldn't it be wonderful if we could get married? Have you ever thought about that? Getting divorced maybe?'

Charles was smitten with terror. No; he had not thought about that. His affair with Lulu had nothing to do with such mundane realities as marriage and divorce. What would happen to his work with Wesley, for God's sake? Or at EMU, come to that? What would he do about Belinda? How could he go on living in Leamingworth—she, presumably, would keep the house? Of course, if she died things would certainly be easier in that department. Then he shook himself mentally. How could he even think such thoughts? He *liked* Belinda. Couldn't, when it came down to it, imagine life without her. 'You don't want to marry me,' he said. 'You'll find someone your own age. Believe me. Not that I want you to,' he added hastily.

Lulu made no reply to this. Instead, after a while, she said, 'By the way, be careful of Wesley. I've been meaning to tell you.'

'What d'you mean, be careful? Does he suspect about us?'

'No, no, nothing like that. But he's been getting very funny recently.'

'How d'you mean, funny?'

'Touchy. Secretive. Like he's got something to hide. Though don't ask me what.' She turned back to him. 'Maybe we'd better not talk. Actions, not words. Talking doesn't improve things any, haven't you noticed?'

CHAPTER 6

Lulu departed at six, leaving a thoughtful Charles behind her. He had made her promise that she would not do anything so silly again. Whatever the rights and wrongs of their relationship (a subject from which he tried to avert his mind until he should feel slightly stronger), he was quite clear that it was not one his conscience would allow him to pursue in her parents' guest-room. He had only to imagine how he would feel if, to take an exactly comparable situation, he should discover that Caroline and Wesley . . . That, of course, was unthinkable. Caroline was a matter-of-fact young woman much taken up with her current boyfriend, an upright young fellow in some branch of usury, or investment banking, as he preferred to call it. As for Wesley, he was far too preoccupied with the pursuit of honours and reputation to devote much energy to the more inconvenient and distracting aspects of sex. But all that apart, *if* Charles and Belinda happened to discover that something was going on between them, Charles knew that this discovery would not be enhanced by being made in their own house at Leamingworth. If there was one thing Charles disliked it was the abuse of hospitality. It was hard enough to face Wesley and (especially) Essie as things were.

Seven o'clock. Charles got up, showered, dressed, descended to the kitchen where he found Wesley making coffee. Charles normally didn't eat much breakfast, but today he felt starving, it being as far as he was concerned almost lunch-time. Wesley's speciality was hotcakes; now he turned out a pile of them and added some sausages. Charles munched. Wesley bent proudly over the stove, wearing Essie's apron. He was tall and blond with a neat yellow beard, now greying, a big, broad man who was becoming a little heavy. It was the physique of a bully, of a man who knew he could always push through by sheer force what he could not achieve by subtler means. Beside him Charles felt weedy, clearly a man whose only recourse would be to intellect.

Wesley filled his own plate with hotcakes and sausages and liberally sprayed the heap with maple syrup. Within a remarkably short time he had engulfed the lot and was pouring his third cup of coffee. 'I thought perhaps you'd like a tour of the labs, see what everyone's up to, and then maybe we can have a talk,' he said.

'Sounds good. The trouble is, I really don't know what I'm up to at the moment.'

'Well, naturally. You just got off the plane.'

'It's not just that.' Charles had not yet explained to Wesley the real reasons for his sudden decision to come to Jones after all. He didn't know whether he should or even could explain, because, when you came down to it, his reasons were entirely negative. This was an act of protest, a snook-cocking exercise, a furious sulk because he wasn't being allowed to do exactly what he wanted. 'I don't even know how long I'm going to be here,' he concluded weakly.

'Well, relax. There's no panic. I've got some plans, and I think you'll find them interesting. Really.'

'One thing I'd like to do is find somewhere to live. And some wheels.'

'What's the rush? You can stay here for a while. No sweat. You know how Essie enjoys your company. You'd be doing her a favour. Really. I've got to go away next week for a few days, and she gets lonesome.'

'Yes, but you know how it is. I'd prefer to find somewhere.' If you only knew why.

Essie still had not appeared as Charles led the way out to the garage. It was a bright, crisp morning, a nip of frost dispersing as the sun gained strength. They climbed into Wesley's car and drove towards the campus. The psychology labs, Charles remembered, were on the further side, facing the lake which was used for rowing and windsurfing in the summer. As they drove, Charles noticed a picket line circling in front of the administration building, a nineteenth-century monument to the immutability of stone. They were carrying placards, but at this distance it was impossible to read them. With a sudden drop of the stomach, as though someone had just punched him in the solar plexus, he realized that one of the circling figures was Lulu. He nodded towards the picket as casually as he could. 'What's all that in aid of?'

Wesley glanced towards them and frowned. 'Some sort of half-assed protest. I've told Lulu before, I wish she'd keep out of that kind of thing.'

'Tough on her, being always under your eye here.'

'Some tough. I wish I'd had things tough like that when I was her age.'

'What's the protest about?' inquired Charles, eager to change the subject. He knew all about how Wesley had worked his way through college.

'Some stupid thing. A coal-mining strike, for chrissakes. What's that got to do with Lulu? Can you see her going down a mine?'

'I doubt if that's the idea.'

'Whatever the idea is, I wish she'd drop it.'

'Afraid she'll turn into a pinko?'

'I don't think that's so funny, as it happens.'

They drove on in silence. Charles had had conversations of this sort with Wesley before, and they continued to worry and surprise him. Why was that, he wondered now. Why should he expect all fellow-academics to share his own kneejerk liberal tendencies? Possibly because in Britain most of them did. But Wesley, having pulled himself laboriously up by his bootstraps—his father had been a car worker in Detroit, and none of his family had ever been to college before—felt only impatience with underdogs. If they chose to remain that way, then so much the worse for them. Charles remembered how astonished he had been when, fairly early in their acquaintance, these attitudes of Wesley's had emerged. Until that moment he had more or less assumed that everyone he knew shared his own world-view, though, since this was largely unspoken, this hypothesis had rarely been put to the test. But he would have been shocked and surprised to find that any of his friends actually voted Conservative. Then Wesley came along, who shared so many of Charles's interests and obsessions—and was a conservative, though, being American, not, of course, a Conservative; and Charles was duly shocked and surprised. Essie, who did not share Wesley's views on politics, laughed at his innocence. But they had remained friends for the same reasons as Wesley and Essie remained married—because, in spite of everything, they liked each other and did not see too much of each other. Goodwill plus inertia: the same glue, when you came down to it, as cemented Charles and Belinda—and how many other married couples? Keep off politics, that was the thing.

They pulled up in front of the psychology labs. Wesley slid the car into a reserved parking bay and led the way into the building, a stone and glass block now five years old whose erection had been largely the result of his energetic propaganda work among rich alumni. The air-conditioning serving countless computers whirred as Wesley led the way from one purpose-built complex to another. From time to time he would stop and chat with white-coated figures, urging, encouraging, noting, suggesting. These were the stuff upon which Wesley's dreams of glory were founded. He instituted lines of inquiry, he oversaw their pursuit, he rushed round the world raising funds and generating publicity. How could all this fail to redound mightily to his credit?

Charles, whose empire had recently expanded from two rooms to two and a half, viewed this activity as one might view a Martian. It was alien and inexplicable to him. Voluntarily to give up the quiet and pleasurable pursuit of knowledge for this orgy of organization—how could anyone bear to do it? However, he did not therefore kid himself that Wesley was without intellect. He was a powerful and sometimes original thinker. It was simply that he was increasingly unable to face the inevitable prerequisite of most thought, viz., solitude and quiet. To be alone for any length of time made him uneasy.

Wesley now opened a door at the end of a suite of rat-lined labs and beckoned Charles into his study. Here all was light and civilization—bookshelves, plant-encrusted windows. He shut the door behind them and locked it, so that the only means of access was now through his secretary's room. He stuck his head through her door and said, 'Hi, Ellen. I want to talk with Charles here for a while. Can you make sure no one disturbs us? Any crises, I'll be free by midday.' Then, carefully shutting this door also, he turned to Charles.

CHAPTER 7

'Peace at last,' said Wesley, and threw himself into his chair, his feet on the desk. Charles sat down more cautiously in an armchair facing the window. He felt uneasy, as though he were on trial in some way. On the lake opposite the window an eight was practising. He felt an irrational yearning to be out there—anywhere but in here.

'So tell me what happened,' Wesley now said.

'What happened?'

'Yeah. One day you give me the brush-off. Life's good. The day after that you call to say you can't get here quick enough. *Something* must have happened.'

'Well, you know that work I've been doing with Bertha—' and Charles told Wesley the whole sad tale of the frustrations of working, or trying to work, at EMU in the present political climate. 'Though I can hardly expect you to sympathize,' he added. 'They're your sort of people.'

'Only in some ways. Well. Poor old Chuck.' Wesley lay back, considering.

'So that's me. What about you? Here I am, and I still don't know what you were so excited about.'

'No-o.' Wesley was uncharacteristically hesitant.

'Well, come on. What is all this? I thought it was supposed

to be so mind-blowing. You can't suddenly feel shy about it now.'

'Nope.' Wesley still seemed at a loss for words, however. 'It certainly is exciting,' he finally agreed. 'It's a breakthrough.'

'So what is it?'

'What was the really interesting thing about this work you were going to do?' Wesley said.

Charles was taken aback. 'I don't know—it was all—I suppose, the chance to work with the girl. To really find something out—'

'Well, that's just what I can offer you.'

'How d'you mean?'

'I'll tell you. But first off, let's get a few things straight. What I'm going to tell you is strictly between us. OK? It isn't to be talked about. Period. Not to anybody at all.'

'All right.'

'OK.' Wesley gestured towards the door which led to the rat-room. 'Working with rats has its advantages, right? They're not bulky, they breed fast, they're intelligent and adaptable. But there comes a point when you have to move on.'

'True.'

'So what happens then?'

'Depends what you're doing.'

Wesley sighed, as if he was dealing with a not very bright pupil. 'So why did you choose to work with Bertha all that time?'

'You couldn't do that kind of work with rats. What I'm interested in is how people's brains work.'

'So you chose a chimp because that's about as near as you can get within what's allowable.'

'That's right.'

'And what's the advantage working with the girl has over working with a chimp?'

Charles stared. 'What d'you mean, the advantage? The whole point is to find out what happens with people—what people are capable of. I might have been able to help her to see—though exactly what sort of seeing I don't know.'

'But she'd have been able to tell you.'

'Yes, of course.'

'Well, that's it, isn't it?' said Wesley. 'Human beings can speak. They can tell you what's happening to them. You don't have to deduce it.'

'Yes.'

'You still don't see what I'm getting at?'

'Not really.'

'OK. Why do we waste our time on rats and chimps? Why don't we just work with people?'

Charles stared. 'Are you seriously asking me that?'

'Sure.'

'Well.' Charles enumerated the reasons on his fingers. 'One. Not being Nazis with access to concentration camps full of untermenschen, we neither have the facilities to experiment on people, nor would we if we could. Two—well, that's the beginning and the end, really. But there are other smaller reasons. It isn't easy to find control groups of people with the kind of conditions we're interested in. If we do, it's a sort of freakish gift—like that hospital full of people who'd got encephalitis in 1920. How often d'you find something like that?'

'It isn't that easy to find chimps these days,' Wesley pointed out. 'They're an endangered species. Not to speak of all those animal rights freaks.'

'Then we'll have to think of something else. Computer simulations.'

'It's not the same.'

'No, it's different. Look, Wesley, what is all this? If this is leading where it seems to be leading, I'm not sure I want to hear any more.'

Wesley shook his head. 'Don't be silly. I'm not some sort of monster. I'm not proposing to dragoon long-term prisoners into acting as guinea-pigs for dubious experiments.'

'Then what are you proposing? You still haven't told me.'

'The fact is,' said Wesley, 'that there are some areas where it's simply not possible to work with animals.' He removed his feet from the desk and leaned forward over his desk, looking serious. 'With the best will in the world, we can't do it.'

'Such as?'

'I'll give you a for instance. Memory. Where it is, how it works.'

Charles stared at him. 'That's an old chestnut, isn't it? I didn't know you were interested in that.'

'A lot of people are interested in that.'

'So it seems,' said Charles, remembering his conversation with Peter Fischer. He recalled, too, Fischer's insistence that he, Charles, should not rely on the indefinite continuance of his cosy working conditions. He was already feeling uneasy; now he began to feel almost frightened. Too many things seemed to be slipping into place: he had the sensation that he had been living in some kind of illusory world whose main feature—also illusory—was the sensation he had hitherto entertained that he was acting of his own free will. He hadn't responded to Fischer's offer at that lunch. Indeed, he had clearly showed that he was most unlikely to be tempted by anything emanating from that particular source. No doubt that had come as no surprise. Too much had emerged about the routine surveillance of politically awkward customers during the past few years for him to imagine that his own support for anti-nuclear and civil liberties movements had gone unnoticed. He had made no secret of any of that— why should he?—nor of his instinctively anti-militaristic and anti-authoritarian attitudes. Charles knew that some people—his daughter Caroline, for instance—thought all that side of him was rather childish, a harking back to the rebel-littered 'sixties of his youth. Wesley probably thought so, too. So, as voluntary means had failed, the coercion at which Peter had hinted had become necessary. Pressure had been applied through Harold Hawkins. Charles wondered if Harold was aware of what was happening. He thought probably not. He wouldn't have needed much urging— probably nothing had given him more pleasure recently than laying Charles's carefully-laid research plans in ruins. As for Wesley, he must be in on all of this, too.

'What made you ring me up like that all of a sudden?'

Charles now inquired. 'Who told you I might be interested?'

'Someone mentioned your name in some connection,' Wesley replied. 'I don't recall just who. What d'you think this is, some sort of conspiracy?'

'Not really,' Charles lied. 'It's just that I had a conversation about—memory—not so very long ago with someone else. Must be in the air.'

'Oh? Who was that?'

'No one you'd know. Not in our field. Anyhow, go on. What's become so interesting about memory all of a sudden?'

'Transplants.'

'What?'

'You heard. Transplants.'

Charles got up and stood in front of the window. The rowing eight was still on the lake. The sun was shining. Trees were beginning to bud. It was the same normal, apparently sane world he had imagined he himself inhabited—until he stepped into this madhouse off the rat-room.

'Wesley,' he said. 'I can't believe I'm really hearing this. I've known you for most of my adult life. We may not agree about everything, but I know you're a damn good neurobiologist, just like I know I'm a good psychologist. And we both know that memory transplants are like— like—' he searched for a metaphor—'like the tooth-fairy. People like to believe in them, but everyone knows they can't exist. Even if there was some way of dealing with the purely technical problems, nobody thinks memory's like that any more. It isn't like speech or smell or something, located in one particular part of the brain. It's everywhere, cells firing all over the place. Different memories in different places. I don't know why I'm telling you all this. You know it as well as I do.'

'Yup. I know all that.'

'Well, then, what are you talking about?'

'*You* know it. *I* know it. But there are a lot of people out there who don't know it and what's more don't want to.'

'There are a lot of people who believe in spirit guides and life after death. What have they got to do with us?'

Wesley swivelled his chair round so that he, too, was looking out of the window. 'Charles, why was it you came over here?'

'I told you. Things became impossible.'

'When you say that, you mean that you realized you wouldn't be able to go on any longer the way you were. Doing your research and a little congenial teaching on the side.'

'More or less, yes.'

'Do you think many people are able to do that? To do just what they want?'

'Some. I don't regard it as an indictable offence.'

'Absolutely. But generally speaking, that's more the way things were than the way they are now. Wouldn't you say so? You may think that's altogether a bad thing. I probably agree with you. But if we're just talking about facts, that's a fact.'

'I suppose so.'

'OK. Now, I guess you think on the whole things are different here.'

'There's more money around.'

'There is, though not as much as you'd think. Most of the big universities are publicly funded, and we all know about the federal deficit. And most of the private ones, like Jones, are enormously in debt. Two million this year at Jones, can you believe it? So it's not too dissimilar, though I agree one doesn't get the feeling that the government's actually against education the way they seem to be in Britain. But the pressures are there. Hardly anyone has money to burn these days.'

'When you say hardly anyone, do I take it you mean there is someone?'

'A few. Texas oil millionaires. And the military. But that's about it.'

'And which of those is interested in memory transplants?'

'You got it. In fact it's the military.'

Charles felt that cold shiver again. He heard Peter Fischer's voice saying, 'I've made it my business to keep informed about you.' He said, 'Why, particularly?'

Wesley shrugged. 'Why does any general want anything? Because he thinks someone else has got it already.'

'Well, in this case he's wrong, isn't he?'

'I don't know. They seem pretty convinced.'

'Who seems convinced of what?'

'The guys I spoke to—that's to say, the guys that spoke to me. They are convinced that the other guys have done it already.'

'Which other guys? Not the Russians these days, surely?'

Wesley said nothing.

'But . . .!' The pictures this conjured up were at the same time so preposterous and so appalling that Charles could, for a while, think of nothing to say. This would explain Peter Fischer's sudden interest in the subject, no doubt. 'But I thought we were all supposed to be friends these days,' he offered weakly. 'No more cold war. No more spies.'

'Perhaps they're thinking of someone else,' Wesley observed impatiently. 'How do I know who the enemy is these days? I'm not a general.'

'But what use . . .? Militarily? I don't see it.'

'It sure would be an efficient form of debriefing. I'm not necessarily talking about transplants. But in order to do that you'd have to know all about the exact location of memory, and the mechanism, and once you know that, why, then you can access it. In the right conditions. I guess that's their thinking.'

'You sound almost as if it's yours.'

'I'm neutral on this. My experience tells me I agree with you, it's fairy-tales. But these are guys who generally know what they're talking about. But that's not the point.'

'No? So what is the point?'

'The point is that this is the last repository of the old academic life.'

'What? The military? Making you sign papers to keep everything secret?'

'Not that bit of it, I agree. But the last chance to be left in peace with your inquiries. Here's the cash, there's your research, just carry on and see what you get. And this isn't a dictatorship, after all. If you don't get the results, there's no come-back. You don't get shipped off to Siberia or someplace. Maybe you won't get another contract, but that's always the chance you take. And, and. No worries about teaching, student assessments, tenure, all that drag. And no limit on the facilities. How does that sound?'

'I should have thought you had all the facilities you needed already right here.'

'Yeah. That brings me back to where we began. Suitable experimental subjects.' Wesley sat for a moment in silence, swivelling his chair thoughtfully from side to side. 'You see,' he began. 'The fact is. Well, there're a hell of a lot of people who are only too glad to offer themselves as material for experiments.'

'What on earth d'you mean?'

'You know how it is,' said Wesley, warming to his theme. 'Maybe you hit hard times for a while. Or maybe you want a little extra for something special—to put a kid through college, let's say. Anyhow, I can tell you that—well, maybe they aren't standing in line exactly, but there's no shortage of people who would be only too pleased to help us. And that's a fact. I've talked to them.'

For a while Charles could think of nothing to say. There seemed no response he could make that would be remotely appropriate either to what Wesley had just been saying or to what he felt about it. After a while he said, 'It all sounds highly unethical.' The words echoed weakly round the room.

'What's unethical about it? This isn't some Dr Mengele operation. These are people who know what they're in for and they're only too happy to cooperate. They know what's on offer. In some cases, it means security for the rest of their lives. It's a big thing for them. And it could be a big thing for us, too. Think about it, Charles. It's a wonderful opportunity. We can do the army's work, but we can do our own as well. I wanted to share it with you. You're my oldest friend.'

'I don't know what to say,' said Charles. 'It's very kind of you, of course. But I can't see myself doing it.'

'What's the alternative? Spending the rest of your life

doing Harold Hawkins's dirty work at East Midlands? Do me a favour, Charles. Don't be hasty. You're committed to a few months over here anyhow. Just let me show you round. You'll like what you see. I promise.'

CHAPTER 8

Charles spent the next couple of days finding somewhere to live and procuring some wheels. He found himself quite well-off, because in addition to his usual salary in England Wesley had found some money to pay him for a short time from an overseas visitors' fund attached to his department. He was at present quite uncertain how long he would stay. His instinct was to head straight back across the Atlantic; but, as Wesley had pointed out, there seemed little to be gained from doing this. Meanwhile he felt an urgent need to find a place of his own, both so that he could take a more independent stance vis-à-vis Wesley and so that he could see Lulu. He knew he ought not to encourage her, especially after that unnerving conversation about Belinda and what was to be done about her. She ought to have a boyfriend of her own age. Nevertheless, logic does not rule on these occasions and Charles kept finding his mind dwelling longingly on other aspects of their encounter in the Mitchell guest-room. He keenly looked forward to an independent bedroom and telephone. Perhaps affected by guilt, he had phoned Belinda a couple of times. It seemed so improbable that she could be the object of the kind of cool speculation in which Lulu had been indulging. Everything seemed to be going on as usual in Leamingworth. Belinda told him that the weather was lovely. She seemed pleased to hear that he was getting on well and that Wesley had some interesting (unspecified) projects afoot. She did not say how much she missed him or that the house felt empty without him, neither did she suggest that she might fly over to join him if this turned out to be a prolonged visit; on the contrary, she seemed at pains to assure him how well she was managing on her own. Charles registered these facts in a vague sort of way.

He was due to view an apartment some way away at eleven o'clock; it was now a quarter to, and Essie, who was going to drive him there, was shouting from the car. They ought to be on their way.

They drove to the apartment, one and a half rooms in a fairly seedy part of town. Essie looked at it doubtfully. 'You know there's no need. You could stay with us, no sweat.'

But it was cheap, and Charles did not propose to spend much time in it. He said, 'I'll take it.'

'You must come and have lots of meals with us. Keep me company when Wesley's away.'

'I'll do that.'

Two days later he was installed, and an old Ford occupied the apartment's parking spot. The place was impersonal: it contained a bed, a table with two chairs, an easy chair; in the kitchen there was a stove, a fridge, a worktop with units under. Both rooms faced on to a street lined with similar apartment houses. There was mustard-coloured shag carpet and a matching mustard-coloured telephone, without shag. Essie had lent him some knives and forks and a bright blanket to cover the bed; he went out and bought some cheap Japanese crockery, some glasses and some liquor. He sat down in his new kingdom and called Lulu's dorm. She was out; he left his number and went to find Wesley at the lab, as they had arranged.

Wesley was anxious to show Charles the delights and temptations of the new project as soon as possible. But this was not easy to arrange, because Wesley's calendar, in contrast to Charles's, which was largely blank, was tightly packed with engagements made months before. He was due to speak at a conference in Canada next day; thence he would fly to Florida and on to Mexico City. Then he was back at Jones for a week before paying a visit to France, where he was coordinating a duel project with a laboratory at the University of Montpellier. Then back to Jones for two weeks before another date in California . . . 'But, Wesley,' said Charles, 'when do you ever have time to do any work?'

'I see my job primarily as coordinator, ideas man. It's important to keep the profile high. You get good people, you raise funds.'

'But what do you *do*? I see your name on a hell of a lot of papers.' Charles, like everyone else, knew the rumours about Wesley's lab, but he couldn't believe that anyone would be allowed to exercise seigneurial rights over other people's work to quite this extent. What was in it for the workers?

Wesley said amiably, 'Look, without me there wouldn't be this place here, none of these people would be here, there simply wouldn't be any work getting done. It's down to me: in the end it's my responsibility. By the way, Charles, I have some interesting news for you.'

'What's that?'

'I came across a boy with exactly the sort of lesion you were describing. Happened to be talking to his physician at a conference. Now if you'd be interested, I could put you in touch. It happens to be quite near where we've got to go to see that project I was telling you about. You could do the work over here just as well as over there.'

'That's very interesting, of course. But I'm not interested in it being published under your name.'

'Come on, Charles, don't be silly, of course there's no question of that. These are very junior people, my name helps them get published. Surely you realize that?'

So Charles agreed to meet the boy and his physician; Wesley would introduce them, and this would happen in two weeks' time, when they would make their trip to the project. As to where that was, Wesley was not saying. All Charles knew was that this work did not take place at the Jones psychology labs, and that none of the staff there knew about it. 'It's top secret,' Wesley said. 'You're the only person I've told. We're only interested in a few particular people.' Once again Charles was reminded of Peter Fischer: 'We're only interested in the best,' he had said.

*

Left to himself over the next few days, Charles felt rather out of place at the laboratory. Everybody else, though friendly enough, had his or her own project. Charles had been allotted a small office. It contained a desk and a phone; he sat there and felt redundant. Lulu had not called him back: perhaps he had offended her in some way that first night. It wouldn't be surprising, the way he'd felt. He felt, among other things, homesick. He wondered what Belinda was doing now; even the prospect of Harold Hawkins and his boring chores was better than this. He told himself that unless something of remarkable interest transpired, he would go home after the projected trip with Wesley. The whole thing sounded rather distasteful, to put it mildly, but he could hardly refuse to go now, and anyway, he felt curious. And there was this boy. It would be nice to do the work Harold had tried to stop. He suddenly felt a deep desire to talk to Belinda. He lifted the phone and dialled the number of the house in Leamingworth, but there was no reply. He let the phone ring for a long time, imagining it belling on as it sat on the old chest in the familiar hallway. He looked at his watch. Eleven-fifteen; that would make it quarter past four, she was probably out in the garden if it was a nice day.

Soon he could stand it no longer and wandered out into the campus. Walking towards the library his heart missed a beat: there was Lulu, walking towards him. She was with a girlfriend, but at least no young man was in tow. As they drew level it seemed as if she was merely going to smile and pass by. What would he do then? Turn and run after her? In his present state of mind he almost felt he would. 'Hi, Charles,' she said brightly, and then, 'Josie, Charles and I have to discuss something. I'll be right along.' Charles felt he had never heard words sound so musically in his ears.

'Did you get my message?' he asked.

'Your telephone number? Sure I did. I've been rather busy. So you got a place of your own?' She gave him a bright smile.

'I thought that would be a good idea.' Lulu, for some

reason, wouldn't meet his gaze. 'I thought you loved me. Those were your words.'

'I do,' she muttered, still not looking at him. 'But I thought I'd better try not to, maybe. Like you said, we're not getting anywhere.'

Had he said that? Charles felt as though he had been slapped, hard, across the face. Perhaps he was going to cry. His last link with sanity was about to break. 'Please,' he said. 'Don't talk like that. You can't break it off now. I couldn't bear it. I only got this place because of you. At least come and see me in it.'

Lulu hesitated, then gave in. 'OK, I guess we ought to have a talk. I don't usually bother with lunch, but why don't we live dangerously and break the precedent? You can give me lunch.'

Charles wrote out the address. 'Do you have wheels? It's a bit of a way.'

'Sure I have wheels, I have a bicycle. I'll see you later.'

Lulu disappeared in the direction of her class. Charles walked towards State Street and its varied provision shops. His homesickness had vanished miraculously, banished by the prospect of an afternoon with Lulu. Talk about being in love––he was clearly as much afflicted by the condition as she was. Perhaps she was right. Perhaps he should cut his losses and his ties and marry her. What use was it living half a life?

When he got home, the phone was ringing. He rushed to it. Must be Lulu: something had happened, she couldn't come. He found to his dismay that his heart was pounding as hard as if he had just sprinted a hundred yards. So much for middle-aged indifference and disapproval.

Wesley's voice said, 'Oh, hi, Charles, I was just about to give up. Look, I had a cancellation, we can visit the project earlier than I thought.'

'Oh.'

'Like I thought we could take off straight away, if that suits you.'

'Oh—well—'

'You got something fixed?'

'I've got a lunch date.'

'Can you cancel it? I'd like to get off as soon as we can.'

'I'm afraid not. I've got no way of reaching the person I'm lunching with.'

'OK. I can see it's rather short notice,' Wesley allowed. 'Will you be through by two? I'll come and pick you up. You'll need an overnight case.'

'My date's not till one.'

'Sorry, Chuck. You'll have to make it a quick lunch. Science calls.'

Charles looked miserably at the brown paper sacks of delicacies littering the table beside him. He'd even bought a lobster. There hadn't been any need for hurry. Why had he rushed home, then rushed to answer that damned telephone? Then he reflected that if he hadn't taken the call, there was a fair chance Wesley would have come round looking for him, and interrupted him and Lulu—well, the thought didn't bear thinking. As it was, he'd have a job explaining why he hadn't mentioned his date with Lulu, should this ever transpire. Not that it was any of Wesley's business. He wondered again how he'd feel if he discovered that Wesley and Caroline . . . Well, that was different, somehow. The thought of Caroline as a sex object was not an easy one to conjure up. She was so sensible. Surprise would be his chief emotion, he decided; that and a certain— well, relief was not too strong a word—at this proof that his daughter, too, was capable of lapses. But he had to admit that this reaction was almost certainly tempered by his own circumstances. Wesley's views about himself and Lulu would probably be quite different. Anyhow, that was one embarrassment that everyone could do without. For a moment he wondered how quickly it was possible to eat lobster mayonnaise; but that, too, was not only impractical but a waste. Far better to make Lulu a present of the lobster and rush out to the deli for a quick corned beef sandwich.

He looked at his watch. It was nearly one o'clock. He unpacked the paper sacks and sorted the contents into perishables and long-term prospects. Lobster, fruit, cheese—Lulu would have to take all that with her. Crackers, a jar of olives, little cans and jars of delicious oddments, all went into his fridge; the rest he returned to the sacks. Then he took up his position by the window, ready to intercept Lulu the moment she arrived.

But in fact he wasn't aware she was in the building until he heard her footsteps outside his door. She must have parked her bicycle round the corner where he couldn't see. He opened the door.

'Hi, Charles,' she began brightly.

'Look, Lulu—' Not only no time for serious talks. No time for lunch, either. 'Let's go out. We can't eat here. I'll explain in the deli. There's one just round the corner.'

'What is this?' She sounded, not unreasonably, both annoyed and surprised. 'In my parents' house I could understand it, but here—? What have you got, hidden microphones? Don't tell me. Wesley's bugged the place.'

'Not as far as I know, but almost as bad. He's on his way round. There's some trip he and I were going to do in a couple of weeks and he's suddenly set on starting off this afternoon. He called just as I got in.'

'Oh God. Just as we managed to get together.' They hugged each other, then let go. No good starting on that— time would pass without them even noticing. Charles felt like a starving man before whom a delicious feast is displayed, just out of reach. 'Let's go,' said Lulu. 'We'll meet again just as soon as you get back.'

CHAPTER 9

Charles returned to his apartment to find Wesley's car parked at the front door and Wesley himself leaning impatiently out of the window. It was five past two.

'Thought you'd skipped out on me.'

'I told you, I had a lunch date. You can't expect everyone to jump every time you have a change of plan,' said Charles crossly. Lucky Lulu had left her bicycle around the corner.

'I'm sorry, Charles. I know that's what it must seem like,' said Wesley, not sounding very sorry at all. 'But you know what my schedule's like, and I'm so keen that you should see this place, it just seemed like a wonderful opportunity. Did you pack a bag?'

'No. I had to leave just after you called.'

'OK, well, we have ten minutes. You just need stuff for a couple of days.'

'Where're we going?'

'Just to New York. Shall I wait down here?'

By three-thirty they were at Boston airport; by four, in the shuttle.

In the car on the way to the airport the two men had scarcely spoken. Each had been lost in his own thoughts. Now, sitting in the plane drinking vodkas and tonic, Charles began to feel better. Perhaps this was what he needed—to get right away from all of them, Hawkins, Lulu, the lot of them. Hadn't he, only that very morning, sitting in his empty, eventless office, been wishing he were anywhere but Southampton, Mass? Then again, he was irredeemably fond of old Wesley in spite of his unspeakable politics and his steamroller ways—because of them, almost: they were part of the conscious act, the manufactured front, which Wesley offered the world much as the hermit crab offers a whelk's shell. That there was another Wesley—a far more complex and considering creature—he felt certain, if only from the delicacy and persistence of his work in the days when Wesley used to do his own work, when, indeed, they used to work together. When Lulu and Caroline were babies and Charles and Wesley thankful refugees from the domestic life.

'So tell me all about this place,' he said.

'Which place?'

'For Christ's sake, Wesley. The place we're going, of course.'

'Sorry. I was miles away. Yeah. Well, you know what I was talking to you about. Memory.'

'You mean this is where they do the transplants?' Charles hooted with laughter.

'Shh.' Wesley looked round nervously.

'Sorry. I'll be more respectful in future. But it's such a load of rubbish, isn't it? Be honest. I won't tell.'

'Look, do me a favour, Charles, keep your voice down. You never know who's listening. As for rubbish, I'm not so sure, and nor will you be, when you see what's going on.'

'You mean they're actually doing them?' Charles remembered the other thing Wesley had talked about, using human subjects. He started to feel uneasy and a little sick. Maybe he should lay off the vodka. 'Where is this place?'

'You'll see.'

When they arrived in New York, Wesley surprised Charles by taking the airport bus into the city. That wasn't like him—it would have been more normal for him to take a taxi, or rent a car. But he brushed off these suggestions, saying that the bus was just as quick. Well, maybe it was; or maybe—Charles conjectured—he wanted to cover their tracks, make sure no cab-driver or car rental company would be able to produce any evidence that Wesley Mitchell was here. That sounded paranoid, but Wesley was behaving in a thoroughly paranoid way. Charles had even caught him glancing over his shoulder, as if to make sure they weren't being followed—or possibly to make sure they *were*. Charles glanced over his own shoulder. No very obvious follower was in evidence, but then they wouldn't be, would they?

They crowded on to the bus and rattled off, and Charles tried to put these rather absurd thoughts out of his mind. Instead he concentrated on looking out of the window. Even after all these years of transatlantic visits he always enjoyed his first glimpse of the famous New York skyline. Yes—there it was, the magical towers against the pale blue sky: he felt a surge of excitement, as he always did. Wesley, beside him, was deep in some technical journal. Charles felt rather childish.

The bus dropped them at Rockefeller Center, and Wesley plunged into the subway. They took a downtown express, and changed to a local at Jay Street. Now Charles was quite lost—Brooklyn was, as far as he was concerned, a desert

wilderness. Names of stations meant nothing to him—
Bergen Street, Atlantic Avenue, what were they?

After about twenty minutes Wesley led them off the train
and out of the subway. Charles missed the name of the
station; he was too busy making sure he didn't lose Wesley,
who was walking very fast—another manifestation of paranoia? They emerged at the corner of two wide, grey
thoroughfares. The streets here had, to Charles's eye, no
distinguishing marks: they could have been any city streets,
anywhere. The north–south arm of this crossroads seemed
distinctly seedy, lined with run-down druggists and food
stores whose windows were protected by thick meshes of
metal. Wesley turned right along the western arm, however,
and this, as they walked along it (still at high speed) became
more salubrious. There were a number of specialist food
shops—a cheese shop, a bagel shop, several well-stocked
fruit and vegetable shops run by Koreans, some of these
with large displays of expensive-looking flowers outside.
The streets running off on either side were lined with trees,
and contained brownstone houses with steep flights of steps
up to the front door. Several of them had builders' skips
outside: signs of a neighbourhood on the way up, reinforced
by the presence of a number of antique shops along the
main avenue. Wesley marched along at a brisk pace.

They passed a forbidding-looking place, a high school,
shut up now for the night—no evening classes today, or
maybe at all—its doors and windows armoured as if to repel
an army. This sinister dark grey hulk recalled a battleship,
squatting toad-like along its block. Across the road, as if to
point up the comparison between the bad old world of the
neighbourhood's previous history and the brave new one of
its latest wave of occupants, stood a marble-clad skyscraper,
its ground floor occupied by a bank. This, apparently, was
Wesley's destination.

A bank? Well, maybe Wesley felt he needed more cash.
But no: it was not the bank entrance he was making for,
but a door towards the back of the building. Wesley approached this with the assurance of long acquaintance and
held it open for Charles.

They were inside the vestibule which served the rest of the building, the offices and apartments (if any) which occupied the upper floors. Charles looked at the board on the wall by the elevators (there were three of them) to see where they might be making for.

Several different companies appeared to occupy the lower floors of the building. There was a firm of lawyers, a PR firm, one or two establishments whose names revealed nothing of what they might be engaged in. Floors 4–14, however, were all occupied by a single lessee, announced by the board as the Prospect Psychodynamics Center. That was all. There was no fifteenth floor.

Wesley called an elevator, one of two marked as serving floors 4 and above. 'Here we are,' he said, his first words, Charles realized, since they had entered the subway. They got in: Wesley pressed the button.

'Only one button?'

'That takes us to the reception area. There's a private elevator serving the rest of the building.'

'So we're going to the Psychodynamics Center, whatever that is?'

'I think you'll find it a most interesting place.'

They stood waiting while the elevator rose. The doors opened on a cream-carpeted area, as thickly set about with plants as the great grey-green greasy Limpopo River with fever-trees. Behind a cream-coloured desk a perfectly-finished girl sat typing, her silver-blonde head nodding to the rhythm of her gold-painted fingernails. She looked up as they entered.

'Why, hi, Wesley, I didn't know you were coming today.'

'It was kind of an impulse. Sue-Ann, this is Charles Watson, a colleague from Britain. He's going to help us with some work here, I hope.'

'Hi, Charles,' said Sue-Ann, flashing him a brilliant, impersonal smile.

The gates of the elevator closed softly behind them.

PART 2

CHAPTER 10

It felt like some sort of homecoming, Andrew Taggart reflected, as he pushed open the door of the temporary hut which had for the past fifteen years housed the Psychology Department at East Midlands University. He had been driving back to London from Nottingham, where he had been investigating a local government scandal for *New Politics*; and seeing the signs to Leamingworth, had decided on an impulse to revisit EMU, which had been the starting-point for one of his more spectacular journalistic coups. Not many of us are privileged to witness the reawakening of the dead, but this had been Taggart's lot when, in Santa Barbara, California, he had seen the delectable Dr Becky Ryan produce the apparently living body of the recently murdered Jasper Hodgkin live on stage. Both Becky and Jasper had been leading lights of EMU Psychology, and rumour had it that Jasper was still to be seen around the department from time to time. So, since he was passing (at least within twenty miles) Taggart, always compulsively sociable, thought he would drop in on the off-chance. It would be interesting to know what had happened to Jasper and even more interesting to find out about Becky, the object of his nostalgic lust. The last he heard she was going to get married; but marriages, and especially marriages to Texans, are not the enduring things they reputedly once were. There was always the chance she might be visiting the old place on her own, or even resuming her career as a single woman there (though he had to admit this was probably unlikely).

So here he was; and here, as he had really known all along she wouldn't be, she wasn't. Nor was Jasper. Nobody in the department could recall having seen him for some months. The general consensus was that he had finished his book about his adventures and had gone off to London or possibly California to sell it advantageously. Taggart had to admit defeat, and was just about to return to the car when he passed a door marked DR CHARLES WATSON.

At the back of his mind a memory stirred. He stood and stared at the door. Now what was it? Cogwheels rotated rustily in his brain. Finally a picture flashed before his mind's eye: the imposing entrance of the Reform Club in Pall Mall, and, descending the steps, that unlikely pair: Charles Watson, an intellectual inclined to left-wing causes, and Peter Fischer, whose path Taggart had crossed more than once at the Ministry of Defence, never to their mutual advantage. That had been the day he'd followed Fischer to Juliette Correa's flat. *That* affair—the Correa affair in general, not the particular one between her and Peter Fischer—had come to an end not long afterwards, on account of her abrupt translation to Rome, where, she was said to have asserted, she had been offered more interesting work. At any rate, her name had disappeared from the headlines and the gossip columns, for which many gentlemen were no doubt truly thankful.

Thinking about that unlikely conjunction again—the Watson/Fischer conjunction—Taggart's seasoned nose sniffed a story. And since he was here . . . He knocked on Watson's door. No reply. He tried it and found it locked. He looked up and down the corridor. No one was to be seen: the place seemed quite unpeopled. However, from the room next door he could hear voices. He knocked and opened the door. The voices stopped. Inside were two women, one young, one middle-aged, both obviously bored out of their minds with the piles of typing before them and eager for any distraction. 'I'm looking for Dr Watson,' Taggart said.

'Well, I'm sorry,' said the elder of the two women. 'He's away on sabbatical.'

'D'you know anyone who would know where he is?'

'I would if anyone did,' replied his interlocutor somewhat pettishly. 'I'm his secretary.'

'Ah. But you don't?'

'No. I said, nobody does.'

'Wasn't he going to America?' put in the younger woman.

Olive, Charles's secretary, looked annoyed. 'He was. But he isn't at his office there. I rang it.' She appeared to be outraged by life's cheek.

'Might you be able to give me the number?'

'Are you a friend of his?'

'My name's Andrew Taggart. Yes, I'm an old friend of his.'

At that moment the phone rang on Olive's desk. She picked it up, said, 'All right,' to it, and put it down triumphantly. 'Sorry, I must go,' she said. 'That was the professor.'

'Wouldn't he know . . .?'

'You'd better not mention Dr Watson's name to him,' said the younger woman, as Olive left the room without replying. 'They're not at all on good terms.'

'Does he have any family? Or have they all gone with him?'

'I wouldn't know,' said the girl. 'He did have a house in Leamingworth, I believe.'

Taggart retired. No doubt, if he persisted, he could get the American number. Olive could hardly refuse to give it to him. But Olive was occupied; and in the meantime he might as well try the Watson residence. If there was anyone there they would know Watson's whereabouts, or he might well be there himself for all anyone at the department seemed to know or care.

In a booth near the porter's lodge Taggart located a phone directory. Watson, C. Of course there was no guarantee it would be as simple as that—people list their phone numbers under the most unlikely initials, or else don't list them at all. But this might be it. C. W. Watson, West Street, Leamingworth. Taggart dialled the number. After a few moments someone picked up the phone. 'Hello?' said a woman's voice.

Bingo! Taggart pressed another 10p into the slot and said, 'Is that Mrs Watson?'

'It is.' The voice sounded wary: probably thought he was a double-glazing salesman.

'Mrs Watson, my name's Andrew Taggart, *New Politics*. I wondered if I might come round and see you? I'm in the area.'

'What about?'

'It's a bit complicated to explain on the phone.'

'Well, I suppose you could come round. It isn't as though I've anything very pressing to do. D'you know how to get here? We're just off the High Street.'

'I'll find my way,' Taggart assured her.

Driving to Leamingworth, he considered how best to approach her. On the whole he inclined towards the plain facts. It wasn't as though he had any axe to grind.

Leamingworth: the kind of place Taggart could not imagine living in. If the word 'provincial' meant anything, it meant this. A small town where streets of carefully-done-up period properties faced one another, only the occasional waggle of a lace curtain to give any indication of life within, while on the pavement comfortable matrons gossiped piercingly in the flat local accents. He parked on the main street and walked up and down until he located West Street.

Belinda Watson opened the door wearing her wasp-striped gardening sweater and faded jeans. 'Andrew Taggart?'

'It's awfully kind of you to see me, Mrs Watson.'

'Is it?' She seemed pretty crisp.

'Well, you don't know me—'

'I know your by-line. And frankly, in a place like this, any touch of real life's always welcome.'

'Why did you stay here then? I understand your husband's in America. Or is that an indiscreet question?'

'Not particularly, as far as I know. I didn't feel like going. Who wants to be a campus wife? Anyhow, Southampton, Mass., isn't very much more throbbing than Leamingworth. Provincial life's provincial life wherever you lead it.'

'Don't you like it?'

'It's where I live. Would you like a cup of tea? Then you

can tell me what all this is about.' She led the way into the kitchen. Taggart wandered over to the window.

'You've got a lovely garden.'

'That's one of the reasons I stayed.' She poured out two cups of tea and sat down expectantly.

'It's a bit of a long story and not very conclusive.'

'Go on.'

'Well, a few months ago I happened to be walking down Pall Mall and I saw a man I know slightly. Man called Peter Fischer—he works in the MOD. D'you know him?'

She considered. 'I think I used to. If it's the one I'm thinking of we used to work in the same place, about twenty-odd years ago. But I never saw much of him. I seem to remember he and Charles didn't get on.'

'You were in the MOD?'

'No, but I was in the Civil Service for a while years ago, before I married Charles. That was the time when the Civil Service was still very funny about employing married women. In case they got pregnant and wasted all that expensive training. Which I did.'

'Well, Fischer's someone I'm interested in. He's a very slippery figure. In charge of something called Special Projects.'

'What are they? I don't expect they existed in my day.'

'I expect they did, one way or another. They're not very tightly defined. They're what you care to make them, really—what Fischer cares to make them. Lines of knowledge which it might be interesting to develop further. Potentially useful possibilities.'

'And?'

'And last time I saw him, he was with your husband.'

'Charles?' She thought a moment. 'I seem to remember he did say something about meeting some civil servant who wanted him to work on some defence project. But he wasn't interested. Could that have been it?'

'I expect it might have been. I was surprised to see them together.'

'D'you know Charles?'

'Vaguely. I've seen him at the odd meeting. The occasional action committee. You know what a small world all that is.' He paused. 'But he wasn't interested, you say?'

'He's been very preoccupied with his own work recently. It would have taken something exceptionally interesting to tempt him away from that.'

'What work was that? Anything in particular?'

'The regeneration of the visual cortex. Doesn't sound like anything Peter Fischer would be interested in, does it?'

'And you think you'd know if he'd been doing anything different?'

'I suppose so. Though you can never be sure. Well, look what's happened now.'

'What has happened now?'

'Charles suddenly haring off to America like this. I mean, you can never tell when something's just going to get too much for somebody. For ages the professor's been trying to get him where he wants him, but he couldn't, because Charles's bit's more or less autonomous—or so I understood. But now because of all the government cuts it seems that Harold's won. No more time for research, nothing but dreary old teaching. So Charles gave him the two fingers and went off to the States.'

'Where exactly?'

'Jones College. It's in Massachusetts. One of those rich private foundations. He's got an old mate there—well, a friend of both of ours, really—who keeps on urging him to come over. All the facilities for research he wants, you know the kind of thing.'

'How long's he gone for?'

'Who knows? Depends how things turn out, I suppose.'

'But you don't fancy going there yourself?'

'Not in the least. Why should I? America doesn't suit me. Anyhow, the children are over here. I'd rather be near them and my garden.'

Taggart got up. 'It's been kind of you to see me, Mrs Watson. I'm sorry to have troubled you. You know how it is, one thing leads to another. I was in the department to try and find an old friend, and I saw your husband's name, and I suddenly remembered seeing him and Peter Fischer and I thought—well, it's always worth checking up on Fischer. You never know what you might not come across.' He fished a dog-eared card out of his wallet. 'Anyhow, here's my number. If you should ever want to get in touch.'

'If you ask me, there's nothing in it. Charles has seen the writing on the wall for ages, it just makes it neater to have a scapegoat. But if anything surfaces I promise I'll let you know.'

Taggart drove back to London feeling dissatisfied. There was something there—he was sure of it. But short of button-holing Fischer, which would clearly be entirely counter-productive, he could as yet see no way of finding out what it was. And short of his finding something out to back up his hunch, there was no way *New Politics* was going to find the money to send him to America to speak to Charles Watson. That was not the sort of operation it was. Its horizons were large, but its funds ran strictly to local government in Nottingham. One could have principles or one could have cash. And quite soon, thought Taggart, the way things are going, there won't even be the option. Cash or nothing, it's going to be quite soon.

Meanwhile, perhaps he should keep in touch with the crisp Mrs Watson. There was something about decisive, slightly derisive ladies that he had always found rather attractive, even if not in the knock-down manner of large blondes. And there she was all alone in that big house . . . He checked his book to make sure he had noted down the Watsons' phone number. He had.

CHAPTER 11

Now began a very peculiar interlude in Belinda Watson's life. It was a sort of punctuation. Until now, she had been able to define herself fairly easily in one way or another. Schoolgirl; student; civil servant; lover; wife and mother. It was true that the last two roles had, so to speak, faded somewhat over the past few years, but they were still extant for the purposes of self-description. But now—what? Now, all that seemed to be in abeyance.

To begin with there was, after an initial phone call and postcard to let her know he had arrived safely, no word from Charles. Normally this would have worried her. She knew that it ought to worry her now. But she was unable to make herself worry. This was because the absence of any indication of Charles's existence somehow confirmed the limbo in which she now found herself, quite alone in the big old house, her daughter in London, her son in Africa (he was taking a year off between school and university), her husband—who knew where? 'Doesn't it worry you, being all by yourself in that great big house?' friends and neighbours would ask her from time to time. But it did not worry her. On the contrary, it left her able to concentrate on the unexpected new development in her life: the entry into it of Andrew Taggart.

There was a curious disparity between the myth and the reality of Andrew Taggart's sex life. He himself colluded with his friends and acquaintances in putting about the story that it consisted almost exclusively of the fruitless pursuit of scornful Brunnhildes. There was of course more than an element of truth in this. Such indeed was the stuff of his fantasies, and, like most fantasies, they remained (with brief and usually unsatisfactory exceptions) unrealized. Both Taggart and his friends derived a certain amount of amusement, meanwhile, from the mere notion of a small, dark, grubby man panting yearningly after a succession of dismissive statuesque blondes. But this picture bore little relation to the facts; the facts being that Taggart was often rather successful with women. And this was not as surprising as it might have seemed. For, as everyone knows who has observed the process in action, a man's chances of success with women have almost nothing to do with his external appearance and almost everything to do with the application and enthusiasm with which he addresses himself to the task in hand. And if there were two qualities with which Taggart was liberally endowed, they were application and enthusiasm.

These qualities Taggart now devoted to the pursuit of Belinda. Driving back to London, he found he could not get her out of his mind. She was attractive, she was available—well, her husband was in America, so it could be assumed she was available—and she represented a challenge. Taggart liked challenges. A few days later, he phoned her.

'Mrs Watson? Andrew Taggart here. I find I've got to be round your part of the world again in a couple of days. I wondered if I might offer you some lunch.'

'Oh. Well, that would be very nice.' She sounded slightly stunned.

'Any good places you know?'

'It isn't exactly a hotbed of gourmets, but I expect I could think of somewhere if I tried.'

'All right, then, I'll come and pick you up at twelve-thirty. Day after tomorrow. Why don't you book us in somewhere?'

How long is it, thought Belinda, as she sat in the dining-room at the Falcon, since I've been in a situation like this? It was as unfamiliar to the present-day Belinda as the surroundings—red wallpaper, black beams, soup of the day, steak and Stilton—were familiar. To be regarded as a new and desirable person, an object of sexual interest even, rather than old Belinda always going on about her bloody horticulture, Mum to be confided in, Mother who was an embarrassment when she wasn't being an irresponsible nuisance, that rather terrifying Mrs Watson. She looked across at Taggart and regretted that he wasn't more attractive. Still, one can't have everything. If he had been God's gift to women, would he be sitting here now in a Gothic-horror provincial pub opposite a, well, a fading middle-aged lady with the remains of an excellent mind. And legs. And there was a certain glamour about lunching with someone whose by-line she'd read so often. And he was good company, no doubt about it. Over the soup he'd been regaling her with inside stories of some current and not-so-current political scandals. Some hair-raising episodes from his own career had followed with the steak. And now, as they sat over the cheese and a last glass of wine, giggling over some antique joke she'd dredged out, he suddenly said, 'You're a very attractive woman, Mrs Watson. Has anybody told you that lately?'

Had she been expecting it? It was at once the most and the least surprising thing in the world: the least, because it had been apparent from the start that he was intending to make a pass at her; the most, because of the extreme crudity of the ploy. And yet, what should he do? More to the point, what did she want to do? Various reactions were open to her. A shocked pretence that she did not understand and did not wish to understand what was going on? Well, that would be ridiculous. Of course she understood: that had been plain from the moment she accepted his invitation. She wasn't fifteen any longer, or starving. The only question was, were they or were they not going to end up in bed? If not, this was the moment to make it perfectly plain. All she had to say was, 'You're a very nice man, Mr Taggart, but I really don't want to go to bed with you. I just thought I'd make that clear now—'— or words to that effect.

Was that what she was going to do? Taggart's eyes twinkled at her from across the table. They were nice eyes, clever, crinkled with laughter. She couldn't remember when she'd last laughed so much as over this lunch. What had she got to lose? Her virginity?

'Not for a very long time,' she said. 'That isn't the kind of conversation I usually have with people these days.'

'Pity,' he said. 'Never mind. Have it with me. Where shall we go on with it? Your place?'

Some hours later, when they were both lying back contentedly contemplating the prospect of getting up for dinner, she said, 'Tell me. At home, is there a special dim light you use when you're trying to get someone into bed?'

Taggart flushed slightly. 'Well, as a matter of fact . . . How did you know?'

'I just guessed,' she said. 'From your opening gambit. Think nothing of it. It doesn't matter.'

Other considerations—such as those which had brought Taggart to visit her in the first place—receded into the background. Belinda found that she enjoyed Taggart hugely, in bed and out. She enjoyed not only everything they did together but the unfamiliar thought that it was she, Belinda, doing these things which would doubtless astonish her neighbours and family, if they hadn't been so busy doing their own version of them themselves. Relaxed and exhilarated—'It's excellent exercise,' Taggart assured her. 'Very, very good for you'— she found herself talking to him as she had talked to no one for years—indeed, ever: when had there ever been anyone she could talk to about Charles, to whom she could not talk; about Stuart, whom she loved so much but saw so little; about Caroline, who was a closed book to her? She talked a lot about Caroline, who worked in the City and was living with her banker in tension-filled luxury. There was a photograph of Caroline in a frame on the piano. Taggart had studied it from time to time. She looked very much like Belinda—Belinda as she had been when she married Charles: the same high cheekbones and rosy complexion, the same fine, straight brown hair—but whereas most photos of Belinda in her youth showed her smiling broadly, Caroline evidently preferred to keep her teeth to herself. Her expression as she confronted the camera was almost severe.

'She sounds terrific. I like stern ladies. That was what first got me really excited about you. You were so crisp and dismissive that first time I called.'

'I shouldn't bother to try, not with Caroline. She hates beards, and she'd insist on ironing your shirts. And she certainly wouldn't let you eat so many biscuits.'

Taggart preened the fringe of beard whose blackness emphasized the indoor white of his complexion, and helped himself to another biscuit. 'Health, who needs it. Still, she does sound wonderful.'

They met one morning, not by arrangement. Taggart and Belinda were sitting over a companionable cup of coffee— Taggart had a couple of days between stories and was spending them with Belinda—when the doorbell rang. 'Must be the postman,' said Belinda and, barefoot in her dressing-gown, went to open it. A young woman's voice said, 'Mother! Aren't you well?'

'Caroline, darling, of course I'm well, I just wasn't expecting anybody. You didn't tell me you were coming. Aren't you supposed to be at work?'

'Oh, I just couldn't—' said Caroline, and at that moment entered the kitchen and broke off abruptly at the sight of Taggart, clothed only in a pair of jeans, seated at the kitchen table drinking coffee. He gave her a pleasant smile which was not returned.

'This is Andrew Taggart,' said Belinda.

'I see.' Caroline looked as if she would have liked to leave immediately. She hovered on the threshold like a bird contemplating flight but uncertain of its power to achieve lift-off. If she had had some suspicions about her mother's current goings-on and had decided to try and catch her *in flagrante* she could not have arranged things better, but Belinda did not think this was what she had had in mind at all. It sounded more as if Caroline was in some sort of trouble and had wanted to talk about it. Belinda felt deeply guilty. She said, 'I'll just go and get dressed. Have some coffee, darling.'

When she got down, however, Caroline was still standing, though she had now moved to the window, and it was clear that not a word had been exchanged between her and Taggart, who now said, 'I'll see you sometime, Belinda. I must go.'

'Please don't,' said Caroline coldly. 'Not on my account.'

'No, I've got an article to write. Perhaps we'll meet again sometime.' He held out a hand, which was ignored, and left hurriedly with a wave to Belinda.

Whatever Caroline had come to say, she was clearly not going to say it now. She stood staring at her mother. 'Who was that?'

'I told you, Andrew Taggart. He's a journalist, you've probably heard of him.' Belinda put an arm round her daughter's shoulders, which Caroline shrugged off. 'Sit down, darling. Unwind. Have a cup of something. Would you prefer tea?'

'I don't want anything, thanks.' Caroline sat and stared miserably into space.

'Usury paying off nicely, then?' It was always the same. First Caroline made Belinda feel guilty, then angry, and then there would be these wretched exchanges which she ought to be grown-up enough to bite back, but never could.

'Mother, I do wish you wouldn't use that horrible word. I'm perfectly aware you don't like what Jonathan does, but somebody's got to do it, and why not him? What's wrong with being a banker anyhow?'

'Sorry. Things all right with the two of you?' Belinda suspected from the shrillness of her daughter's tone that they were not. Perhaps the affair with Jonathan was coming to an end. If so, that would be hard, because they worked in the same office. Perhaps that was what Caroline had come to talk to her about.

'Quite all right, thanks. Why?'

'Oh, I just wondered.'

There was a silence. Then Caroline said meaningfully, 'I wondered if you'd heard from Dad recently.'

This was the third or fourth time she had raised this particular question since Charles's departure, and Belinda found these inquiries increasingly irritating. Resentment, as usual, fuelled by guilt, the mixture as before. She was not upright, faithful, orderly, responsible, as Caroline was and would have wished her mother to be. Nor was Charles, of course, but that was beside the point. Where Caroline was concerned Charles could do no wrong. Belinda could do no right—a state of affairs not likely to have been improved by this morning's events. The point now was that Belinda had plenty to feel guilty about.

'No, as a matter of fact I haven't. Have you?'

'Not a thing. Don't you think we should do something about it?'

'What on earth d'you mean? I can't quite think of anything much one could do.'

'Mother, he left in April. It's September now. I'm sure you've got lots on your mind,' said Caroline sarcastically, 'but I'm almost beginning to think you really don't care whether or not you ever hear from him again. Don't you think about him sometimes? After all, you've been married to him for twenty-odd years.'

'I can't say I'm particularly exercised, darling. I mean, no news is good news, isn't it, really? I'm sure we should have heard if something was wrong.'

'The truth is, Mother, you just don't care about him, do you?'

'Oh, I wouldn't put it as strongly as that. But if you mean does he fill my every waking thought, well, no, I'm afraid he doesn't, not any more. You wait till you've been with Jonathan as long as I've been with your father. Either you live your own life or you're an adjunct of somebody else's, and I've had enough of being an adjunct. I don't expect it'll ever happen to you, you don't have the kind of illusions I had at your age.'

'You could try ringing his office in America.'

'Why don't you, if you're so worried?'

'I did. There was no reply.'

'Well, then, there doesn't seem much point me doing it, does there?'

'Mother. You can't just sit there living off Dad's salary and not even give a thought to what's happening to him.'

'I do wish you wouldn't take this self-righteous tone all the time, darling. What else am I supposed to live on?'

The conversation ended in mutual dissatisfaction. Caroline accepted a light lunch and left without divulging the original motive for her visit. Belinda went out miserably into the garden and began to poke around with a trowel, but this activity did not bring with it the usual peace of mind. It was a lovely September afternoon, the kind of afternoon she lived in the country to enjoy, but she did not enjoy it. About half an hour after Caroline's departure, the phone rang. It was Taggart.

'She still there? Poor old thing, I'd have stayed if I'd thought it would do any good.'

'No, she left in a cloud of self-righteousness.'

'Oh dear.'

'She's always been very attached to Charles . . . And I suppose we didn't leave much to the imagination.'

'No. Still, that's hardly your fault. You're entitled to your own life. If your husband will go haring off to America . . .'

'That's another thing. She's always going on about have I heard from Charles.'

'Haven't you?'

'No.'

'Really? Not at all?'

'I had a card to tell me he'd got there, and a phone call. He told me he'd got a place to live and an office. Then I had a letter from Essie, the wife of the friend he's gone over to work with, saying he and Wes had gone off somewhere. And since then I suppose I haven't thought about it. Too much else to think about. You know how it is.'

'I know how it is.'

'Enjoying my long-lost youth at the age of forty-five. When I was young I was too busy being grown-up and responsible.'

'You were wasted,' said Taggart, with the assurance of one who knew what he was talking about. 'I should say you had a definite gift for irresponsibility in all its forms.'

'Thank you.'

'How long is it since you heard from Charles?'

'What is it now, September?'

'The tenth.'

'Months. Not since May. I suppose it is a long time, looked at like that.'

'Looked at any way at all. Your daughter does have a point. I suppose I should have mentioned it myself, but it's hardly my worry. I'm in no hurry for him to come back.'

'I suppose if I'm honest I've simply been averting my mind from him. Hoping all—this—could just go on and on. Of course I knew it couldn't, really. Apart from anything else, he's due back at the department. He only had a term's sabbatical.'

'Doesn't that make it even stranger, not hearing from him? I mean, either he's coming back any minute, in which case he'll want you to meet him at the airport or something, or he's decided to stay over there, in which case he'd have to let a few people know. Wouldn't he?'

'Mm. Yes, you're right. What d'you think I should do?'

'Much as it goes against my own interests, I think you should make a few telephone calls.'

'What, now?'

'Why not? What's the time? Quarter to seven, it'll be quarter to two on the East Coast. Try his office. Let me know what happens.'

Belinda by now felt not merely worried but almost panic-stricken. All the anxiety she had failed to feel over the past months flooded through her, its effect magnified by the guilts which assailed her on all sides—all those guilts which she had felt, hitherto, as little as she had thought about Charles. She hunted through her diary and dialled the endless strings of digits needed to connect her telephone with that on Charles's office desk on the other side of the Atlantic. As usual when she was flurried, she misdialled, then misdialled again; but finally, with the usual feeling of surprising ease, the phone could be heard braying at the other end. Then someone picked it up. Belinda's heart missed a beat.

A woman's voice said, 'Hello, psychology, Anita Frame speaking.'

'Is that Charles Watson's office?'

'No, I'm afraid it isn't.'

Belinda stared down at the number written in the diary in front of her. 'Are you sure? 2059?'

'This is 2059, but it's my office, and my name isn't Charles Watson. It may have been his; I've only been here since the beginning of the month. But I had the impression that before I came it was unoccupied,' said Anita Frame with that infinite politeness which distinguishes the American telephone manner and which is always so surprising to naturally boorish Europeans.

'I'm terribly sorry to bother you,' said Belinda, feeling the panic rise like bile. 'Do you happen to know where I might find Dr Watson?'

'I'm sorry, I don't know anyone of that name here.'

'Is that Wesley Mitchell's department?'

'That's correct.'

'Do you happen to know if Dr Mitchell's around today?'

'Yes, he is; he should be in his office. Would you like me to try and connect you? In case we get cut off, the number is 2033.'

After two interminable minutes another phone could be heard ringing. It was picked up almost at once. 'Mitchell,' said Wesley's voice, its tone indicating that he was a busy man loath to be interrupted.

'Wesley? This is Belinda Watson here.'

'Oh, hello, Belinda. Nice to hear you. What can I do for you?'

'Wesley, do you know where Charles is?'

'No, I'm afraid I don't. Don't you?'

'Why don't you? He went over to work with you, didn't he? And of course I don't. Would I be having this conversation if I did?'

'Now, Belinda, calm down. Sure I asked Charles to come here, and sure, he came. But then it seems he got interested in some other project and decided to move on. That would be about May. I haven't heard from him since.'

'Why didn't anybody tell me about this?'

'Hell, Belinda, I assumed he'd tell you. Am I some kind of nursemaid?'

'Sorry. I'm just rather worried. What was this other project? Have you any idea?'

'I'm afraid I don't. I'm afraid people like to keep secrets in this business. Science just isn't that open any more.'

'But, Wesley, he can't just have disappeared.'

'Well, of course he hasn't.'

'But he *has*! Nobody's got any idea where he is. How else would you define disappearing?'

'Belinda, I really wish I could help you.'

'Can't we do something? Get on to the police?'

'Are you kidding? An adult man decides to move on to a new job, that isn't a crime here yet. It isn't even a crime not to tell your wife, though I agree it's pretty darned stupid.'

'So what do you suggest I do?'

'I don't know. Get a private detective?'

'Thanks for being so much help.'

Taggart picked up his phone almost before it had begun to ring. 'So what's happened?'

'Apparently he left Jones last May. Wesley has no idea where he is. He doesn't seem a bit worried. The bastard! Fine sort of friend he is.'

'Be reasonable. You weren't worried yourself till about half an hour ago. What did he suggest?'

'Getting a private detective.'

Taggart had been thinking while Belinda had been making her transatlantic call. He hadn't asked about Charles much, simply assuming that Belinda was routinely in touch with him. But if she wasn't, then the whole business became suddenly more interesting. People don't just disappear for no reason. So what could Charles's reason be? Romance? That had been the reason Belinda hadn't divulged his failure to communicate. It was possible—what's sauce for the goose—but Taggart didn't believe it. To be passive—to fail to be communicated with—is one thing, but not to make a routine phone call, write the odd postcard, is quite another. If all that had happened was that Charles was having an affair with someone, then on the contrary, he would have been *more*, not less, assiduous about domestic routine. Or Taggart would, in his place. So it was something else. What? Taggart's mind went back to Pall Mall, to that unexpected conjunction that had caught his eye on the steps of the Reform Club. Was this something to do with Peter Fischer—some job Charles was doing for him, perhaps? Something that had gone wrong, maybe? Once more the scent of a story wafted before his nostrils. He said, 'I could go.'

'What d'you mean?'

'What I said. Much as it's against my interests. I'd back myself against a private detective any day.'

'But—'

'Listen. The way it would work is this. I've got to go over to the States anyway soon. There's some conferences I'm covering for *New Politics* and a couple of other papers. I always like to pick up a nice lot of stories when I'm there—make the most of it, and it's a chance to see some old friends. So why don't I combine that with having a look for Charles? Maybe there's a good story there, too.'

'Would you really?'

'I would, really. Now stop talking as if the world's about to end. We'll probably find he got an offer he couldn't refuse from a rival establishment down the road and your friend Wesley's so furious he can't bring himself to speak about it. Anyhow, admit it, you'll be sorry to see him back.'

'First I shall be glad,' said Belinda. 'First I shall be inexpressibly relieved. After that I shall be sorry.'

CHAPTER 12

The conference Taggart was attending on behalf of his employers turned out a lot more interesting than might have been expected from its subject—the new developments on the international scene and their impact on Western economies. This was not on account of any blinding revelations in the subject-matter, but because two of his fellow conferees turned out to be Peter Fischer and—Juliette Correa.

Taggart could hardly believe his eyes or his luck. Fischer—that was not so very unexpected. But La Correa? Surely Fischer wouldn't have been so indiscreet as to import her so publicly? Anyhow, wasn't she supposed to be in Madrid? Taggart went up to her, hand outstretched. 'Hello, Miss Correa. Nice to see you. Andrew Taggart—we met a couple of times in the House of Commons. Perhaps you don't remember—'

'Oh yes, of course.' God, she was gorgeous! Wonderful figure, shining black hair, and that extreme beauty of feature and complexion, the best of Indian and European worlds, which are found in some Goans. 'How nice to see you again.' She even lied delightfully. Taggart cast a glance across the room towards the place he had last glimpsed Fischer. He was still there, staring fixedly towards them. He looked horrified. Perhaps he hadn't been expecting her, then?

'I thought you were in Madrid.'

'I was, for a while, but then I was offered an even more interesting job here. I'm a political assistant to Congressman Collins.' She smiled brilliantly at him. 'He's just over there. This is one of his areas of particular interest.'

'And how do you like Washington?'

'Oh, I love it. Though of course there's nowhere like London.' Taggart made a mental note of this remark: he was already putting together the delightful piece he would soon file.

'Still, I expect you meet lots of old friends over here,' he said encouragingly.

'Oh yes, lots.' She smiled again, brilliantly and vaguely, and drifted away in the direction of her congressman. Taggart, too, drifted round the room, restraining himself from too obvious a glance in Fischer's direction.

This morning they were discussing the relations between international policy and the built-in inertia of the military–industrial complex—how the latter affected the former and whether the former could ever affect the latter. Not a new subject, but one of continuing interest to Taggart, and possibly the one where he and people like Fischer least saw eye to eye: Taggart seeing it as his duty to expose and undermine such relations, Fischer as *his* duty to stop Taggart doing any such thing. Generals droned on about the civilian benefits of military research and what a calamity it would be for the world should its shadow ever grow less. Taggart glanced at his watch. This particular get-together was not a long affair, simply an exercise in briefing and background. The presence of Miss Correa was a definite bonus but nothing worth delaying for unduly. A small excuse to continue with the persecution of Peter Fischer, an exercise he always enjoyed, but not one to be taken to excess. More to the point, should he speak to him about Charles Watson? The approach direct sometimes yielded results—but not, he suspected, in this case, where he would sacrifice all the advantage conferred by the fact Fischer didn't know Taggart had seen them together. After all, if Charles was doing some clandestine job for Fischer, then was he likely to tell Taggart all about it just because he asked? No, he wasn't.

At this moment he saw the very man making his way across the room towards him. He waved cordially, but Fischer did not look cordial. 'What are you doing here?' he asked, in the tones of a park-keeper who has caught a small boy stamping on the flowers.

'Reporting the conference. It's a subject of great interest to my paper.'

Fischer looked at him with dislike, even hatred. 'You'd better be careful what you say. I shan't hesitate to use the libel laws if you give me the slightest opportunity.'

'I can't imagine what you're talking about.'

'Huh!' Fischer, evidently unconvinced, turned on his heel and walked away.

Back to his hotel room after this and file his piece. Then he had a couple more interviews to do in Washington, a meeting with an old friend in New York, a couple of days pursuing the American end of a story about drugs and police payoffs, and then he would go on up to Jones to oblige Belinda. And possibly himself. But not Peter Fischer.

The general came to the end of what he had to say and a round-table discussion began to which neither Taggart nor Fischer contributed. Then there was lunch, after which would come the winding-up session. Enough was enough. Surreptitiously Taggart slid out of the building into the crisp sunshine. If the general was right only one in ten of the citizens presently seething around him did not make a living in some way influenced by military research. Who would want to kill off or divert the source of so much innocent well-being? Who did the general think he was kidding? Taggart made for the nearest telephone to see if he couldn't bring forward his interviews.

Two days later he arrived in Southampton, Mass.

He had deliberated for some time over what he should do once he arrived here. The obvious thing, of course, would be to go and see Wesley Mitchell. But Taggart felt curiously reluctant to do the obvious thing. Why should he think that the approach direct would get him any further than it had got Belinda—who, after all, had so much more obvious right to be making inquiries about Charles Watson's whereabouts? And Mitchell hadn't been able to help her. Or at any rate hadn't helped her. Why, then, should he help Taggart? No; snooping was called for. But where to start?

The hotel was set back among trees on one side of a wide street. On the other side was the Jones campus. It was mid-afternoon. Taggart decided to take a walk. He couldn't have fewer ideas than he had at the moment: perhaps something would come to him. He left the hotel and crossed over the road, sauntering along until he came to one of the monumental gates leading into the campus. Groups of girls and boys dressed in expensive casuals sauntered about. The girls were ravishing, enjoying the brief interlude of genuine youth which they would no doubt spend the rest of their lives trying to recapture. Taggart's heart beat faster. He heard Belinda's voice in his head: she had her own peculiarly bracing form of pillow-talk.

'I sometimes wonder about you, Andrew.'

And himself replying sleepily: 'Glad to hear there's still some mystery left.'

'No, really—the way you *fantasize* about women. All this bit about tall, masterful blondes.'

'What's wrong with that?'

'Well, it's like a schoolboy, somehow. Nothing to do with real life. A way of avoiding thinking about *people*. I sometimes wonder—Are you sure you're not gay?'

'Are you seriously asking me that? After—?'

'Oh, that's got nothing to do with it, not necessarily. The one doesn't preclude the other, not always, in fact quite often not, I believe. It's a question of where you feel emotionally engaged. I mean, all that sounds to me as though what you're doing is trying to distance yourself from real women.'

'Aren't you real?'

'I'm married. I'm safe. I'm not in the running. I just happened to be here, and this happens to rather suit us both. I'm certainly not a tall, masterful blonde, anyhow.'

'No, but you're so *stern* . . .'

At this moment his attention was distracted from both this remembered conversation and the delicious girls who had occasioned the memory by the sight of a man just entering a building a little way off to the right. The man's back was towards him, but it was a back he knew—indeed, one with which he had only recently become reacquainted as it turned itself ostentatiously towards him, indicating to everyone including Taggart that its owner not only did not wish to speak to him but strongly objected to finding himself in the same room, even. The back belonged to Peter Fischer.

Taggart wondered if Fischer had seen him. It seemed unlikely: none of the paths leading to the building he had just entered approached from a direction facing the point where he now stood: though of course he couldn't be sure. He wondered why he suddenly felt it was so important not to have been seen. The more imaginative chroniclers of the journalist's art would have said that this was the sixth sense which told him he was on to a story, the quality which sets the successful journalist apart from the rest; Taggart thought it more likely that he knew his natural enemies and wanted, if possible, to be the one to steal the march. He stopped a passing girl (a pretext but, alas, no time . . .) and said, 'Excuse me, what's that building?'

'That one over there?'

'The modern one.'

'Yeah—that's the psychology labs.'

'Psychology . . .' Taggart suddenly felt a shiver in his spine. 'Does Dr Wesley Mitchell work there, do you happen to know?'

The girl called over to a friend if possible even more gorgeous than himself, 'Marylyn, does the name Wesley Mitchell mean anything to you?' Turning back to Taggart she explained, 'She's majoring in psychology.'

'Sure. He's the dean.'

'Of psychology?'

'That's right.'

'Just one more thing,' said Taggart. 'You couldn't tell me where his office is, could you?'

'Sure thing. You go in the psychology building there, right, then up to the second floor, you'll see some swing doors right in front of you, go in there, through a big room with rats in cages on both sides, there's a door at the end, that's Wesley's room. That's the quickest way from here. Or there's another entrance round the back, if you go that way you go through his secretary's room.'

So. If you want to make an unannounced visit, go round the front. Of course, there was no reason to suppose that Peter Fischer was necessarily going to see Wesley Mitchell—except that he had to be. Didn't he? There were Fischer and Charles Watson coming down the steps of the Reform Club, Watson (if Taggart could remember right, but of course it was more than probable he was superimposing his own subsequent knowledge—still, he had a good visual memory)—Watson looking distinctly annoyed, Fischer bland and unperturbed, with that beatific expression that made you want to hit him. And then Watson had suffered an unexpected setback in his own department—why? Why so suddenly? Why just then?—and had come out here to work with Wesley Mitchell, who had just issued that convenient invitation. And had disappeared. For so long that even Mrs Watson had got a little worried. And now here was Peter Fischer. It was too much of a coincidence to be coincidence.

He thanked his informants and went back to the hotel room. Four o'clock—it would be mid-evening in Leamingworth. He dialled Belinda's number.

'Belinda, it's Andrew here.'

'Andrew! I thought you were in America.'

'I am. Look, tell me again. Exactly why did Charles come here so suddenly?'

'I never was entirely clear. On the face of it, it was because things at the department were changing. Cuts beginning to bite at last. He wasn't going to be able to get on with his own work in his own way any more.'

'And this was quite sudden?'

'Very. Somehow he'd always managed to wangle things before. Thought he'd managed to avert the threats. The professor always resented that—he just resented Charles generally. Then all of a sudden it seemed that Harold, the professor, had got his way. Got Charles where he wanted him.'

'Was this completely out of the blue?'

'Oh, I think so. Completely.'

'You remember the first time I came to see you, we were talking about Peter Fischer and how he must have been the person Charles had mentioned having lunch with. The civil servant who wanted him to do defence work. D'you think he connected the two? The changes in the department and the lunch with Fischer?'

'Oh, I don't think so. Peter wasn't anything to do with education. It was just a lot of hot air, Charles said.'

'Hm, I wonder. Thanks, Belinda, that's very helpful.'

'Andrew. Have you found Charles?'

'No. Haven't really started looking yet. Just wanted to clear one or two things up. 'Bye, Belinda.'

'No, don't ring off. There's something I want to tell you.'

'Oh, surely not. Aren't you on the pill?'

'No, nothing like that. No, it's—something I should have told you before, I suppose, but—Anyway. Look, I think Charles is having an affair with Lulu Mitchell.'

'Who?'

'Lulu Mitchell. Wesley's daughter. Well, I don't *know*. But it was something I sort of picked up when they were over a couple of summers ago, and I think they've met a few times since.'

'Is it still going on?'

'How would I know? It isn't exactly something you can ask, especially when you aren't sure it was happening in the first place.'

'But you think this Lulu might know something.'

'You could try, couldn't you? Anyhow, it didn't sound as though Wesley was going to be very helpful.'

'No, that had occurred to me. OK, thanks, Belinda. You wouldn't know where Lulu might be, would you?'

'She's a student at Southampton. Dad's on the faculty, she gets her tuition paid.'

'OK. Thanks. I'll be in touch.' And Taggart rang off firmly, before he should be bankrupted by a single telephone call.

CHAPTER 13

At least, now, the next move was clear, thought Taggart. Find Lulu. And keep away from Wesley. No friend of Peter Fischer's would be likely to help Taggart.

He found the local phone book and looked under Mitchell. There were a substantial number of Mitchells, including one Dr Wesley; but no L's. Not that that meant anything. If she was a student it wasn't very likely she'd have her own phone. Presumably she lived in a dormitory—not at home, for sure: must be bad enough being in the same town as one's parents, at that age. Well, there must be some central list somewhere of all the students and where they lived— some woman whose life it was to know such things. He picked up the phone book again. Jones University. Easier said than done: Jones had about a hundred different phone numbers listed. Which did he want? He rang the first on the list and explained what he wanted. A patient voice told him to try Registry. Registry . . . He dialled.

'Hello. I wonder if you can help me. I want to get in touch with a Miss Lulu Mitchell.'

'Lulu Mitchell . . . One moment . . .' He pictured the flickering screen; could hear—couldn't he?—the jab of fingers on the keys. 'All right,' said the voice. 'She's in McDonald Dorm. Want the telephone number?'

'Please.'

As easy as that. He dialled the number. Probably no reply: a vague memory arose from his own student days of telephones in corridors ringing, ringing, as people passed by . . . But once again this culture of telephonic efficiency confounded his expectations. Almost at once someone answered. 'McDonald Dorm.'

'Oh—hello—I wanted to speak to Miss Lulu Mitchell.'

'I'm afraid she's not here right now. Do you want to leave a message for her to call you back?'

'She doesn't actually know me. My name's Andrew Taggart. I'm trying to get in touch with her on behalf of Dr Charles Watson. I'm staying at the University Inn . . . I don't suppose you know when she might be available?'

'I'm sorry, I have no idea. Do you want her to call you at the Inn?'

'Yes. I'll be here between six and seven. Otherwise, perhaps she could leave a message to say where I could contact her.'

'Sure. Have a nice day, now.'

He looked at his watch. Nearly five already. Not so very long to wait. Always supposing she would return his call. He brought out his portable typewriter and began to compose a piece about the Washington briefing for *New Politics*. Might call it *The Civilian Subculture*. That was certainly the way a lot of those generals saw it.

At two minutes past six the telephone rang. A girl's voice said, 'Is this Mr Andrew Taggart?'

'You must be Miss Mitchell.'

'That's right. You called . . .' She sounded nervous, and no wonder. No idea how he knew about her and Charles, no idea (or maybe she did have some idea) where Charles was, no idea what he could want.

'It's very kind of you to return my call so promptly.'

'Oh, no, I've been so worried. Do you know something about Charles?'

'Don't let's talk on the phone. How about some dinner? Are you free this evening?'

'Why, sure.'

'Then I'll come and pick you up and we'll go somewhere nice. Tell me where to come. I'll be there at seven.'

There was, Taggart had to admit, not much he could do to spruce himself up, travelling, as he invariably did, with the barest minimum of luggage. Of his two shirts he was wearing the grubby one while the other was dripping dry over the bath. His shoes were scuffed. His hair needed cutting and washing. Well, that at least could be remedied.

He took a shower and towelled himself dry vigorously, then felt the washed shirt to see if it was even remotely wearable. It was not. There was, however, a pair of clean socks—a sheer stroke of providence, that: his previous socks had finally collapsed in holes only two days before and he had bought three new pairs. Comparatively polished, then, he set forth for McDonald Dormitory. This turned out to be a large frame house off-campus—not far from the hotel, in fact. The front door was open, and an apparently continuous stream of tall, casual, heart-stoppingly healthy girls passed in and out. How could anyone be so confident? What had they all got to be so confident *about*? Taggart's heart beat admiringly. Lucky for him European girls weren't mostly like this. He'd never get a stroke of work done. Taking his courage in both hands, he joined the stream and entered, then stopped and looked around. Just inside the door there was a cubicle containing yet another wonderful girl, who poked her head out and said, 'Can I help you?' But before Taggart could reply a voice said, 'You must be Andrew Taggart.'

Lulu's style was rather different from that of the bouncing preppies around her. They were mostly tall and sporty; she was small and slight with her father's blond colouring allied to her mother's unruly frizz of hair and small, pointed face. Not really my type. Taggart noted almost with relief. Things were complicated enough as it was. 'That's right,' he said. 'And you must be Lulu.'

He held the door open and she slipped out under his arm. She certainly was small. Not many girls could get under Taggart's arm without bending double. 'Where'll we go?' she said now.

'Do you have any ideas? I'm a stranger round here.'

'Do you like Chinese?'

'Sometimes,' Taggart lied. Clearly Lulu did, and it was more important that she should be happy than that he should stuff his gut.

Soon they were seated in the regulation semi-darkness of a restaurant, awaiting the arrival of various dishes to which Taggart had assented with the abandon of total ignorance.

Lulu, facing him, leaned forward across the table cupping her face in her hands. Her eyes, Taggart noticed, slanted upwards slightly, or maybe that was just an effect of her posture. 'Now,' she said. 'Tell me who you are. All I know about you is your name.'

'It's hard to know where to begin.'

'At the beginning.'

'Ah, but where's that? All right. I'm a journalist, a British journalist. I work mainly for a weekly called *New Politics*, which is quite small and left-wing. That keeps body and soul together, and if I want something extra, like clothes, say, I do things for other papers or the television or something. OK so far?'

'And you know Charles?'

'Only very vaguely. We meet occasionally at conferences.'

'Then how did you know—' Here she stopped herself and began again. 'Then what made you get in touch with me? I mean, it's my father who's his friend.'

'I know Belinda,' said Taggart gently.

'Oh.' Lulu fiddled with her chopsticks. If it hadn't been so dark, Taggart might have noticed the wave of crimson that flooded across her face. 'Does she—er—'

'She doesn't know anything, but she suspects. Look, it'll be easier if I just tell you what happened. The thing is, Belinda suddenly realized that it was about three months since she last heard from Charles. You know how time passes, she's been rather busy with one thing and another. So she suddenly got in a panic and phoned up your dad. And *he* said he didn't know anything about it, that Charles had gone off somewhere in May and hadn't been in touch since. Well, Belinda thought that was rather odd, so I said, since I was coming over now anyhow, I'd see if I could find anything out. So here I am.'

At this moment their meal arrived, consisting of bowls of rice, a large whole fish gaping on a plate in a vaguely celebratory way, and several satellite dishes of vegetables. There was also a pot of green tea. Lulu helped herself enthusiastically. 'The carp's wonderful here,' she said. 'Do try it.'

'Ah. Yes, it's very good, isn't it?'

'Aren't you going to have more than that?'

'I'm trying to lose a bit of weight,' said Taggart deprecatorily.

'Well, if you really aren't going to have any more . . .' Lulu ate on hungrily.

'So, I wondered if you could help me at all.'

'I wish I could.' Thoughtfully, Lulu picked bits off the fish with her chopsticks. 'Of course, you must have guessed, it's true what Belinda thought. Charles and I, well . . .'

'So I've gathered.'

'So when I heard he was coming over I thought . . . we thought . . .'

'I can imagine.'

'And then—he suddenly went off.'

'And you haven't heard from him since?'

'Not a thing,' said Lulu miserably.

'Do you believe your father when he says he has no idea where Charles can be?'

Lulu thought back. 'No, I don't. I'm sure I don't—now why not?' She thought back to that last hurried meeting. 'Well, of course. It was because they were going off together. There was some work Dad'd been planning to show Charles, and then suddenly off they went.'

'Any idea where to?'

'No, but I might be able to find out.'

'Does your father know about you two?'

'No, neither of my parents knows. Nobody knows. They'd hate it. Anyhow, it just wouldn't cross their minds. They don't put us in the same, well, social frame.'

'Well, I suppose that's something.'

'I'll tell you one thing,' Lulu said. 'Dad wouldn't know that I knew about him going off with Charles. What happened was, he'd just got an apartment, and I was going to have lunch with him there and spend the afternoon together. That was at eleven-thirty, we fixed it all up. Then when I got there at one o'clock, after class, it was all off, Dad had called, they were leaving at two, and what was Charles to do? Say he'd fixed to spend the afternoon in bed and would

Dad kindly leave it until tomorrow? Especially it being me. So we had to rush off round the corner for a sandwich.'

'But he didn't say what this work was or where it was?'

'I don't think he knew. It was just a trip Dad'd been talking about.'

'And is there anybody else who might know something?'

'Here in Jones? No, he hadn't been here very long—didn't know that many people . . .'

'Well, look. I don't know how long I can stay. Can you try and find out about this trip? Where they went?'

'I'll see what I can do,' said Lulu. 'But don't rely on it.'

CHAPTER 14

The trouble with finding out about any particular trip of Wesley Mitchell's, as Lulu explained, was that there were so many of them. 'He's always off on trips,' she told the bemused Taggart. 'He's away more than he's here.'

'So how does he run the lab?'

'From afar, mostly. He plays the conferences. Raises cash and profile. Throws out ideas.'

'But he's here now, isn't he?'

'I believe he is. But how did you know that? Did you go and see him?'

'No, no. He doesn't know anything about me—I hope. But someone I know did—just go to see him, I mean.'

'I feel terrible,' said Lulu. 'As though I'm working against my own father, for God's sake. It isn't just you. I've felt like it ever since I started this thing with Charles.'

'Why, are they enemies underneath it all?'

'No, of course not, they're friends, that's the trouble. They *would* be enemies if Dad found out, I guess—or at least Dad would be Charles's enemy. That's why it's all got to be so secret. I hate it—having secrets from my parents.' She looked earnestly at Taggart. 'I mean, Dad's my best friend. Truly. We're real close. Like, he didn't have a son, so we did all the things together that fathers usually get to do with their sons. We even went on hunting trips together. He taught me how to live in the woods, how to use a gun. And now . . . I feel just terrible about it.'

'That's growing up for you,' said Taggart sagely. 'Everyone has those sorts of troubles.'

'Did you?'

'Well, it was more that I don't think I ever told them anything. I can't really remember. It was a long time ago.' Taggart, saying this, felt suddenly old, of a different generation from this child who was still worried about not telling her parents all. Well, he was a different generation. He was the same generation as her parents. Realizing this gave him a nasty turn. She could be his daughter.

Lulu, when she began seriously to consider how to find out where Wesley had taken Charles so very suddenly that day, found herself at a loss. She couldn't ask directly—how was she supposed to know who Charles had gone off with? And why should she even have noticed? Well, she might have *noticed*. He was an old family friend, after all. Taking Taggart's word for it that her father was presently in the university—their paths rarely crossed—she made it her business to bump into him casually, near the library. She positioned herself by a window from where she knew she could see the door nearest his office at the Psychology Labs and, sure enough, eventually he emerged. Moving with the speed of light Lulu cannoned into him, looking even more dishevelled and absent-minded than usual.

'Sorry, Dad.'

'Think nothing of it. You nearly castrated me, that's all. How's things, Lu? Haven't seen you in a long while.'

'No, well, you know how things are. I'm just fine. Hey, Dad, there's something I've been meaning to ask you. I was looking for Charles Watson the other day—some student thing I promised I'd tell him about—and no one seemed to know anything about him. Wasn't he due to stay this semester?'

'He was, but he had to leave earlier than he wanted. Something came up—he wasn't too clear. I'm surprised he didn't tell you. I thought you and he were good friends.'

Wesley looked at his watch. 'Sorry, hon, I must rush. Let's meet up for lunch some time, right?'

'Sure, Dad.'

Lulu kept her face more or less averted and hurried on, as anxious to avoid her father seeing what she felt as he appeared to be to end the conversation. Surely he must notice that something was wrong? The way her stomach had lurched when he told those lies about Charles? Well, not lies, exactly, but a long way from the truth. Lulu felt terrible. She had felt bad enough, deceiving Belinda and her parents about her relationship with Charles. But now it seemed she was not the only one doing the deceiving. Wesley was at it too. Now that was really bad because it meant that he had something to hide. And that, Lulu's mind rushed on, could mean only one thing. Something dreadful had happened and Wesley was mixed up in it. Lulu felt that she could not bear the weight of this discovery. At the very least she must share it. Her first instinct was to rush to her mother—but that, she told herself, would be stupid. Essie would be sure to divert the conversation on to Lulu and her reasons for being so concerned, and then . . . Anyhow, why upset her mother? Besides, she had a suitable confessor at hand. She ran to the nearest telephone—the one in the library—and called the University Inn.

'Andrew, I've got something.'

'That was quick!'

'Well, it's not anything very definite yet. I met up with Dad and sort of casually asked him about Charles.'

'And?'

'Well, he just pretended he didn't know a thing.'

'Well, that's what he did with Belinda.'

'But, don't you see, it means he's hiding something.'

'Of course I see that. That's why I'm here.'

'Oh.' Lulu was crestfallen. 'Yeah, I suppose that's right.'

'You couldn't believe it until it was thrust under your nose. Well, I don't blame you.'

'I suppose I just couldn't believe Dad would be so—well, it's as if he spent his whole life telling lies and hiding things. He did it just without even thinking.'

'I suppose he does, spend his life like that I mean. If he has all these secret lines of research going.'

'Yeah, I guess so.'

'So what you've got to do is find out where they went.'

'OK, I'll get right on to it. How long are you here?'

'Till tomorrow?'

'Well, I'll try.'

Lulu felt like a fool. What had she thought her father would say? 'Why, sure, Lu, here's his address?' Why tell her when he wouldn't tell Belinda? No, this exercise, she could see it now, had been for her own benefit: she wouldn't believe it until she heard it in person. OK, so now she could get started. If it was a question of pretending, two people could play at that. She sat and thought for a few moments, then picked up the phone again.

'Professor Mitchell's office.'

'Hi, Ellen, this is Lulu here.'

'Why, hi, Lulu, how're you? I'm afraid Wesley just went out half an hour ago and I'm not expecting him back till about four.'

'Well, actually it was you I wanted to talk to. Thing is, Ellen, we've got a project on energy use and one of the things we're doing is a survey of how much people travel and how they travel—you know, airplane, automobile, bike. We've each got to find ten different people we know who lead very different lives and map out their itinerary over six months. So I thought, east, west, home's best, who do I know that really gets around? And who's going to have the details? So here I am, your friendly neighbourhood snooper.'

'You mean you want the details of everywhere your father's been for the past six months?'

'That's about it. It'll be in his diary, won't it? Don't worry,' she added hastily, 'this is all anonymous. It's impersonal research. Intellectual inquiry.'

'Seeing as it's you . . .' Lulu smiled to herself. Ellen had been her father's secretary for fifteen years: their acquaintance covered the entire span of Lulu's conscious life.

'No need for details,' Lulu added reassuringly. 'All I need

is the bare facts. Like June 16, San Diego, plane Boston–San Diego, conference.'

'I'll do it where I can, but I don't always know what it's for. There are some things your father doesn't tell even me.'

'Oh, you know what I mean. If there's a blank, it's a blank.'

'All right, when d'you want this—survey—to start?'

'It's end of September now, right, so I guess the end of April.'

'I guess I could do that. There'll be a blank for the vacation.'

'Don't worry about the vacation, I can fill that in.'

'All right. When d'you want this?'

'When can I have it?'

'I'll do it now, or I'll forget. Come by at the end of the afternoon.'

'Gee, thanks, Ellen. Look, you couldn't manage it for three-thirty, could you? I've got a class at four that won't end till six, and then I've got to go out.'

'I'll try.'

Lulu put down the phone and glanced at her watch. It was ten past eleven. She had already missed a class that morning—better not miss another. Her next was due to start in twenty minutes. She hurried off.

At 3.30 sharp she tapped on Ellen's door and put her head into the office. Ellen, neat and grey-haired, was, as always, at her post. Lulu knew—everyone knew—that it was Ellen who ran the department, not the ever-absent Wesley. Demonstrably—it was demonstrated at least four times every term—the place could run perfectly smoothly without *him*, while if Ellen ever happened to be absent on account of pneumonia or the death of a near relative, everything ground to a halt. 'I shouldn't do it,' she now said, holding out some sheets of paper neatly clipped together. 'Whatever you do, don't tell Wesley. He'd probably eat me.'

'Me, too. I won't say a word. Ellen, you're a friend.'

Lulu rushed back to the phone in the library and called Taggart. He was still in his room—what did he do in there all day, for heaven's sake? (Wrote articles, was the answer. He had now completed two and a half.) 'I've got it,' she told him breathlessly.

'Got what?'

'Sorry. I keep assuming you know what I'm doing. I've got a schedule of Dad's movements for the past six months.'

'How on earth did you get that?'

'From his secretary. We're old friends. She thinks it's for research.'

'So it is. Why don't you bring it over? I'm in Room 45. Up the stairs, turn right, then left. It's about half way along the wing.'

'I'll be there in twenty minutes.'

They laid out the sheets of paper on the table by the window. Everything was typed out neatly, clearly and without ambiguity. In the past six months Wesley had travelled to China, to France, to Mexico, to Brazil, to Japan, and (it seemed) to just about every city in the United States. 'He certainly does get around,' said Taggart. 'Do the airlines give him a special bonus?'

'I expect he tots up a free seat every now and then.'

'Who runs the department?'

'His secretary. Ellen. The lady who gave me this.'

'Does your mother get to go along?'

'Not often. She hates airplanes. She has her own life. I guess it's something they've worked out between them.'

'When I look at what people's marriages are like after twenty-five years I worry less about not being married myself.' Taggart applied himself to the schedule for May. On the second Wesley had flown to Paris for a UNESCO meeting; on the seventh he had returned, spent a week at Southampton, then two days in Seattle for a conference. Then back to Southampton till the twenty-fifth, when he had been absent for three days. Then the ceaseless round of conferences and meetings began again. Taggart pointed at the unidentified blank. 'That must be it.'

'Yes, that would be about right. It was the end of May I last saw Charles.'

'It must have been something he booked himself. Are there any more blanks like that, I wonder?'

'Well, there's a big blank in the vacation, of course. Even Ellen gets to go on holiday sometimes.'

'But here's another, look, end of June. Do you recall him nipping off like that in the vacation? "I'm just off to Timbuktu for a few days, dear, don't wait up," that kind of thing?'

'I wasn't around my parents much this last vacation, so I wouldn't know. But I could see if I could find his credit card bills if you like. There might be something on those. Car rental usually says where the renting office was.'

'Doesn't he keep that sort of thing locked up?'

'I don't think so. He's not at all the careful type. He's much more likely just to have lost them or thrown them away. But he'd need them for his tax returns, so I expect they'd be somewhere.'

'Lulu, you're a daughter in a million.'

'Don't.'

'Seriously, though, I think you're wonderful. How about a movie tonight? I have to go back to England tomorrow evening, so this is our last chance. Make an old man happy.'

'I guess I'd be better off if I didn't make so many old men happy.'

That evening, as they were going into the movie, she said, 'I guess I can try to find those papers tomorrow. Dad's off to Washington first thing, and I know Thursday's Mother's day at her office. She's involved in some kind of social work in Springfield. Her conscience day, she calls it.'

'Lulu, you're wonderful. Can I come and help?'

'I guess so. If you think it would be safe.'

'How else would I pass the morning? My plane leaves Kennedy at nine in the evening. I'm taking the shuttle from Boston around five.'

At ten next morning, Lulu and Taggart walked up to the front door at 704 Wyoming, feeling like thieves. Lulu opened the door and called, 'Hi, Mom!' There was no reply. 'I guess we're safe,' she said. 'Dad left on the eight-thirty plane from Boston—it was the last item on Ellen's sheets. Shall we have a cup of coffee?'

'I'd feel happier if we did the dirty work first.'

'OK. Dad's den's this way.' She led the way through the familiar rooms. It was surprising how normal everything felt. Just like home. The door to Wesley's den was shut, but not locked: why would he lock it? Inside, the desk, the armchairs, the bookshelves, the shaded desk lamp, all looked just as usual. Now where would he keep his bills? Not, it turned out, in the desk drawers: all they contained were a selection of stationery and odd rubber bands and lengths of string. Where, then? Various papers were scattered on top of the desk, but none of them were bills.

'Would he keep them all together in a folder or something?' asked Taggart.

'Might do. Anything on the shelves?'

They turned their attention to the bookshelves that lined the room. Large areas of these were covered with stacked papers, but these turned out to be mainly piles of academic précis. Looking about, Lulu saw a pair of box files standing on the floor. She opened one of these and her heart leapt into her mouth. She was literally unable to speak for excitement. She would never last the course as a detective: she'd die of a heart attack half way through the first week. I must be calm, she told herself. 'Maybe this is it,' she said finally, in a sort of breathless croak.

'Let's see.'

Lulu brought the box file to the desk. It was filled with bills and receipts. As in all archæological finds, the most recent material was at the top. Amex, Mastercharge . . . September, August, July, June . . . Lulu pointed to an item that figured on the June statement. Shuttle, Boston–New York, May 25; shuttle, New York–Boston, May 28. The second had cost just half as much as the first. Two fares out, one fare back. 'Think that's it?'

'I think it may be.'

'New York,' said Lulu thoughtfully. 'Well, I guess that's something.'

They looked at each other. To say it was something was

undoubtedly correct, semantically speaking. But in all other respects it was nearly as bad as not knowing anything at all.

CHAPTER 15

Over a cup of coffee in the kitchen, Taggart and Lulu debated what their next move should be. The trouble with New York was not just that it was so big, but that it was (in American terms) so close. You would pop up to New York from Southampton almost without thinking.

'Does he go there very often?' Taggart inquired.

'I guess so . . . Though I think he visits Washington more.'

'But if Charles is in New York, and if that's on your Dad's account, then perhaps we could assume that if he went to New York at the moment it might well be connected with that.'

'Yeah. But does that get us any farther?' Lulu asked doubtfully.

'It might.' Taggart put another spoonful of sugar in his coffee, to see if an extra shot of carbohydrate might get his brain functioning more efficiently. 'Let's see. Is there any way you could get to know when he goes there next?'

'To New York?'

'Yes. Any reason you can think of that would be an excuse for him to let you know when he's next going to be there.'

Lulu considered. 'It would have to be some specific job, wouldn't it? Something I needed that could only be done in person. I mean, otherwise, why not just have the people mail something, or call you?' She considered, sipping her coffee and staring unseeingly out of the window. At length she said, 'How's about this? I have a friend who works in the law library at NYU. She's on the faculty there. I need some papers that I know she has, and she doesn't want to mail them because they're rather valuable. So next time Dad goes to New York, can he pick them up for me, or let me know so I can have my friend put them in a cab to wherever he's going to be?'

'Brilliant,' said Taggart. 'And then?'

'And then we follow him, I guess. See where he goes.'

'Easier said than done.'

'Not if we know he's going to the law library. Either he comes himself and we can pick him up there or he sends a cab and we follow it. Or get in it. The cab-driver's not going to mind, not if he gets paid.'

'I certainly can't think of anything better. The trouble is, we've no idea when that will be, and I've really got to get back to England just now.'

'No problem. I'll do it.'

'I was hoping you'd say that,' said Taggart. 'Look, when the moment comes, call me. I'll give you my home number and my office number. If I'm not there, you can leave a message at either. I'll be on the next plane over. OK?'

As Lulu had expected, her request, though not exactly received with open arms, was not one that could reasonably be turned down. Wesley, when next she saw him, promised her that he would let her know of his next visit to the Big Apple: promised without enthusiasm, certainly, but promised all the same.

'But don't you get to New York yourself, sometimes?'

'Of course I do, Dad, but I've got some really tough assignments and I'd really like to keep calm and just spend time studying these days. I just figured you'd be going before I would. Pretty please?'

'Well, as it happens I'm going in two days' time.'

This was just a week after Taggart's return to London. Lulu called him collect, first at the office, which he had left, and then at home, which he had not yet reached. She left a message on his answering machine, and then hung around in her room, with strict instructions that she was to be called if there were any calls for her. An hour later her patience was rewarded.

'Andrew!'

'When's it happening?'

'Day after tomorrow.'

'Lulu, I can't manage it. I simply can't do it. I've got a vital interview set up for then.'

'Don't worry, I can manage. I guess it would be easier for me anyhow, because I know my way around the city better than you.'

'So what'll you do? Go up on an earlier shuttle and wait for him?'

'No, he'll be going first thing. Unless I want to get up at five in the morning. No, I'll go the day before and stay with my friend, and then I'll wait at the library.'

'I'll be thinking of you. Let's hope he sends a cab. That way you'll at least get an easy ride.'

Wesley, however, did not send a cab.

Lulu had been skulking around the law library since early in the morning, although of course it was inconceivable that Wesley would get there before ten o'clock at the earliest, since he wouldn't arrive in the city until nine. The place was built on the usual monumental scale, the visitor entering a vast foyer at the end of which carpeted steps led up to the library itself. The parcel which Wesley was to pick up had been left at the library front desk, and Lulu had selected for herself a place in a nearby alcove which would enable her to keep watch on the desk without herself being seen. She had also taken other precautions, such as taming her frizz of yellow hair as far as she could and hiding it under a large turban, and procuring a pair of heavy spectacle-frames. Given that she was literally the last person Wesley would be expecting to see there, she hoped that these would be enough to deflect a passing glance.

The wait seemed interminable. Lulu was terrified that her attention would be elsewhere at the critical moment; yet it was impossible to concentrate on the desk all the time. But of course when the moment came she didn't miss it. Even if she hadn't seen her father she would have recognized his voice asking for a package which had been left for Miss Lulu Mitchell. Lulu slid out of one of the side doors into the foyer while her father was occupied at the desk, and waited for him to emerge.

Now that the moment had arrived she felt surprisingly calm. In the eventuality that Wesley should have a cab waiting for him, she was of course lost. But somehow she didn't think he would. Washington Square, where the Law Library is located, is near a number of excellent bookshops—much better than anything available in Southampton—and Wesley, she knew, was a sucker for bookshops. If he came in person she was betting on this foible: he would go on a bookshop crawl, either before he came to the library or afterwards. Either way she would tail him, or try to. If he took a cab, she would either have to find one herself and tell it to follow, or else try and be near enough to hear the destination he gave the cab-driver. It might work or it might not.

Waiting outside the library for her father to emerge, she noted with relief that there was no very apparent cab waiting for anyone. And when Wesley finally emerged, swinging the briefcase containing her package, he showed no signs of looking for a cab. Instead he walked briskly in the direction of the subway at West 4th Street and disappeared down the steps.

Lulu, heart pounding, felt that her luck was in. Her ruse had worked, and now this! If she couldn't keep sight of her father in the subway, she couldn't keep sight of him anywhere. It wasn't as if he was trying to slip a tail. She had thoughtfully laid in a store of subway tokens, and followed him now to the Downtown Express platform, loitering behind him so as to be poised to slip into the same carriage when his train should finally arrive.

Wesley brought out a *New York Times* and began to read it. Short of bumping into him or tapping him on the shoulder, there seemed to be no way in which Lulu could attract his attention. This was lucky, because the trains at this time of the morning were not particularly full; and if this meant that it was easy to keep him in sight, it also meant that passengers were more likely to notice one another. Lulu cursed herself for not having a newspaper of her own behind which she could hide, but there was no way she could risk losing her quarry in order to buy one now.

Wesley took the A train downtown. He sat in the middle of the carriage. Lulu slipped into the same carriage at one end, taking a seat near the door so that she would be ready to leave when he did. Opposite her, advertisements in Spanish urged the advantages of vocational training; there was also her favourite ad, for the Roach Motel. (They check in, but they don't check out!) The usual panhandlers limped and sobbed and brazened their way through the train. Most of the passengers, including Wesley, buried their faces in their papers. Lulu gave one of them a quarter, which he received with disdain.

At Jay Street Wesley got out and changed trains to a downtown local. Lulu had been to Brooklyn a few times, but not often: she hoped he wouldn't be leading her too far afield into unknown territory. She didn't know whether she would feel able to face somewhere like Bedford–Stuyvesant even in the interests of finding Charles. But she need not have worried. Wesley only stayed on the local for a few stops, and when he got out, Lulu, following, saw that they were in one of the middle-class neighbourhoods near Prospect Park.

Keeping some yards behind him, she followed her father down the grey street, past the antique shops and the specialist provision stores. Her mouth watered: she hadn't had much for breakfast, and a bagel with lox and cream cheese was a tempting prospect. But there was no time to stop now.

Outside the high school, the pavement was crowded with pupils taking their lunch-break. The boys and girls filled the street, loud, noisy and slightly threatening. Most of them were bigger than Lulu. Resolutely she made her way through the tide, but momentarily lost sight of Wesley. When she was able to look for him again, he had disappeared.

For a moment she felt panicked. After all that, to lose him now! But then she reasoned with herself that, after all, he couldn't be very far away. She couldn't have lost sight of him for more than a minute at the most.

A glance down the side streets showed no evidence of Wesley. He might have gone into one of the houses, of course: but he'd have had to move pretty sharply to have disappeared completely inside a minute. The kind of locks people have in New York these days, it takes that long just to open the front door, and there was no sign of any of the doors she could see opening or shutting.

Where else, then? Lulu's glance lighted on the bank. It was a branch of Citicorp, and she knew Wesley banked with them in Southampton. Maybe he'd gone in to draw some cash on his card. She went inside to check, her heart in her mouth and as inconspicuously as she could manage. But she need not have worried: Wesley was not there.

Coming out of the bank, she noticed the door in the back of the building. Better check in there.

She was expecting to be confronted with the usual lengthy directory of tenants. But this, as Charles had noticed before her, was remarkably short. Prospect Psychodynamics Clinic. That had to be it: she felt sure of it. But how to check? She couldn't exactly risk walking in—what if she met her father face to face? Her disguise wasn't so deep that he wouldn't be able to recognize his own daughter.

Lulu left the building and retreated on to a convenient flight of steps to think. What she needed to do was keep the place under observation somehow. Of course, there was nothing to stop her staying right where she was and watching the door. Nothing except common sense, that was. Brooklyn, even in its more benign neighbourhoods, is no place for a solitary girl to hang around a street corner indefinitely.

Lulu looked around her. On the other side of the road the bagel-shop beckoned. Nothing to stop her buying a bagel now: if this was really where Wesley had been making for—and it seemed highly probable—it seemed extremely improbable that he would be leaving this instant. Anyhow, if that *was* where he was, she'd achieved her goal, up to a point. And if it wasn't she'd lost him. Either way she deserved some lunch.

She bought her bagel and wandered out on to the street again, munching. The sidewalk was full of pupils from the school opposite, chewing their lunches, smoking cigarettes filled with who knew what noxious substances, and indulging in the usual teenage horseplay. Lulu looked around for shelter.

Next door was an optical equipment store, its heavily-armoured window full of arcane and expensive lenses.

Suddenly Lulu had an idea.

CHAPTER 16

Lulu finished her bagel and licked her fingers, then pressed the bell which would alert the lens store to a possible customer wishing to enter. A small, suspicious-looking man peeked out of a door at the back of the shop. He looked definitely unwelcoming: presumably he suffered from too many improbable customers ringing his bell during the school lunch-hour. Lulu signalled that she wanted to come in. He looked slightly reassured and emerged from his den to press a button behind the counter which would unlock the door. Feeling like a criminal, Lulu slid inside. She bought a pair of powerful binoculars, which she slipped into the capacious bag she always wore over her shoulder.

'You wanta be careful,' said the shopkeeper, indicating the milling throng outside with his head. 'They don't care what they take.'

'They'll be going in in a minute, won't they?'

'Yeah,' he conceded, consulting his watch. 'I guess they will.' And indeed, as they watched, the boys and girls began to struggle back into the school. Lulu left the shop, crossed the road, and went in with them.

She felt rather nervous, but experience had taught her that if you are going to enter a building where you have no business the trick is to behave as if you own the place. Any nervousness is an immediate indicator of guilt. Anyhow, she had no need to feel nervous here. The place was thronging—the school must have had at least a thousand pupils—and no one took the slightest notice of her. Possibly they took her for one of the younger members of staff, or a secretary, or a social worker—there were a hundred things she could legitimately have been.

The smell of the school, the immemorial odour of dust, chalk, sweat and disinfectant, transported Lulu back to her own not very distant schooldays. But the smell was where the resemblance began and ended. Her school at Southampton, peopled by the children of the wealthy middle class, had been nothing like this. Here the paintwork was dingy and chipped, guards who looked as if they might very well be armed appeared here and there in the thronging corridors, and the atmosphere was distinctly adversarial. Pupils against teachers, teachers against the system.

Lulu made her way purposefully to the side of the building nearest the corner on the other side of which stood the clinic building. She knew what she wanted to find, but she didn't know whether she would find it. The school building was a single unit occupying the width of a block, whose windows faced forward on to the avenue and back on to a small, high-walled yard abutting the gardens of the houses in the side streets. What Lulu wanted was to find a window from which she could see the clinic building. This shouldn't be impossible: the side walls of the school were almost but not wholly blank. The small windows clearly did not belong to classrooms. Washrooms, maybe? Lulu made her way up a flight of stairs and along a corridor which led between two rows of classrooms, from which it borrowed light through a glass clerestory. The corridor was still pretty dark, though, lit here and there by light-bulbs hanging from the ceiling. Not a good place to meet a drug addict if you were alone. Lulu shivered: this school would be unique if it did not have a drugs problem. She noticed two girls disappearing inside a door at the end of the corridor—the door she was looking for?

When she got there she found that she had been correct in her supposition. This was indeed a washroom, and it did indeed have a window which must look across the street towards the clinic building. But it had one drawback she had not anticipated. The window, besides being very small, was set high up in the wall, well above her head. Lulu checked the washrooms on the two floors above. They were identical.

What now? Sitting on the toilet in one of the washrooms (Lulu had never forgotten the childhood imperative to use one whenever you find one handy), she considered her next move. Her aim was simple: to remain in the school after everybody had left and see what she could make of the clinic building by watching through her binoculars. She had ascertained that this should not be impossible, though it would be uncomfortable: she would have to bring in a chair to stand on. None of the classroom windows, which were lower, faced in the right direction. The only real difficulty would be in hiding herself in the school. It was to be assumed that the janitor checked it out pretty thoroughly before he looked up. Before then, she needed to make some preparations. She would need to eat; and she ought to have a notebook and pencil and maybe a camera, though she didn't rate her chances of taking very good pictures from the kind of vantage-point she was going to have. Anyhow, if the camera was going to be at all worthwhile, she'd need a telephoto lens, and those are heavy and expensive and difficult to conceal even in a bag as capacious as hers. No; no camera. But food was imperative. No one can concentrate all night without food.

Having decided this she marched out confidently, just as she had marched in. There was a nasty moment when a boy stopped her in the corridor, but it was only to ask her the time. Lulu felt her heart pounding. She walked past a uniformed guard who barely glanced at her, and out of the building.

Well, so far so good. She felt slightly weak at the knees. Better sit down and have a civilized cup of coffee while she had the chance. She glanced at her watch. One-thirty. She'd better be back inside the school by two-thirty, so as to have time to get nicely lost in the crowd. She went into a coffee-shop and sat down at a window table. While she was waiting for her order she looked across the street to see if there was any sign of Wesley coming back. There wasn't. That didn't mean anything, of course. He might still be at the clinic—if that was where he was; but where else could he be?—or there had been a hundred opportunities for him to walk back down the street without her seeing him.

Her coffee came, with a Danish pastry. Lulu ate hungrily, then set off to buy provisions for the rest of the day. In one of the Korean fruit shops she bought apples and cheese, and in a deli next door, some cookies and chocolate and sliced pastrami. That should keep her going. As for drinks, she'd have to drink water from the tap.

2.25: time to get back into the school. As she marched up to it Lulu felt curiously detached, as if she were taking part in an activity that had nothing to do with real life. That it involved her father and her lover was not so much unbelievable as outside anything she could really envisage. She was brought down to earth, however, when a group of boys, who must have been aged about fourteen, barracked and jeered at her as she entered the school gates. They were real all right, and they were a lot bigger than she was. They probably took her for a teacher. She felt she should probably have asked them, in tones of authority, what they were doing hanging around outside while school was still going on, but that would have been asking for trouble: whatever happened, she must remain as far as possible invisible. She walked past the boys into the school. They didn't follow.

No more trouble, she prayed. Inside the school people were milling about, changing classrooms for the last period. That suited her fine. Soon, in fact with remarkable suddenness, the corridors were empty. The lesson had begun.

What Lulu wanted to find now was somewhere she could hide out while the school emptied and the janitor made his rounds before locking up. Prowling around the corridors, she came upon a door which didn't appear to lead to any classroom. Trying it gingerly she found herself staring into a cleaners' cupboard, containing mops, brooms and all the rest of the usual equipment. That might do. On the other hand, she'd probably be better off in one of the classrooms when the janitor did his rounds. He might well be responsible for cleaning, and the last thing she wanted was to be found lurking like a criminal.

At three o'clock the bell rang to signal the end of school, and an avalanche of pupils poured out of the classrooms, followed some time later by the exhausted-looking staff. In about half an hour the school was nearly empty of pupils, though a few remained engaged in various after-school activities. By half past four these, too, had finished; and by five, the place was empty and Lulu could hear the janitor shutting and locking the various doors. His footsteps echoed round the uncarpeted corridors, so that it was possible to chart his progress.

Lulu had found a room where a large table was set across a stationery cupboard door. The cupboard itself was empty—presumably all movables such as stationery were kept centrally under lock and key these days—and it was not locked. By moving the table a little she found she could squeeze into the cupboard, which she did, pulling the door to after her when she heard the janitor's footsteps drawing near. He was opening and shutting doors as he came along the corridor, presumably checking to see that no one was still inside the school. She heard him approach the room she was in, come a little way inside, stop while he looked round to check the place was empty—and leave, shutting the door behind him. He evidently didn't do an in-depth check every night, or maybe the table, still pulled across the cupboard door—you couldn't see that it had been moved forward unless you came up fairly close—was enough to convince him. Lulu breathed again, realizing that while the man had been in the room she had literally stopped doing so. Some time later she heard him pass by the door again, then go down the stairs. Slipping out of the cupboard she ran to the window, and saw him let himself out. The door clanged behind him with a heavily-locked finality. He turned another key in the lock from the outside—a deadlock, presumably—and let himself out by the gate in the high wire fence that closed off the front of the school from the road. Lulu was alone for the night. She set off for the top floor washroom, whence she hoped to get a glimpse of what went on in the Prospect Psychodynamics Clinic.

She brought a chair from the nearest classroom and set

it under the window. Why couldn't she have been a little taller! As it was, she had to stand on tiptoe to see out properly, and there was no hope of keeping that up indefinitely. She would just have to stay at her post for as long as she could and rest when she had to. She focused the binoculars and waited.

The school was four storeys high, which put her on a level with the reception of the clinic. She could see across to the reception area window, which was obscured by a venetian blind, and one other. By the time she had finished her meal and got set up with her chair and her binoculars it was after six o'clock, and lights were beginning to be turned on. Luckily for her, the inhabitants of the clinic were not worried about being overlooked. The slats of the blind were set horizontally, and soon a light was turned on in the room next to it. Lulu adjusted her binoculars and stared.

The reception desk was now manned, or womanned, not by the exquisite Sue-Ann but by an older lady with grey hair. She sat there typing and occasionally answering the phone. In the next-door room no activity was visible.

Lulu watched for some time while nothing happened of any interest. She was just about to give up and have a rest when she noticed someone come into the reception area, followed quickly by someone else. She looked down into the street and saw several more people making for the door which led to the Psychodynamics lobby. They were mostly carrying bunches of flowers or small parcels. Of course! It was visiting-time. Lulu glanced at her watch. 6.30. Inside the reception area a group of people had now accumulated. They were talking to the grey-haired lady who was sending them on their way to different parts of the clinic. Some of them, as far as Lulu could make out, didn't stop in reception, or at least she could see no sign of them there although she had seen them going in below. They were presumably the ones who knew their way to whomever it was they were going to visit.

Her calves were beginning to ache, and she got down from the chair to give herself a rest. When she looked again, all was quiet. At 7.30 visiting-time was evidently up: people trooped out, minus flowers and packages. Lulu gave herself another rest.

For a couple of hours nothing much happened, at least while she was watching. Then, just before ten o'clock, she felt her stomach suddenly turn over. A figure she recognized had entered the reception area—one she would recognize anywhere, no matter how many venetian blinds obscured her view. It was her father.

So she had been right!

She stared until her eyes felt as though they were going to fall out. Wesley was evidently talking to the lady behind the desk. There seemed to be someone with him. Lulu strained to see if she could make out who it was. Might it be Charles? But no, as far as she could see this was a dark man. Then Wesley and his companion disappeared from view. Lulu stared down at the street and, sure enough, they appeared a minute later, dimly illuminated by a street lamp. The other man was unknown to Lulu. He was of medium height, with a high domed forehead, black hair slicked across his balding head, round black spectacles. The two men crossed the road towards the school and set off in the direction of the subway.

For some time more Lulu strained at her binoculars. Perhaps Charles would appear? But nothing moved in the clinic. At 10.30 the grey-haired lady left her desk. Only the night staff would stay now until the new shift arrived in the morning.

Lulu got off her chair and almost fell to the floor. She was exhausted. Her legs ached and so did her arms. She felt sweaty, dirty and hungry. She also felt cold. Even though the weather was still warm during the day, the nights were beginning to be cool, and she had no heavy clothes with her. She cursed herself for not having thought of bringing a sleeping-bag. Well, there was no way out now. She was well and truly stuck until morning. Even if she could get out of the door—and without triggering off an alarm, which seemed improbable—there would still be the problem of getting over the fence in front or the wall behind.

Nothing for it but to make the best of things. She made

for the staffroom, which she had located earlier, and which was likely to have some comfortable armchairs in it, or even a sofa. She was lucky: it did have a sofa. She stretched out on it, huddled into her sweater, and waited for sleep.

CHAPTER 17

If she hadn't been so exhausted, both physically and emotionally, it is doubtful whether Lulu would have fallen asleep at all. As it was, she dropped off relatively quickly, to wake, shivering, just after three in the morning. After that there was nothing for it but to wait for the school to open, when she would have an opportunity to slip out. She ate some more of her food, went and had a wash (as far as that was possible with only a roller towel to dry on) and huddled up in the staffroom to wait for the moment of release.

This happened earlier than she had expected, with the arrival of the cleaners at six o'clock. At first she couldn't make out what was happening. Then the clatter of mops and buckets enlightened her. After that it was only a question of making sure nobody saw her and slipping out at the first opportunity. She worked her way cautiously towards the stairs and slid out of the main door like a wraith. There were only four cleaners, one for each floor, so that this was not difficult. Then, feeling like a tramp, she made her way towards the subway and thence to the Port Authority bus station. There was no hurry any more, so no need to waste good money on planes.

By the time she reached Southampton she felt completely drained. She knew she would have to ring Taggart sometime. But not yet. First a shower. Then food, then bed. Perhaps tomorrow she would feel equal to undertaking some violent action such as picking up a telephone. Not today.

Tomorrow came, and with it a new access of energy. But now a new problem arose. Where could she make her call? No question of using the dorm telephone: she didn't want this particular aspect of her life known to all and sundry. No question of the phone at home, either. If she hadn't minded visiting Charles in the guest-bed, she drew the line at fingering her father from his own telephone. Anyhow, the call would show up on the bill.

All Lulu's friends knew that when she was worried she would run her hands through her hair, in the hope, so Wesley teased, that massaging the brain might induce it to work better. Now she did this until she looked like Struwwelpeter in the famous picture—and an idea came. Charles, on the day of their abortive lunch, had given her a key to his apartment. There was a phone there. She would use that.

Lulu had not visited the apartment since Charles's departure. Somehow she had not liked to do so, and besides, there had been no occasion for it. There had been the summer vacation, which she had spent in California with some friends. Not much time to think of Charles there. Part of the reason, too, had been the sneaking, unadmitted thought that if he had failed to get in touch with her, this must mean that for some reason he didn't want to. But now all that had changed. Perhaps it was all this melodramatic action she had recently been taking—not that she had any proof that Wesley's actions in New York had anything to do with Charles, or indeed were anything but totally innocent. Why shouldn't he visit the Prospect Psychodynamics Clinic, or any clinic he wanted to? Nevertheless, she had begun to feel scared. Charles's failure to get in touch now seemed very strange indeed. A man doesn't take an apartment if he has no intention of ever living there. And he had taken it largely on her account.

She let herself in surreptitiously, feeling like a thief, and shut the door behind her with relief. No one seemed to have noticed her arrival at the building. The place looked like the *Marie Celeste*. If it were not for the layer of dust covering everything, it might have been vacated five minutes ago. Dirty dishes in the sink. Food on the shelves and in the fridge. The bed slightly rumpled, not very well made after a disturbed night. Lulu's first instinct was to tidy up, throw away the mouldy, stinking milk in its carton, wash the dishes. But she desisted. Maybe the police would need to see the place sometime, and if so, they wouldn't thank her for having cleaned it up. She probably shouldn't even be using the phone. Anyhow, maybe it had been disconnected: Charles hadn't been around to pay his bills for months.

It was not disconnected, however: he must be paying rent and phone directly from his bank account, which presumably was still being fed from Wesley's funds—or maybe the outgoings had been so small that there was still enough to cover details of this sort even if actual income had ceased.

Lulu was about to dial Tagggart's home number when she realized that in this case the call would appear on Charles's phone bill, which might not be a good idea in this case any more than if it had appeared on her parents' bill. So she called collect, and, to her intense relief—there had been complications enough already—Taggart was there. At first she was almost incoherent in her desire to tell him everything, to be relieved of the solitary possession of this knowledge, but gradually she calmed down, and eventually she had told him the whole story.

'That's terrific!' he said admiringly when she had got to the end of her tale. 'You ought to be in my job. You're born for it.'

'I don't know that I could bear the strain.'

'Oh well, the secret is that one isn't usually so personally involved. Look, I'll get on a plane as soon as I can and call you when I arrive. Could you get back down to New York?'

'I expect so.'

'OK, I'll need you to show me where this place is.'

The call came two days later, and Lulu, who had been dreading it—the last thing she wanted was to revisit that long, grey avenue in Brooklyn or ever see that school building again—was almost relieved. It had been impossible to concentrate on anything while she was waiting for it. She agreed to meet Taggart at midday next day on the steps of the New York Public Library.

They found a quiet hamburger joint in the East 30s and Taggart made her tell him everything all over again. When she had finished he said, 'Visiting time sounds the best bet.'

'What d'you mean?'

'Well, now you've so resourcefully discovered this place, the next thing is to get in there. Right? And that's one for me. You're altogether too noticeable. We don't want any descriptions of you getting back to your Dad. No, I thought you'd agree with that. So in I go clutching a bunch of flowers.'

'But what will you do then? Anyhow, there's absolutely nothing to connect Charles with this place. Did you realize that?'

'Sure I did, but we've got to start somewhere, haven't we? Anyhow, I've got a feeling in my bones. Peter Fischer's involved in this somewhere, and he's a nasty piece of work. I don't know how long he's been involved with your father, but I do know he is now. He's current—and so is this place, whatever it is. Psychodynamics—I'm sure that's the kind of thing Charles did. Does.' He glanced at Lulu to see whether she had registered his slip, but her small, set face was giving nothing away. 'Well, we shall have to see, shan't we?' he finished lamely.

At 6.30, then, Lulu watched Taggart as he joined the group of visitors in the Psychodynamics lobby. Then she turned and headed back to Southampton, as he had sternly instructed her to do.

As the elevator doors opened, Taggart, contrary to appearances—and entirely contrary to the impression he had given Lulu—felt his heart beating wildly. Not that he was particularly worried at this stage. Even if his cover was broken and he was exposed as an interloper, there was nothing to connect him with Wesley Mitchell or Charles Watson. But why should it be broken? The scene was just as Lulu had described it. A grey-haired lady sat behind the reception desk instructing those who did not know their way where they might find their relatives. The others made their way directly to wherever it was they were going. Taggart followed these. Once they had disembarked in the reception lobby they simply turned to where two more elevators, evidently serving only the clinic, waited to convey them to the upper floors.

Clutching his bunch of flowers, Taggart stood in the elevator with a fat lady somewhere in her forties and a nervous-looking young man. The fat lady pressed the button marked 9. The young man requested the sixth floor; Taggart, the tenth. The numbers on the elevator panel went up to 12.

The elevator doors opened on to the tenth floor, and Taggart stepped out. He was standing in a corridor, one side of which contained elevators and washrooms, the other, a row of numbered doors with small glass windows set in them. The corridor was lit by a window at each end (although by now, of course, it was dark outside).

Still holding his flowers, Taggart peeped inside one of the numbered rooms. It contained a lady propped up in bed and staring at the television which stood on a swivelling shelf attached to the opposite wall. Beside her stood a table containing a vase of fresh flowers (she must have had her visitors yesterday, or perhaps earlier that same day—maybe there was a lunch-time visiting-hour as well) and a plate of fruit. The next door room was dark; but the one after that contained another patient, this time a man in late middle age who was lolling back asleep on his pillows.

A door opened, and a nurse bustled out. Taggart walked purposefully towards the elevators and pressed the call button. The nurse bustled on past him just as the elevator arrived. Taggart stepped inside smartly. It was empty. He pressed button 12. Not surprisingly, the twelfth floor presented much the same scene as the tenth, though here, most of the doors were dark. Perhaps they filled the place from the bottom up.

Taggart looked about him thoughtfully. While he was peering into one of the lit rooms, a door opened in the wall behind him and a white-coated figure came through—presumably one of the medical staff. The doctor (if it were a doctor) bade him a polite 'Good evening' and pressed the elevator call button. Taggart meanwhile walked on slowly down the corridor towards a lit room at the end.

The elevator came and the white-coated man got in. When he had safely disappeared Taggart went to inspect the door from which he had emerged. It led, not to a washroom, but to some stairs. He considered these thoughtfully, then shut the door, entered the washroom next door and disposed of his flowers in a large trash-can conveniently situated there. Then he called an elevator, descended to the clinic lobby, and left the building.

CHAPTER 18

When Taggart arrived back at his hotel he was suddenly struck by exhaustion. It hit him like a blow to the stomach. Jetlag. Nothing for it but to succumb. He lay down on his bed and passed out.

When he awoke it was three in the morning. He willed himself to go back to sleep again, and this time made it until five. He then read till seven, when he allowed himself to get up and go out to get some breakfast and make one or two small purchases. After that he returned to his room where he shaved off his beard, carefully and painfully. Taggart hated shaving—that was why he wore a beard. His skin was soft, white and tender and he hated scraping it. He had considered going to a barber-shop for this ordeal, but had shirked it at the last minute. Even the most skilled barber couldn't have the same tender consideration for his face as he would have himself.

By the time he was through with all this it was 9.30. Almost time to go, if his guess was correct. He checked that he had everything he needed and left his key at the desk. Then he plunged into the subway.

He arrived outside the clinic three-quarters of an hour later. Everything was quiet, no movement in or out. Well, he wouldn't expect anything for an hour at least. He went into a coffee-shop and ordered a second breakfast, which he ate at leisure over the *New York Times*. He ordered more coffee, and leaned back. From the window by which he was sitting he could see the door behind the bank which led to the clinic.

Time passed. Nobody in the coffee-shop took much notice of him. The place was half empty: presumably they filled up at lunch-time. Quarter to twelve: that must be soon now. A few more people drifted in, and then, all at once, a great wave of children spilled out of the high school. Taggart got up and wandered out.

Yes: his guess had been correct. A few people were entering the clinic door, one or two of them carrying the usual invalid-visiting paraphernalia. He drifted across the street and into the door with them, and rode up to the fourth floor in the elevator. This time there was a glossy girl at the reception desk, who smiled encouragingly at the visitors as they entered the lobby. Taggart smiled back and made purposefully for the internal elevator, where he pressed the button for the twelfth floor. Once there, he made for the men's room and locked himself in one of the cubicles.

He now brought out a flat packet he had brought with him and opened it. It contained a white coat of the type worn by doctors, dentists and male nurses. He zipped himself swiftly into it, and immediately felt protected. If you were wearing a white coat people didn't bother to look at your face.

Now for it. He took a deep breath and stepped out of the door. While he was nerving himself to open the staircase door, a nurse came out of one of the rooms opposite. She gave him a brilliant smile, said 'Hi!' and went on her way. Clearly a white coat will get you anywhere.

Feeling reassured, Taggart pushed open the door and climbed the stairs to the thirteenth floor which, conforming to superstition, was labelled fourteen.

The thirteenth floor, at first sight, was just like all the others. Numbered doors on one side, services on the other, a window at each end. He crossed the corridor and began to peer cautiously into the rooms.

The first room Taggart came to, which was No. 143, was

empty; but No. 142 was brilliantly lit, daylight plus powerful artificial light. He walked up and peered inside. What he saw was an operating theatre, with what seemed to be an operation in full swing. A number of figures, capped, gowned and wearing surgical masks, were grouped intently round the table, upon which lay an inert white-draped figure. The surgeon, who to judge by her physique (for of course her face was all but invisible) was a slight young woman, was intent upon some delicate process, peering through what seemed to be some sort of long tube into part of what must be the patient's head. Not that it was possible to be certain of this; but what was clear was that everyone was clustered around that end. Quite a number of people seemed to be standing round not doing anything much. If I only had a mask, thought Taggart, I could be in there too.

A mask. That would be a good idea anyway. He cursed himself for not having thought of it when he had been doing his shopping. Where might he find one? On an off-chance he went back to the unlit door and tried it. Inside was another theatre. He went in and found a small room leading off it with sinks, soap, towels: a scrubbing-up room. On the wall was a white cupboard. Taggart opened it. He was in luck. It contained neat piles of surgical caps and gloves, in plastic envelopes; and in another pile, also in sterile bags, masks. He took a couple and put them in his pocket. Then, as an afterthought, he unwrapped one and put it on, together with a cap. You can never be too safe.

He returned into the corridor. The next question was, how to get into the theatre? Once he was in, he was confident he would not be noticed. He waited awhile, thinking. Then the lit door opened. Had they finished? But no, only two people came out—a couple of nurses, by the look of it. Once outside, they removed their masks and began talking. They passed Taggart with scarcely a glance.

Well, nothing for it: he'd better take his chance. If people could come out, people could go in. He walked up to the door and entered quietly but firmly, as if he was meant to be there. No one took any notice.

The main reason for this seemed to be that their attention

was totally directed elsewhere—that is to say, to the operation, which seemed to be at a crucial stage. The patient was deathly still. A sheet covered his or her head, cut away to reveal a gap where the skull had been opened, and within which the surgeon was working. The long tube appeared to be some sort of television camera, which transferred a picture to monitor screens set around the room at different angles, so that everyone could see what was going on. These showed a highly magnified picture of the patient's brain, within which the surgeon was operating with some slender implement, perhaps a surgical laser. For the most part she, too, watched the screen, guiding her own movements with references to the magnified picture; occasionally—perhaps for particularly tricky bits—she watched through the camera tube itself. As to precisely what she was doing, it was impossible to tell. Cutting something out? Welding something in? There was no way in which a watcher could have said. But whatever it was, it required the intensest concentration, and of the most unremitting kind. On and on it went, a microscopic movement here, a long pause, another microscopic movement there. The theatre was rapt. Taggart slipped out, unnoticed as he had slipped in.

He shut the door quietly behind him and began to walk back along the corridor towards the men's room. The strain of the past half-hour had given rise to an overpowering need to pee. He was also aware that he was sweating profusely, and looked forward to a splash of cold water on his face. Then he realized that he was not alone in the corridor. A man and a middle-aged woman were coming towards him, both wearing white coats. The woman was wearing a nurse's cap. They took in Taggart's surgical mask. 'Hi,' said the man. 'How's it going in there?'

'OK. Fine,' said Taggart. His voice seemed to encounter some obstruction in his throat, around which it emerged thin and strangely falsetto. The man seemed about to ask another question. Taggart hurried on before he could formulate it and slid through the door of the men's room. At least being caught short seemed a convincing reason for a hurried departure.

He locked himself into a cubicle and slid the surgical mask and cap into his pocket. Sitting on the toilet seat, he pondered his next move. Now he was in here, he must make the most of it. As far as he could see, it was purely a question of keeping his nerve. He took a deep breath, left the cubicle, and splashed cold water on to his profusely sweating face. Then, retaining the white coat, he slipped out of the men's room. The coast was clear: no one in sight.

Down the corridor he heard the sound of something being wheeled along. He walked towards the sound. It proved to be a trolley laden with coffee, juice, cookies and doughnuts. Mid-morning snacks for the inhabitants of the corridor. It was being wheeled by an impassive Mexican woman, the first non-white Taggart had met in the building. She barely glanced at him. Probably all whites look alike to her, thought Taggart with relief. She knocked perfunctorily at a door, poked her head in and said, 'Coffee?' Evidently the answer was in the affirmative, because she re-emerged, poured a cup, added sugar and took it in together with a doughnut on a paper plate.

He moved on down the corridor and glanced in through the window of a door past which the coffee-lady must already have passed. Inside a plump middle-aged man was finishing his doughnut. He didn't look as if he needed doughnuts, but then any distraction is welcome in hospital. The man, so far as Taggart could make out from the door, had a scar on his head: he was balding, and the scar, on one side and towards the front, was very noticeable, neat, three sides of a square, as if a flap of skin had been hinged back. Taggart opened the door and walked in.

A television was on in one corner of the room. On it a woman was shouting at a man. The plump man didn't seem to be watching it; in fact he didn't seem to be doing anything much, just sitting. Taggart said briskly, trying to sound like a doctor on his rounds, 'And how are you feeling today?'

'OK.' The man sounded bored. Well, anyone would be bored. Perhaps that was part of what they were trying to do here. See how long it took actually to bore a person to death. As far as Taggart could see, the television was the only form of distraction in the room.

'Not too bored?'

The man looked surprised. This was evidently not one of the questions he was used to being asked. 'Bored? Nope. I just sit here.'

'Time hang heavy?'

'It passes.'

'Operation seem to have any effect yet?'

'What do you think?' the man returned, showing no visible emotion. 'You got the machines.'

'But what do you think?'

'Seems much the same. Can't remember nothin', but then I guess I never could remember much.'

'Scar not hurting?' Better say something which might sound authentic.

'Draws a little bit.' The man seemed to find it hard to say anything, his words driven out across seeming mists of sleep. He shut his eyes. His head nodded. He was asleep. Taggart recalled d'Alembert, who slept fifteen minutes longer each day until the day came when he never awoke at all. He left the room, shutting the door quietly behind him. Perhaps the man had seen him as if in a dream. Perhaps there was no difference for him between sleeping and waking.

Taggart went on down the corridor. No one appeared to be living behind the next door. From the room after that, however, he heard voices.

He was about to hurry past the door when, glancing briefly through the window, he caught sight of one of the people in the room. He had seen a photograph of that person in Southampton—Lulu had shown it to him. It was Wesley Mitchell.

Taggart looked around. The sound of voices was tantalizing—he could almost, but not quite, make out what was being said. If he put his ear to the keyhole he would no doubt hear better, but that was to assume that nobody would come along the corridor or open the door. Yet he had to know what Mitchell was saying—it was his best hope yet of finding out what was going on here.

He tried the door into the next room. It was not locked, and the room was uninhabited. He shut the door and put his ear to the wall. Nothing but an indistinct murmur. He looked around for something that might lead into the next room—a pipe, for instance—but none was immediately visible. Then he noticed a door in the wall. He opened it, and revealed a cupboard. Perhaps there would be a corresponding one next door? He stepped inside and found that, when he put his ear to the wall, he could hear quite distinctly what was being said. Always cautious, he shut the cupboard door behind him and settled down to listen.

CHAPTER 19

For the moment, though, he was out of luck. 'So long,' he heard Wesley Mitchell say. 'We'll be seeing you.' Then there was a sound as of chairs being pushed back. Whatever conversation had been taking place had now evidently ended. Then the door of the next room opened and shut, and he heard the sound of footsteps passing his door and receding into the distance.

Well, he was getting somewhere, though not very far. All he had ascertained was what they already knew—namely, that Wesley Mitchell visited this place from time to time. And that this was one of his times. That was a bonus. And that he took a particular interest in the person in the next-door room. And who was that? Anyone Taggart might recognize? There was one easy way to find out. Slipping noiselessly out of his cupboard and then out again into the corridor, Taggart, gowned and masked, passed by the next room again and glanced once more in at the little window.

The inhabitant, however, was of no apparent interest. He (for it was a man) was of medium height, dark and stocky, with a neat black beard. He was sitting in a chair by the window, leafing through a paperback book. Taggart had never seen him before. Wesley Mitchell and whoever had been with him had meanwhile disappeared. They had been walking in the direction of the door leading to the staircase. Taggart now made for this. At the bottom, the lights on one of the elevators showed that it had just reached the reception area. By the time he got down there Mitchell and his companion would no doubt have left.

What now? He could give chase, but there didn't seem to be much point in that. Mitchell might lead him somewhere else, but even if he did (and Taggart was by no means confident that he would succeed in following him—that wasn't his speciality, and this wasn't his city) they would be no further. The quarry they were after was not Mitchell, but Charles Watson. Mitchell was of interest only because he was the last person who could be directly connected with Watson. They had come to New York; and if any clue was to be found to Watson's disappearance, it seemed likely to be somewhere here, in the Prospect Psychodynamics Clinic. To which he knew Mitchell would be returning.

But when?

If he knew, he could wait. Or come back. But he did not know. So what should he do?

Taggart mentally went through his diary, or what he could remember of it. This was Thursday. He had various meetings arranged for next week, at least two of which he would be loath to miss. They were for the Wednesday and the Friday. That gave him a week. No, less: to get back and be ready for Wednesday morning, he really ought to leave New York Monday night at the latest. All right: he had five days. That's how long he could wait for Mitchell. If nothing happened in that time, he could reasonably feel he had fulfilled his personal obligations so far as Belinda was concerned. He would tell her everything he knew, and if she wanted to set a proper detective on the job, or confront Mitchell herself, she could. Meanwhile, he would wait. Taggart was used to that. It was part of the job.

That, however, did not make it any the less tedious. Taggart, like Lulu, reckoned up what he would need to keep him going during his vigil. He could, of course, go out for meals if he wished: but quite apart from the risk of missing something, he felt he would do better to draw as little attention to himself as possible—which meant appearing as little as possible. All right, then. He would need iron rations and—possibly even more important—reading materials. There was a bed, there was a washroom, the place was, like all hospitals and indeed like every public building he had ever entered in America, heated to boiling-point. So there would be no problem about basic bodily needs. All he would need would be caution and patience. And luck.

He negotiated an unobtrusive exit successfully: the lovely receptionist took no notice of him, and by the time he returned, during the evening visiting-hour, laden with fruit (for the friend he was visiting) and a briefcase filled with bars of chocolate and paperbacks, the grey-haired lady who took her place in the evenings was safely installed. He had left his white coat and his masks in the cupboard of the room he proposed to occupy (and let's hope they don't suddenly wheel in an urgent case, he prayed). Returning to the thirteenth floor, he noticed that the washroom was even equipped with showers, should things get too squalid. He was surprised that more of New York's disadvantaged street-dwellers didn't try their luck in places such as this. Or maybe they did. How was he to know?

So far, so good. He settled himself down to wait. Time passed. Luck, however, did not seem to be with him. He was ready for anything, but nothing happened. Thursday evening, Thursday night. Well, he hadn't been expecting anything so soon. Friday. Every time steps passed his door, his heart entered his mouth. People seemed to be continuously tramping up and down the corridor. He had stationed himself just inside the door, so that he could not be seen from the outside, and thought up a story (he would pretend to be a frightened foreigner, unable to understand what anyone was saying, and hope that they would throw him out: he had prudently left his passport and travellers' cheques at the front desk of his hotel). But nobody came into his room. Occasionally, someone would enter the room next door. When that happened, he would run across to the cupboard and stick his ear to the wall. But it was never anything interesting: just meals being delivered, as far as he could make out. The man next door watched television a lot. Taggart could understand that. He couldn't remember a time in his life when the minutes had passed so slowly.

Saturday passed, and Sunday. Roll on Monday. Perhaps he needn't wait all day. Most of the fruit and chocolate was gone, and he was beginning to feel seriously hungry as well as bored. Something he hadn't reckoned with was that, when darkness fell, he couldn't turn on the light to read without the risk of drawing unwelcome attention to himself. And darkness fell early, these winter evenings.

Sunday evening. The place was deathly quiet. Fewer footsteps than usual passed his door. Well, naturally: most of the staff were at home. Surely it would be safe to turn a light on now, give himself a break? The man next door was watching a ball game. Even though he was completely uninterested in sport of any description, Taggart envied him.

Footsteps coming down the corridor. Two people. Heavy steps, sounded like men.

They approached, slowed: Taggart's heart was in his mouth. They stopped—and entered the next-door room.

This was it. This had to be Wesley. Who else could it be?

It was Wesley. It was the same voice he had heard last Thursday.

'Hi,' it said. 'Time for our little discussion. Took a little longer than I expected to get things sorted out.'

'OK,' returned another voice. It sounded English. Taggart listened intently—so hard that his ear felt as though he would never be able to detach it from the wall. 'What now?'

'That's up to you,' said Mitchell's voice. 'Depends how confident you feel.'

'Up to me?' The English voice spoke again. It seemed familiar. Taggart was almost sure he recognized it. Or did he? It was years since he had heard Charles Watson speak. Was this the same voice? Or was he imposing associations upon it? Not that he could see how Charles Watson could possibly be in the next room. Unless, of course, the second pair of footsteps belonged to him.

'Sure,' said Mitchell.

'Well then, I'd like to go home,' said the Englishman. 'Back to Leamingworth. See my wife and family. They must be getting worried. See my colleagues, though I don't expect they are.' It *was* Watson, then. Taggart was beginning to recall his voice. There was a certain urbane hesitancy about it that was very characteristic. And yet . . .

'That should be most interesting,' said a third voice. And this, too, was an English voice—and one that Taggart most certainly recognized. It belonged to Peter Fischer. 'I was just thinking about that lunch we had together at the Reform Club. Remember?'

'When I pooh-poohed the whole thing.'

'That's the one.'

'You had the advantage of me there. But nobody likes being browbeaten. You should learn a little tact.'

Fischer said blandly, 'It was sheer impatience. I couldn't wait to see what would happen.'

'Anyhow, we got there in the end,' Wesley interjected.

'That's right,' said Fischer. 'So when d'you plan to come back?'

'As soon as possible, really. There's some loose ends I ought to tie up at Jones first, I suppose.'

'You mean the apartment,' said Wesley.

'That kind of thing.' Charles agreed. Taggart wondered, not for the first time, how much Wesley knew about his daughter's activities.

Wesley said, 'Don't worry about that. I'll deal with it. I feel kind of responsible for this whole thing.'

'You could fly back to London with me if you want,' said Fischer.

'All right,' said Charles.

'How're you feeling?' Wesley asked.

'A little nervous, I have to admit.'

'You'll wow them,' said Wesley incomprehensibly.

There was a noise of people getting up and moving around. Peter Fischer said, 'I need fortifying after all this.

Something to eat and preferably drink. You coming with us?'

'I'll stay here, if you don't mind. There are one or two things I want to think through.'

'All right, I'll get Sue-Ann to fix the tickets.'

Footsteps; a door opened and shut. Taggart, from his cupboard, heard the steps pass the door of the room he was in and recede. When silence was re-established, he took his shoes off and crept out of his cupboard. Silently he opened the door of his room, stepped out—no one in sight—and closed it behind him. Then, slowly, cautiously, and as soundlessly as he could, he tiptoed up to the door of the next room and peered in through the little peephole. If Wesley Mitchell, Charles Watson and Peter Fischer had just been talking next door, what had happened to the bearded man?

He was still there. He lounged on the bed facing the television, which stood on a shelf fixed to the opposite wall. But he did not move to turn it on again. Rather, he seemed to be deep in thought.

Taggart was rooted to the spot. He could not take his eyes off the man on the bed. There had been Mitchell, there had been Peter Fischer, and there had been—this man. Who was preparing to pass himself off as Charles Watson. To take up his life. But without—it seemed—making any effort to *look* like him. No wonder he had felt some hesitation about assigning that voice to Charles Watson. Now that he knew it *wasn't* Charles, he realized that the timbre was slightly wrong. The accent, even the intonation, were similar, but the whole voice was slightly—lower? It was hard to say precisely. An ineradicable American undertone, perhaps. Did Americans find it as hard to do British voices as British did to do American ones? Taggart tried to think of instances, but could recall only Marlon Brando as Fletcher Christian in a film about Bligh of the Bounty. That had sounded British all ight. And so did this man. It was just . . . The fact was, Taggart had to admit, that it was just that this man wasn't Charles Watson. He sounded just like him, he spoke lines from Charles Watson's life, but he *wasn't* him. Was he?

What now? Taggart tiptoed back into the next-door room, put his shoes back on, and sat down on the bed to think.

As far as he could see, there were two options. He could confront 'Watson' now, or at any rate talk to him; or he could cop out, get away from the clinic, and return to England to await developments. Curiosity urged the first course; professional instinct, the second. He wouldn't get any more out of 'Watson' if he confronted him, either as a journalist or as a pseudo-doctor, than he had gathered by eavesdropping. On the other hand, if he confronted him now, there was always the chance that 'Watson' would recognize him when—as he intended to do, for both private and professional reasons—he met him in England. The bearded man couldn't help noticing his accent if he spoke to him now; the white coat was merely protective colouring, no help in person-to-person situations. And it would not be a good idea, Taggart considered, for anyone to know he had been visiting the clinic. There was the question of his personal safety—something pretty strange was going on, and it was something Mitchell and his friends might prefer to keep to themselves. Then again there was the long-term view. He didn't want the whole operation to close down before he had a chance to find out what it was about. And he hadn't even had the elementary sense to bring a camera with him. Not that photographs would have revealed very much. What had he seen, after all? The sign outside, whatever *that* might mean. Surgeons performing an operation on somebody's brain. A zombie who appeared to have undergone an operation similar to the one he had witnessed. A man who was Charles Watson in everything but appearance. What was one to make of that? Pretty circumstantial stuff. As to what the circumstances pointed to—well, that was in such stark contrast to everything he thought he knew about science that Taggart preferred, for the moment, to set it aside. He needed to take advice.

He slipped out of the room. On an impulse he turned, not in the direction of the stairs but the other way along the corridor, peeking in at the windows of the doors he passed. Most of the rooms were empty. In one there was a black woman, in her forties, Taggart judged; in another, a thin young white woman with stringy blondish hair. In one was a young white man with the vacant stare of a drug addict. Charles Watson, or the person who had been Charles Watson, was not, however, in any of them.

Taggart found himself back where he had started, at the door leading to the stairs. He walked down to the next floor, then took the elevator to the foyer, which was now almost deserted. Indeed, it contained only two people apart from the glamorous receptionist: Wesley Mitchell and Peter Fischer. They were engaged in animated conversation. As Taggart entered they glanced round and lowered their voices. They didn't look at him twice.

Taggart made for the door. He would walk down the stairs to the ground floor—far rather that than stand around waiting for an elevator with Peter Fischer sitting three yards away. As he opened the door, Fischer looked up, and Taggart heard an indistinct exclamation. Damn! Glancing at his watch—if he *hadn't* been rumbled, there ought to be some explanation for his sudden turn of speed, and perhaps they might think he was late for something—he slid out of the door and ran down the four flights of stairs to the bottom so fast that his feet scarcely seemed to be making contact with the ground. Just as he reached the ground floor, he heard an elevator door open behind him. Not waiting to see whom it might disgorge, he rushed out into the street and ran in the direction of the subway.

He arrived, breathless, and, just before he plunged into its depths, glanced behind him. Nobody seemed to be following him. Had Fischer seen him? Perhaps he hadn't. After all, Taggart was just about the last person he would be expecting to see. And he didn't have a beard, and he was wearing his white coat. As far as the beard went, one couldn't be sure. There were some people who simply didn't notice the presence or absence of facial hair, but just recognized the person. You had to know the person quite well, of course, but Taggart was sure Peter Fischer knew him well enough for that. And that shout he'd given . . . But maybe he was wrong. Or maybe Fischer had convinced himself that *he* was wrong. Let's hope so, thought Taggart.

It took him a long time to reach his hotel. He had been shaken by his close encounter, and as a result found it hard to concentrate on where he was going; the result of *that* being that he kept finding himself headed for strange places whose names meant nothing to him and which were probably instant death the moment you stepped into the street. British journalist mugged in Harlem. In the end he manœuvred himself to 57th Street and got off, regardless of the fact that this was miles uptown and east of where he wanted to go. But he preferred to walk. At least on foot in Manhattan you can't get lost.

Safely back in his hotel room he threw himself down on the bed and went to sleep. When he woke up it was eight o'clock. He picked up the phone and keyed the number of Lulu's dorm.

'Can you leave your number? I'll get her to call you,' said the voice of whoever happened to be on telephone duty that evening.

'Look, this is very important. Can you just check if she's there? It really is important.'

His voice must have carried a genuine ring of urgency because, after a moment's hesitation, the girl said, 'OK, just hold the line, please,' and could be heard walking away from the phone. And after a long, long pause, there was Lulu.

'Who is this?' She sounded terrified.

'Me. Andrew Taggart.'

'Andrew! Thank goodness you're safe.'

'Why shouldn't I be?'

'I don't know. That sinister place . . . Did you find Charles?'

'Yes. No. Sort of.'

'What d'you mean, sort of?'

'Hard to explain.' And you can say that again. 'Look, Lu, I've got to get back to England. Now, at once. I'm going to Kennedy now. I'll call you as soon as I can, or write. I just wanted to thank you. You were wonderful.'

'Was Charles there? Had he been there?'

'Yes, I think so,' Taggart said evasively. 'I think that was certainly the place.'

'He isn't dead, is he?'

'No. Not dead. I don't think so. But I don't think you'd recognize him.'

'What d'you mean, not recognize him?'

'Well, he's—changed. I think you should put Charles out of your mind, Lulu.'

'But what's happened to him.'

'If I'm not mistaken, that's something we'll all be finding out in the near future,' said Taggart unsatisfactorily, and with that he rang off.

CHAPTER 20

Sitting in the plane, Taggart drew breath for the first time in what felt like several months. He had got a standby ticket almost immediately, and had been able to board the plane late because he had no baggage apart from his briefcase. It was a Pan-Am flight, and it did not, as far as Taggart could see—which was not very far, because this was a jumbo, and full—contain Peter Fischer or the bearded man. And it seemed improbable that they would have made it to Kennedy before him. Indeed, there was—assuming that Fischer *had* seen Taggart, and had therefore concluded that things, whatever those were, were not quite as secret as he had hoped—a serious possibility that Fischer would abandon the whole plan. Whatever *that* was. If the new Charles—Charles the Second—did appear, then it would be fair to assume that everything was going ahead in spite of Taggart.

Anyhow, it would be prudent to act as if events would go ahead in spite of everything. In which case, Belinda Watson had to be told. Should he call her, Taggart wondered, from

Heathrow, or could he wait until he got home? At some point she must be warned of what was in store for her. If he waited, he might be too late. But if he didn't he might condemn her to an unnecessarily bad time; for how much could be said from a public call-box, especially from one of those dreadful phone-carousels at Heathrow, where you could never hear a word that was being said in the constant uproar and where there were always queues of people jiggling impatiently behind you. On the whole, he thought he'd wait till he got home.

Filthy, familiar London seemed homely and welcoming after Brooklyn. Naturally it was raining. Taggart put his head back and drank in the damp. He took a taxi to Hoxton. The old witch next door stuck her head out of the window.

'Been on one of yer trips then, Andrew?'

'Just a short one, Mrs Jenks.' The fewer people who knew he'd been in America the better. Taggart smiled at Mrs Jenks and let himself firmly into his house, shutting the door behind him. Now was not the moment for an hour's nice relaxed gossip.

He felt distinctly nervous as he dialled Belinda's number in Leamingworth. The phone rang five times. He was just about to put it down when the other end answered.

'Belinda, it's Andrew. I was just going to ring off, thought you must be out.'

'Sorry, I was in the garden.'

'In the rain?'

'It smells so nice out there in the rain . . . You're back.'

'That's right. Has anyone been in touch with you?'

'What about?'

That was all right, then. 'Well, it's about Charles, actually.'

'Did you find anything out? Has something happened to him?'

'Well, yes, it has.'

'Go on, Andrew. What?'

'It's hard to explain.'

'Is he ill?'

'No.'

'And not dead or disappeared?'

'No. No, not really.'

'What d'you mean, not really?'

'Well, it all depends what you think of as the essential Charles.'

'D'you mean he's lost his mind?'

'Not in the way you mean. But literally, I suppose that's just what he has done.'

'He's gone mad?'

'Not at all. I'm sorry, it's terribly hard to explain.' Taggart was going to add 'over the phone,' but he omitted this, realizing that it would be no easier face to face. 'What's happened is that his mind seems to have been transferred to someone else.'

'What on earth do you mean?'

'Just that.'

'Andrew, I think it's you that's lost your mind.'

'Well, don't say I didn't warn you. You're going to have a terrible shock, Belinda.'

'When?'

'When this person turns up.'

'When's that going to happen? Andrew, how do you know all this? What's been going on?'

'I think I'd better come and see you. Let me get a bit of sleep. I'll be with you tomorrow afternoon.'

Driving towards Leamingworth, Taggart tried to analyse his feelings. They were certainly a mixed bunch. There was some sense of worried personal involvement, his relations with Belinda being what they were. Though whether they *still* were he somehow doubted. Too much had happened that involved his professional curiosity, and it was difficult, Taggart always found, to combine the personal and the professional. In any contest the professional always won. That was the story of his life. Ace investigative reporter, personal life unsatisfactory despite genuine capacity for affection. Preference for intelligent women of a certain age. That was just his luck: nicely settled, and then the object of his attractions turns out to be at the centre of the hottest story of his life. He couldn't help thinking that even feelings deeper than Belinda's for him would be rocked by a request for her reactions to the return of her husband encased in another body. Exactly what did you feel when you realized what had happened, Mrs Watson?

That was another worry, of course. Would he be in time to witness the event? How much of a hurry would Fischer be in to test out the new creation *in situ*, always presuming he was still proposing to test it out? On the whole, Taggart thought he would still try, and the more he thought about it, the surer he was of this. After all, if some man who was not—and yet was—Charles Watson suddenly turned up claiming to be him, that was hardly an event which would pass unnoticed. And, since Peter Fischer and Wesley Mitchell were no strangers to the way the world worked, then it could reasonably be assumed that it was intended to be noticed. In which case, what did Taggart know that would not soon be common knowledge anyway? Well, the place and the personnel; but maybe that wasn't going to be a secret either. Wouldn't Wesley want to claim credit for any new breakthrough he had made? Mastermind, fixer-in-chief, the new Frankenstein? But maybe he wouldn't want to lay any proprietorial claim to this particular monster. As for Peter Fischer, he would adapt his game to the circumstances. That was his forte.

Belinda's house, at any rate, looked much the same as when he had last seen it. No obvious earthquakes had rocked it. 'Nothing's happened yet,' said Belinda, first thing when she opened the door. He'd been right about that one, anyhow, reflected Taggart ruefully. None of these fancy endearments, how are you feeling, how nice to see you, how about a quick one. None of that. Her mind was elsewhere.

'No, well, I didn't think it would have, yet.'

'Tell me all about it,' Belinda said, leading the way into the kitchen. She filled the kettle, made a pot of tea and set it on the table, together with a packet of chocolate digestives. At least she remembered that much.

Taggart suddenly felt very tired. Jet-lag biting as it always does, in mid-afternoon. And one always feels depressed when one is tired. 'Well, I went to find Lulu Mitchell,' he began bitchily. 'It was quite true what you suspected, by the way. Anyhow . . .'

He started at the beginning and went on until he came to the end. Then he stopped. It was almost dark outside. He must have been talking for hours. He looked at his watch. Just over an hour and a half, counting breaks for tea and biscuits and the odd interjection. But Belinda had not interrupted much until the end, when she had wanted to know, in the minutest detail, exactly what this person who seemed to *be* Charles—but was not Charles—looked like.

'You'll know soon enough,' Taggart assured her.

'Yes, but I want to be prepared. As much as it's possible.'

At this point the phone rang.

'Perhaps this is it,' said Taggart.

Belinda was dry-mouthed. She could hardly bring herself to lift the receiver. 'Blin?' said Charles's voice, using his old pet name for her. 'Darling, it's me.'

CHAPTER 21

Covering the mouthpiece with her hand, Belinda said, 'Can you go somewhere else. Another room. I don't feel like an audience for this.'

'Is it him?' She nodded. Taggart, sadly, left the room. He could understand how she felt—of course he could—but he was disappointed nevertheless. He couldn't even listen in on an extension, because there wasn't one. One of Charles's foibles was a dislike of telephones by his bed or indeed anywhere. He accepted that you had to have one in the house, but one was enough.

'Hello?' said Charles's voice again. 'Blin? Is that you?'

'Charles? Is it really you?'

'Darling, I'm most awfully sorry. You must have thought I'd vanished into thin air.'

'I did, rather. What happened?'

'To tell you the truth, I can't really remember. I seem to have a sort of gap.'

'How long for?'

'It's October now, isn't it? Well, I remember getting to Southampton—it was the spring then, May. I got an apartment—I remember that. And then—nothing.'

'There must be something. Where are you now?'

'One of those hotels near Heathrow.'

'But where did you come from?'

'I don't know. America, I suppose.'

'But—are you all right?'

'Perfectly, except for that damned gap. Are *you*? What's been happening to you? You must have been worried sick.'

'Well, yes, I was a bit worried.' The conceit of men would never cease to amaze Belinda. 'Things go on. Nothing much changes.'

'How're things at the department?'

'No idea. I haven't been there.' Oh dear, and there it was already—that old sparring tone. You'd think it would be possible to let that drop.

'Shouldn't think much has changed there, either.' He sounded faintly depressed.

'So when are you coming home?'

'Now, I suppose. I assume I can get out of here—I still seem to have my cheque-book and credit cards and things. I just thought I'd give you a ring first. Give you a bit of warning.'

'How will you get here?'

'By train. I checked, there's one leaves St Pancras at eight, gets to Leamingworth at ten to ten. Could you meet it?'

'Yes, of course.'

'OK, then, I'll see you there.' And he rang off.

Belinda called, 'It's all right, you can come back now.'

'Was that him?'

'Charles, yes.'

'What's happening?'

'He's coming back tonight. Wants me to meet him at

Leamingworth.' She looked hard at Taggart. 'Andrew, I think you've been under the influence or something.'

'What d'you mean?'

'That was *Charles*. I should know. I've spent twenty-five years living with him. All this nonsense about science fiction. You should know better than that.' She looked at him reproachfully. 'I don't know what you're trying to do, alienate me from my husband or something?'

'I expect I would quite like to do that, but I promise you, that's got nothing to do with this. Still, I don't blame you. When's he due?'

'Ten to ten. I'm meeting his train.'

'Shall I come with you?'

'Don't be silly.' She sounded horrified.

'No, I suppose not.' Taggart jingled his car keys in his pocket. 'Look, I'm pretty whacked. I haven't got the energy to drive home tonight. I'm going to find a hotel and go to bed. There's some sort of motel on the way to EMU—know the one I mean? Well, I'll be there. If you want me, give a ring. OK?'

'All right, though I can't think what I'd want you for. Sorry, but you know what I mean.'

'To help explain the situation to your daughter, for a start. Look how she reacted when it was just me. And I wasn't even pretending to be her father!' Belinda's face fell, and Taggart added hurriedly, 'Just a joke.'

'I know.'

'All right.' Taggart suddenly felt so tired that he didn't know if he could manage it even as far as the motel. He squeezed Belinda's hand and left.

It was by now six o'clock. Nearly four hours to wait. Belinda felt nervous. Too much was happening all at once. She couldn't really take in what Taggart had been telling her, let alone believe it. Clearly the relentless search for new scoops had gone to his head with dire results. On the other hand, something was clearly up. She didn't know what to think about this story of amnesia Charles had just told her. An easy way out of an awkward corner was what it sounded like to her. Perhaps he'd been off on a spree with Lulu—or more likely, with someone else: Taggart seemed to have been the one spending time with Lulu. But it wasn't like Charles just to duck away from reality like that.

Belinda ran a bath, then had something to eat. It was still only eight o'clock. She played the piano for a while, a habit of hers when she was waiting for time to pass; then tried to read, but failed to concentrate. Eventually the hands on her watch reached half past nine. Time to go.

The train was late, of course. Fifteen minutes: it wouldn't arrive till five past. The night had turned cold and windy. Belinda huddled into her coat and watched the passengers coming through the barrier. Seven minutes past ten: this must be Charles's lot. She strained to see into the passageway behind the barrier, but could see no sign of Charles. Eventually the stream slowed to a trickle. Then nobody. No Charles.

A stocky man with a black beard was looking at her. Eventually he came up to her. 'Blin?' he said, in Charles's voice.

Belinda fainted.

She came to lying on a bench in the station waiting-room. The dark man and the ticket-collector were bending solicitously over her. 'There, she's coming round,' the ticket-collector said as she opened her eyes. He sounded relieved. 'She'll be all right now.' He disappeared.

When Belinda found herself alone with the dark man, she began to shake violently. 'Don't be afraid,' he said in Charles's voice, with Charles's intonation. 'It's only me.'

'But . . . but . . .' Belinda couldn't speak: she couldn't think what to say. She pointed to the man, to his person that was so entirely the antithesis of Charles.

'I know,' said Charles's voice, soothingly, disconcertingly, speaking through the unknown mouth. 'But it's only me. Really.'

'But what happened?'

'I told you,' said the bearded man. 'I can't remember. I just woke up one morning and there I was.' He smiled at her. 'Is it that bad?'

'It's quite a shock.' Belinda sat up. 'How do I know you're not just some impostor?'

'Do I sound like one?' asked Charles's voice. 'Anyhow, why would anyone want to impersonate me?'

'I don't know. But then I wouldn't, necessarily, would I?'

'I'm not, though.'

He sat there on the bench, looking at her calmly. He felt solid and reassuring in a way she realized that Charles—the old Charles—never had. 'Better be getting home,' he said. 'D'you want me to drive?'

'No, I will. I feel OK now.' How would he know the way? Or the car? Belinda led the way out and across the road to where she'd parked. She ought to want to catch him out, see if he really could drive back home with no prompting. That was what Andrew would do. But somehow she didn't feel like doing that. She felt—it was hard to define how she felt—thoroughly well-disposed towards this person: more than she had towards Charles for years. The old Charles, that was. For some reason, into which she was not at present strong enough to probe, she was not just prepared but positively wanted to believe that this man was who he said he was. Charles, but in another body. She was prepared to be convinced: and if she was happy, why not everyone else?

They got home and she made a cup of tea. He seemed to know his way around the place well enough. He asked her about herself, about the children. All this time Belinda hardly said a word. She simply stared at this man; stared and stared, until after a while she began to get used to his presence. He took away the teacup and then took her hand. Charles's hand—Charles's *old* hand—had been long and thin and nervous. This new Charles's hand was, like the rest of him, solid, strong and comfortable.

'Shall we go to bed?' he said. 'I'm feeling pretty knocked out.'

She heard him moving around in the bathroom, and then he came into the bedroom wearing pyjamas—Charles's pyjamas, naturally: they were not quite big enough across and rather long—switched off the light and climbed in beside her.

For a long time they lay in the dark, not speaking. Then he reached across and took her hand. 'Don't be frightened,' he said.

And Belinda, sniffing the strange smell of this new body, hearing the familiar tones of the old voice, suddenly found that she wasn't frightened at all—or not very much. Fright, she realized, was fairly low on the list of emotions she was feeling at present. It was more that she was interested—very, very interested—and excited. They were two emotions she had not experienced in her husband's presence for about twenty years. The hand pulled her towards him, and she let herself roll over with a sense of delightful anticipation.

PART 3

CHAPTER 22

Taggart, alone in his hotel room, found himself, in spite of his tiredness, waiting for the phone to ring. Surely it must— that, or the whole episode in Brooklyn had been nothing but some strange dream or nightmare. Not that this seemed so very improbable. On a windy October night in Leamingworth, the very existence of the Prospect Psychodynamics Clinic seemed unlikely. But the phone did not ring. He did not know what to make of this. As far as he could see, there were only two possibilities. One was that he had indeed been grotesquely mistaken and the Charles who had appeared was the Charles of old. But in that case why had he reappeared so exactly on cue, just when the new-look Charles was due to make his public debut? The other was that in the end 'Charles' or Fischer or Mitchell had lost their nerve, and he had not appeared at all. In that eventuality he might have expected Belinda to get in touch, but not necessarily. She might have thought it was too late, or might not have wanted to talk about such an anticlimax so soon after its occurrence. The truth—that Belinda, after the first shock, was finding her new-look husband considerably more appealing than the one he had replaced—never occurred to him for a minute. So Taggart suffered in silence, not liking to telephone in such a potentially awkward situation (this was one of the drawbacks of getting personally involved: if he had been nothing but a journalist, such scruples would not have bothered him). And when, next morning, he did call her, the result was most unsatisfactory. Yes, Charles was back; she was delighted to see him again; as for the rest, she resolutely refused to enlarge upon it. He was very well, slightly changed—that much she would admit—but not at all for the worse. And with a happy wifeliness which pointedly excluded Taggart more effectively than any words could do, she rang off.

Various alternatives now faced Taggart. One was the traditional journalist's method of camping on the doorstep. Not being equipped with bugs, there was no way he could monitor what was going on inside the Watson house. But he could at least see who came in and out. For at some point Charles Watson, in whatever form, had to emerge. However, although this on the surface seemed an obvious strategy, it presented problems. One was that, short of renting a room opposite and peering from behind the net curtains, Taggart could see no way of maintaining this surveillance without Belinda's knowledge. The Watsons' street presented no very obvious cover otherwise. He could buy a pair of binoculars and lurk in his car, of course. But he felt curiously disinclined to do this, partly because of the terrible boredom involved, partly—he had to admit—because he didn't feel like facing Belinda if she caught him at it. Anyway, even if the man with the beard did come out of the house while Taggart was watching, what did that prove? Only that Belinda admitted bearded men to her house; and whose business was that? No one's—unless Taggart chose to confront him with the accusation that he was passing himself off as Charles Watson. In which case where—if Belinda was making no fuss—did Taggart come in? The answer was, in various roles, none of which he relished. The supplanted lover—no. The investigator of Wesley Mitchell, Peter Fischer and their suspicious dealings—possibly; but was this the moment to break that story? Taggart felt that it was not. When he revealed all he wanted to do so with maximum effect, and being premature never achieved that. No; if the bearded man was really going to pass himself off as Charles Watson, then Taggart, as far as he could see, had no need to demean himself in any of these unsatisfactory ways. The imposture, if that was the right word, would quickly come to public attention. And only Taggart would know the inside story. That would be the moment to get weaving.

Meanwhile he could leave things to take their own pace or he could speed them up, for instance, by alerting one of the Watson children to the situation. That would have to be Caroline, for the boy, as far as he knew, was still in Africa. And here once again personal feelings intervened. He knew that Caroline did not get on with her mother, and he was reluctant to hand her a rod with which to beat Belinda's back. But even if he did nothing, sooner or later Charles—or 'Charles'—would have to go back to work; and then the fat would be in the fire. Taggart wished his old friend Becky Ryan was still at EMU. In a way his whole involvement with all this was her fault—he would never have visited Belinda in the first place if he hadn't been there seeking news of Becky. And if she had been there she could have tipped him the wink. As it was, it seemed improbable that the arrival of a substitute Charles Watson would not make the newspapers somewhere. He resolved to get in touch with the cuttings service, and also to telephone the department from time to time asking for Charles. That way he should know pretty soon what was going on.

In fact Taggart need not have worried. There was no chance that he could miss the next development in the story. It screamed at him from the headlines four days later. **BOFFIN CHANGES BODIES**, announced the *Mail* in letters an inch high; or, as *The Times*, preferred, **PERSONALITY TRANSFER ALLEGED AT EAST MIDLAND UNIVERSITY**. The substance of the story was simple. Charles Watson, Reader in Mind Sciences, had returned—late—to his department at EMU from a sabbatical term spent in the United States. Only the Charles Watson who had returned in October was not the Charles Watson who had left in April. He sounded the same, his work was the same—the inner man was, it seemed, the same—but the outer shell was entirely different. This was, to all appearances, a quite different man. But—what were appearances? Were they everything—were they, indeed, anything? The man in question averred that they were not. His story was a fantastic one. Charles Watson, he said, had been particularly interested in the location of memory, and had gone to the States in order to pursue that topic. He was interested in the possibility of memory transplants, and thought he had evolved a way, in conjunction with a colleague, of achieving these. The time had come when no more could be done without using human guinea-pigs. Feeling that no one had the right to impose such a risk on someone else, Dr Watson had requested that his colleague conduct the experiment on himself. The current Charles Watson was the result. In all essentials he was Charles Watson. Mrs Watson accepted him as such. As he said, 'My interest is in the mind. Frankly, I see the body only as a vehicle.' As to the details of the operation or the colleague with whom he had been working, he could—or would—give little satisfactory explanation. One result of the operation, he explained, appeared to be an amnesia covering the whole of the period immediately preceding it. The ostensible reason for his American visit had been to work with Dr Wesley Mitchell of Jones University. Dr Mitchell confirmed that Watson had indeed paid him a short visit, and that he was indeed concerned with the location of memory, but he was not working on memory transplants, whatever those might be. He doubted whether any such things were possible, though of course it was never wise to be dogmatic. Watson—the original Charles Watson, that was—had stayed at Jones only until the end of May. After that he had disappeared and Dr Mitchell had no idea where he had gone. This was the first he had heard of him since then.

Reading these stories, Taggart's first reaction was to telephone Belinda. But of course her number was engaged, and the operator confirmed that the telephone was off the hook. It had in fact been off the hook since seven that morning, when Belinda had received a telephone call from her daughter Caroline.

'What's all this rubbish in the papers about Daddy?' Caroline demanded.

'It's not rubbish. It's true,' Belinda protested.

'Really, Mother, I've been wondering about you for some time, but now I know you've finally taken leave of your senses.'

'What d'you mean? Don't you think I'm the person best qualified to know who is and who isn't your father?'

On the other end of the line, to Belinda's horror, Caroline burst into tears.

'Darling, don't. Don't cry. Something's wrong, isn't it? That's what you came to tell me that day, and you never did. What is it? Is it Jonathan?'

'Don't mention his name to me.'

'Why, what happened?'

'He moved out. He found someone he liked better.'

'But what about your job? Doesn't that mean you see him . . .?'

'I've just found a new one. It's still hard enough, with the mortgage. We're trying to sell, but the market's collapsed and it doesn't look as if we'll get what we paid for it, even. I thought at least I had my family. And now you're trying to make me believe that some strange man is really my father! Aren't you even interested in what's happened to Daddy?'

'I suppose I should be,' mused Belinda, 'but to tell you the truth, I really think I prefer him the way he is now.'

'Oh, God! How can you say something like that?'

'Well, it just makes a lovely change, after twenty-odd years. Like when everybody moves round two places at a dinner-party after the main course, well, sort of. Some people get closer over the years, but somehow that never happened with us. It's like another chance.'

Indeed, Belinda did not know when she had been happier. The contrast between her own delightful situation and that now facing poor Caroline could hardly have been greater. She felt guilty on that score, but on no other. The man now living with her undoubtedly was Charles, in that he spoke Charles's thoughts in Charles's voice. Only the body was different, and this Belinda found extremely exciting. It was like having an affair, but with your own husband. Whether in response or because the new Charles simply fancied Belinda as much as she did him, the two of them were having a wonderful time. Belinda wondered what she could do to help her daughter. Should she invite her home to stay, to get away from everything for a while until her flat was sold? As things stood, that hardly seemed a practicable solution.

'Ooh!' said Caroline while her mother was still pondering. 'It's no use talking to you!' And she rang off and Belinda, realizing that Caroline would merely be the first of many callers that day, none of whom she wanted to speak to, left her phone off the hook.

Taggart mused on what to do next. One possibility was to join the mob who would undoubtedly be assembled round the Watson house and the Psychology Department at EMU. But on the whole there seemed little point in that. He would only find out what he had known long before anybody else. As for phoning, presumably the department secretary's line would also be permanently engaged, and anyone who could tell him what he wanted to know would have handed out instructions that they weren't taking calls from journalists. He would just be referred to the university press officer, which would be worse than useless. On an impulse he dialled what had, when he had known her, been Becky's office number at EMU, and which might now belong to whoever had taken over her office in the hut. A woman's voice answered.

'Is that the Psychology Department?'

'Who is this?' The woman sounded suspicious. Naturally enough—the place must be besieged.

'My name's Andrew Taggart. I'm an old friend of Becky Ryan's—used to work there.'

'She hasn't been here for years.'

'No, I know. The fact is, I'm a journalist, I work for *New Politics*—'

'I thought I knew your name.'

'Well, I rather hoped Becky's phone would still belong to someone in the department.'

'Oh God.'

'There's really only one thing I wanted to know.'

'What is it?' She sounded resigned.

'How does this new version of Charles Watson cope with the work?'

'There hasn't been a lot of time to find out,' his interlocutor responded tartly.

'No, I can imagine that. But does he seem like an impostor? I mean, could he possibly be Charles?'

'It's hard to say.' Taggart relaxed: she sounded quite interested now—at least, enough to prevent her ringing off. 'I mean, I didn't—I don't—know Charles very well. He has his own little group that he tends to work with most of the time.'

'And you're not one of them?'

'No . . . But I know them, of course. And apparently he's quite convincing as far as that's gone.'

'What happened? Did he just turn up?'

'Yes, last week.'

'Must have caused quite a sensation.'

'You can say that again.'

'Is he in now?'

'No, I believe the university is considering its position.'

'I can believe that. Well, thanks very much. You've been extremely kind.'

'Not at all. Give my love to Becky if you see her.'

'Sure.' Taggart put down the phone and thought longingly about Becky for a few minutes. Then, resolutely putting her out of his mind, he considered what to do next.

CHAPTER 23

The first thing Taggart did was to switch on his word-processor and start to write a piece about the affair. But he quite soon switched it off again. Because, of course, there was a gaping hole at the centre of it. The fact was that although he was remarkably well-informed about the peripherals of this affair—and indeed, even some of its more central aspects—he still hadn't interviewed any of the principals other than Lulu and Belinda. And not only were they not the central figures, but the most basic loyalties prevented him saying much of what he knew about them. How could he tell the world that Lulu had been having an affair with Charles? It wouldn't be so bad for her, though it would be bad enough. But for Belinda; for Lulu's mother; for Charles's children—No, he couldn't do it; anyway, it was hardly central to the real story. And could he really use what Belinda had told him in that last conversation, about being in love with her new husband? *That* was certainly interesting, but to print it would hardly be the action of a friend. No; he would have to speak to one of the others. Fischer? He dismissed the notion. All he wanted to do was keep out of Peter Fischer's way until the piece was safely set up in type, preferably out and distributed. Wesley? He didn't know him. That left just one person: the new Charles Watson, Charles the Second.

But he would not do this immediately. Things were still too hot: he'd never get the kind of relaxed interview he wanted and that he might well be able to arrange in a couple of weeks' time. Accordingly, it was half way through November before he tried phoning Belinda again, on his return from covering the Party conferences. Nothing, he decided then, could be more unreal, or maybe surreal was the word he wanted, than those megalomaniac talkfests at run-down English seaside resorts. It was time to return to the real world.

Belinda appeared to have had her phone reconnected. She even answered it, after a while.

'Belinda, it's me. You can't hold me off for ever. Not after all I've done for you. I want to come and interview your new husband. After all, didn't I go rushing off to America to find him for you?'

Belinda sighed down the phone. 'I suppose I've been expecting you.'

'Well, of course you have! You're not stupid. What else would you expect?'

'All right, Andrew, you can come down tomorrow. Let's get it over with. And after that I don't want to see you again. Not for a while, anyhow. It's nothing personal.'

'Nothing personal!'

'Oh, you know what I mean. Come for lunch?'

'That's a bit early. I've got one or two things to do in the morning. I'll come around half past two, three. OK?'

Next morning was a fine, blue day, with that crisp late-autumn sparkle. A day to get out of London. Taggart decided to give himself a treat and abandon the various boring odds and ends which needed clearing up. He would go to Leamingworth at once, give himself lunch in that nice pub by the river which they'd visited together so often during the summer, and descend on Belinda and Charles 2 rather earlier than they were expecting him. That should unsettle them a little, which would be all to the good. What was more, he would do himself a favour, he wouldn't drive but would go by train. That way he'd avoid the long road back in the dark. He packed a small rucksack with work to do on the train, got on a bus which would take him to St Pancras, and felt his spirits rise as he left Hoxton behind him.

They rose even further as the train approached Leamingworth. In the Leam valley most of the leaves were off the trees, and the lacy branches stood out against the blue sky and the rich brown ploughed fields. Taggart stretched and prepared to leave the train. He glanced at his watch. Ten to twelve. Excellent. He'd go straight to the pub, which stocked a really excellent local bitter, order their meat and two veg lunch, take a short walk and then go and beard Mr and Mrs Belinda. There was a walk down by the river he always enjoyed, and it looked as if he wouldn't be coming here much after this. You couldn't blame Belinda. Nobody wants a ghost at their feast, and there isn't a lot in it for the ghost, either.

This plan he proceeded to put into action. He finished his lunch just after one and set off on his walk. The pub stood near a bridge beside which a path led down to the river bank.

The river path, as usual, was almost deserted. There didn't even seem to be the usual fishermen, crouched under enormous umbrellas. Perhaps it was the sunshine that was putting them off. No point in bringing out your umbrella on a day like this. Which way should he go? Upriver in the direction of Belinda's house—the end of her garden would then be just opposite him—or down the other way, out of the town, when he would end up in the first of a series of fields full of cows? Probably best to keep away from Belinda—he didn't want her to think he was spying on her. On the other hand, he felt reluctant to quit Leamingworth without one more glance at that garden and its ridiculous pavilion. He'd got very fond of it. It represented many happy hours for him. He set off upriver.

When he got there, he paused for a while looking across. It was hard to tell, but there seemed to be some people in the pavilion. Belinda and her new Charles, presumably. On a day like this she'd probably persuaded him to take their lunch out there, slightly frigid, but so scenic! Suddenly overcome with embarrassment in case they should spot him staring across, or with jealousy, or with some other indefinable emotion, he turned on his heel and walked back fast in the other direction. The only other person visible was a dogwalker moving slowly in the same direction as himself. By the time he reached the field of cows he had calmed down. All around was silence, broken only by the sound of tearing grass. You couldn't even hear the traffic here, except for a crack that sounded like a car backfiring.

He turned the corner of Belinda's street just after two. But here things ceased to go as he had anticipated. As he turned the corner, he saw that there was a great commotion taking place just about by the Watsons' house. There was an ambulance, police cars, a gawping group of bystanders. He walked on down the street, and saw that Belinda's front door was open. 'What's up?' he asked a woman whom he vaguely recognized from previous visits as living opposite, and who was now deep in whispered conversation with another woman, similarly grey-haired and iron-permed, whom he did not recognize.

'I *think* someone's died,' she said in the hushed tones of reverent confidentiality. 'They just took a stretcher into the ambulance, and the blanket was over the head.'

Taggart found that he could neither move nor speak.

Something seemed to have closed up in his throat, and at the same moment all strength had left his legs, so that he almost fell over. Belinda, he thought. The bastard's killed Belinda. What harm did she ever do? He rushed unsteadily towards a policeman who was standing about outside the house. 'What's happened?' he asked, and then, because no understandable words had actually emerged, repeated the question.

'I'm sorry, sir. I'm afraid I can't talk about it, and you certainly can't go in there,' the policeman added, barring the front door through which Taggart was trying to barge his way.

'But Mrs Watson's a friend of mine! I want to find out if she's all right!'

'Perfectly all right, sir, I believe.'

'Oh, thank goodness for that. I thought . . .' and Taggart's voice trailed away lamely.

At this moment Belinda, closely followed by another policeman, came into the hall. 'Andrew! I thought I heard your voice! Oh, thank God,' she said, and fell, sobbing, into his arms.

'Are you a friend of Mrs Watson's, then, sir?' said the second policeman—at least, Taggart assumed he was a policeman, although he was not wearing uniform.

'Yes. She was expecting me,' said Taggart, marvelling, the moment after he had said this, at the kneejerk reaction even of experienced cynics like himself necessitating that he explain himself in the presence of a policeman. He patted Belinda's heaving back and stroked her hair. 'There, there,' he said. 'It's all right now. Whatever's happened?'

'Oh, Andrew. Someone shot Charles.'

'Shot him? When?'

'We were having lunch in the little summer-house, you know, at the end of the garden, and there must have been someone on the other side of the river. There was this bang and Charles just fell down. There was—' But here speech left her and all she could do was indicate her head with her hand.

Taggart remembered the people he had glimpsed in the

pavilion, and the crack he had taken for a car backfiring. That must have been the shot. Whoever had fired it must have been lurking around while he was standing there. Taggart shivered.

'All right, Mrs Watson,' said the policeman. 'We shall have to talk to you again later, but I don't think we need bother you any more just for the moment. If you wouldn't mind keeping away from the summer-house for the moment until the photographer's finished. He won't be long. Would you like us to get in touch with anyone to look after you?'

'No, thank you,' she muttered. 'Andrew can stay with me.'

'All right, sir. If you wouldn't mind just answering a few questions. Matter of routine. Then we'll leave you in peace.'

'Yes, of course. Might I know who I'm talking to?'

'Certainly, sir,' said the man evenly, and produced a warrant card which informed Taggart that he was talking to Detective-Inspector Rogers, Leamingworth CID. 'Now.' He led the way back into the sitting-room, sat down and produced a notebook and pencil. 'If you wouldn't mind giving me your name and address.'

Taggart did so and described what he had been doing that day.

'Down by the river, were you, sir. I suppose you didn't hear the sound of a shot?'

'As a matter of fact I think I might have. I was in that field with the cows, you know, if you walk along the river path in the other direction, and I heard what I thought was a car backfiring. But it could have been the shot. It was about the right time. At least, I know nothing had happened ten minutes before that, because I'd walked down in the other direction first and I noticed that there were some people in the pavilion.'

'You couldn't tell me who they were, or how many, could you, sir?'

'No, I'm afraid I couldn't. They were inside the pavilion. All I could make out from the other side of the river was that there seemed to be people moving in there.'

'And would you mind telling me exactly what were you doing looking across like that, Mr Taggart?'

'I told you. I had some time to spare, so I thought I'd walk down by the river for a few minutes. It's very pleasant on a day like this.'

'You're familiar with this part of Leamingworth, are you, then, sir?'

'Yes, Mrs Watson and I are old friends. I've often stayed here.'

'And I suppose you didn't notice anyone carrying a shotgun when you were in the pub? Or by the river?'

'Not that I can remember.'

'No. Well, perhaps we'll be in touch with you again if we need any further help.'

'Certainly.'

'Thank you, sir. Goodbye now, Mrs Watson. Look after yourself. Ah, here comes the photographer, he must have finished. So we'll leave you in peace.'

'Can you get those people to go away?' said Belinda.

'I'll see what I can do.' A moment later, they heard him urging the assembled neighbours to move along, now, please. The ambulance had left some time before. The police car drove off. They were alone.

Belinda was quite collected now, though she couldn't stop shaking. Taggart made a pot of tea. He put a lot of sugar in Belinda's cup. Belinda said she'd already been given a cup by the police, but she accepted another one meekly enough. 'We were just sitting there,' she said. 'It was such a lovely day, and it's very sheltered there, the sun comes through the glass and makes it lovely and warm. Well, you know what it's like. So we thought we'd have a cup of coffee there. And then—'

'Someone shot through the glass?'

'Charles was sitting right by the window over the river.'

'Did you notice anyone hanging around there? See them running away or anything?'

'There may have been someone—you know how it is, there are always people walking their dogs and so on, they're just part of the landscape. You don't really notice them.'

'Did you see me? I was standing on the opposite bank just before it must have happened.'

'No, you see, we didn't even see you. One just doesn't notice anything.'

'And you didn't see anyone running away?'

'No. All I could think about then was Charles. And there's that clump of trees—they could easily have hidden in there till they saw me running back to the house.' Just as they'd presumably hidden there until Taggart had moved off and the coast was clear. That must have spoiled their plans, some idiot coming and standing, staring, just when they were ready to go. Whoever they were.

Belinda looked up at Taggart, her grey eyes staring in a face whose skin suddenly seemed to be drawn tight over the high cheekbones. 'Who could have done it, Andrew? Why would anyone do a thing like that?'

Taggart shook his head. 'Perhaps it was just some maniac. No reason at all.'

'D'you think so? In a way it would be nice to think that.'

Taggart shook his head. 'No, I suppose I don't, really. There've been altogether too many strange things going on for me to think that. But don't ask me what *did* happen. I haven't the faintest idea.'

Belinda said, 'Andrew, you can't stay here. You're a busy man—you've got too much to do. Don't worry about me, I shall be all right.'

'But I do worry about you! What d'you take me for? I tell you what, why don't you come back to London with me? You could stay at my place for a while if you wanted.'

Belinda had visited Taggart's house a couple of times. She shook her head firmly. 'No, thanks, it's sweet of you, but I'd rather be here.'

Taggart remembered the piled up plates in the sink, the accumulated dust, the heaps of papers everywhere, the grey sheets—all the things which were so familiar that, as a rule, he didn't even notice them. 'Perhaps you're right,' he conceded. 'But you can't stay here all by yourself. What about Caroline? Or Stuart? Is he still away?'

'No, he's back. But he's started his term. I'll tell him, of course—have to ring his college, I suppose.' She sighed. 'Caroline will organize me. And she won't be a bit sorry that this has happened. She terribly disapproved of—of—'

'I can imagine,' said Taggart, thinking of his own meeting with Caroline. 'Has she met him?'

'She was here for dinner last night, as a matter of fact. It was perfectly clear what she thought.' Belinda shook her head. 'Poor kid. I know what you think, but I feel sorry for her. She had everything all sorted out. She had this wonderful job, and Jonathan, and the new flat. She never did think much of the way we organized things, Charles always leaving everything to me, and she and I—well, anyway, she'd just got herself established on her own account, and suddenly it all evaporates and she doesn't even have her old family to fall back on.'

'You can't blame yourself for that. Come on, we've been through all this before. Get her over. You've got to have someone. Here, phone her now. Or I will, if you want.'

'No, no—that would be even worse.' Belinda picked up the phone and dialled. Taggart heard it ringing at the other end, then the click of an answering machine. No one was at the flat. Belinda didn't leave a message. This wasn't exactly the kind of situation you could explain coolly into a machine. 'I expect she's at work,' she said dully.

'D'you know her work number?'

'No, I don't think I do, actually . . . She's just changed jobs.' Belinda sounded quite relieved at this. She clearly did not relish the prospect of being comforted by her daughter.

'Wouldn't you like me to stay over?'

'No, thank you, Andrew. You know how it is. I mean, where would you stay? No, I think I'd rather be by myself. Don't worry about me.'

CHAPTER 24

Of course Taggart worried—how could he not? Nevertheless, in the end he acceded to Belinda's insistence and went back to London. His first idea had been at least to keep her company over supper, but she assured him she didn't want any supper, which was not hard to believe. No; there was nothing he could do, she assured him, more than he had already done; so he made sure she had some sleeping pills (not too many) and eventually, reluctantly, returned to London.

When he got back to his flat he automatically played over the messages on his telephone answering machine. Most of them were routine, but one made him sit up.

'Hi, Andrew,' said Lulu's voice brightly. 'I wanted to surprise you, but you weren't here, so that's just bad luck. Here I am in London, whaddaya know. Dad had some work to do here, and Mom wanted to come over for some shopping and to go to the theatre, and she said would I like to come with her, as it's my birthday. So here I am just over the weekend. Are you around? Why don't you call my hotel.' And she gave a number and rang off.

Taggart felt very tired. He didn't know whether he could face calling Lulu just now, with all that would entail in the way of explanations. Anyhow, it was highly unlikely she would be in. He glanced at his watch. Nine-thirty: she was almost certainly at the theatre. He'd leave it until the morning. This evening, he had other things to do. Such as roughing out the article he was going to write for this week's *New Politics*. The magazine came out on Wednesday; Friday was the copy-day for features. No time to lose.

The piece, of course, was the one that had been hanging fire for so long, about Charles Watson and Charles 2. There was no putting it off any longer. The whole story was going to blow up again, no doubt about that. No doubt all the stringers in the Midlands were at this moment on the phone to Fleet Street.

But what should he say, and how should he say it? In the circumstances it seemed safest to stick to the facts. But what were the facts? Charles Watson had had a talk with Peter Fischer (he had seen them). Charles had turned Fischer down. He had also turned down Wesley Mitchell's original invitation to America. Then the rug had been pulled from under him at EMU and he had as precipitately accepted. Wesley worked in the area Fischer was interested in. Charles had gone off with Wesley and had never been seen since, at least in his original form. Wesley had no reason to suspect anyone knew about this. Lulu only knew about it by the merest chance. There was no proof that Wesley had taken Charles to Prospect Psychodynamics. But Taggart knew that the man he knew as Charles Watson 2 had come from there: he had seen him there. He had also seen Wesley Mitchell and Peter Fischer there together.

And Peter Fischer had probably seen him.

And now Charles 2 was dead.

At this point Taggart began to feel distinctly nervous.

He had, when he first returned from America, half expected to hear from Peter Fischer. But now here they both were in London, and not a dicky-bird. It wasn't, of course, easy to imagine exactly how the interview would have gone, since, if that *hadn't* been Taggart in the Prospect Psychodynamics lobby, the last thing Fischer would have wanted would have been to put ideas into his head. But if it *had* been him, then (Taggart would have thought) he would have wanted to make it quite clear just how much, or rather just how little, Taggart might feel free to mention without dire consequences. A little indirect probing followed by menaces, veiled or otherwise.

But the fact remained he hadn't got in touch, hadn't issued any dire warnings, and Charles 2 had hit the headlines (as it happened, without any help from Taggart). This argued, as far as Taggart could see, that the whole purpose of Charles 2 was to hit the headlines, and that neither Fischer nor Wesley Mitchell was going to commit suicide if his name was associated with the affair, though left to themselves they preferred it to remain bathed, at least for the moment, in mystery. Certainly neither of them had as yet associated himself with Charles 2—Mitchell, indeed, had repudiated the reincarnation's claim, though not without leaving himself an opening should things turn out to look profitable in that direction—and yet presumably (surely Fischer would have told Wesley why he'd rushed off so precipitately that day, and who Taggart was?) they must have been expecting him to write a piece about it all implicating both of them. From Wesley's point of view this could be viewed as yet another feather in his academic cap, though the morals might be better left unexplored. On the other hand, if Mrs Watson wasn't grumbling, who was anybody else to complain? From Fischer's point of view ... Taggart had thought about this, and had concluded that Charles 2 was evidently something in the nature of a message to somebody. The message being, look what we can do; think if we did it to you! And the somebody being—Fischer's opposite numbers. In which case, the mention of his name could only underline the nature of the message.

So far so good. Taggart had even passed some pleasant moments reflecting how puzzled Peter Fischer must be at the persistent non-appearance of the expected piece. But this had changed everything. Somebody had wanted Charles 2 out of the way, and had disposed of him. Why? The only reason Taggart could think of was that he knew too much, and somebody wanted to make quite sure he wasn't going to say too much. He hadn't, yet; and was presumably under strict instructions not to. But somebody wasn't taking any chances. He had made the desired point, and he was now expendable. In which case, what price anybody else who might also know too much? Even if Fischer hadn't recognized Taggart at the clinic, he might well feel thoroughly paranoid about him. There was the matter of the lovely Miss Correa, for one thing. Now that Taggart came to think about it, she'd disappeared—or been shunted off—to Spain at just about the time when Fischer's name had been surfacing in her connection. And then there she'd been bobbing up again in Washington, the very embodiment of indiscretion. Fischer had certainly been furious about that. A chap in his line of business doesn't need publicity of any kind, let alone that kind of publicity. Did he suspect Taggart of having been the source of that paragraph in the *Eye*? If so, then his chagrin at the Washington meeting must have been something spectacular. Taggart wondered what Juliette Correa was doing now. It might be worth checking, though she was probably safe enough under the ægis of her congressman. If ægis was the word. Anyhow, in that particular connection, maybe Fischer thought it was a case of least said, soonest mended. But that did not apply universally. No, sir!

These thoughts lent wings to Taggart's fingers. His first idea had been to rough out his piece, which he would then finish and polish first thing tomorrow. But suddenly everything seemed terribly urgent. There wouldn't be the slightest point in going to bed before he'd got everything safely on paper, and preferably delivered. He wouldn't sleep a wink anyway until that was done.

By two o'clock the piece was ready. Taggart let himself out. The night was sharp: quite a frost tonight with those clear skies. His car probably wouldn't start. He'd probably do better to cycle, rather than wake the neighbourhood turning the engine over and over and using up the battery. He wheeled out his trusty bike from the hallway where it lived and set off.

An hour later he was back, feeling pleased with himself. The piece was delivered; the ride had been pleasantly bracing; and no hooded gunman had leapt out from a dark corner as he had been half expecting. He let himself back in, wheeled in the bike, shut his front door and went to bed, where he slept the sleep of contented exhaustion.

He was wakened by the pealing of the doorbell. He lay for a moment wondering what was happening, feeling as though someone had just punched him in the stomach hard. Then the doorbell rang again. He looked at his watch. Seven-thirty. No wonder he felt terrible.

He crawled out of bed and pulled on a dressing-gown. The bell rang again. 'Shut up, you stupid bastard,' he shouted, 'I'm coming,' but the shout emerged as a croak, either because his vocal cords were not yet fully awakened or for some other reason into which he preferred not to inquire too closely. Finally he got to the door and opened it. Outside stood a policeman.

'Mr Taggart? Mr Andrew Taggart?'

'That's me.' Taggart wondered what he could have done.

Had someone stolen his car in the night? No, there it was parked as usual on the other side of the road.

'I wondered if you'd mind coming with me, sir.'

'What for?'

'We're making inquiries into the death of Dr Charles Watson, sir, or someone purporting to be him.'

'Yes, I know all about that. I was in Leamingworth yesterday.'

'Quite so, sir, so you'll know what I'm talking about,' said the officer, who seemed to be faintly uncertain of this himself. Taggart wondered how young they were recruiting them into the force these days. Sixteen? Fifteen?

'Mm.'

'And I wondered if you'd mind coming down to the station to answer a few questions.'

'At this time of morning? Couldn't you have left it till a bit later?'

'Wanted to be quite sure of finding you in, Mr Taggart. People often leave for work surprisingly early.'

'Not me.'

'Shall I wait while you get dressed, sir?' The policeman, pre-empting the answer to this question, stepped into the hall. Taggart retreated and tripped over the bike. The policeman beckoned to a colleague who was waiting outside in the car. Suddenly the little house seemed very full of people. 'And then there's just one other thing, sir. We'd like to search your house.'

'What on earth for?'

'Ah, well, I'm not at liberty to say, sir.' The policeman looked enigmatic. Probably didn't have the slightest idea what he was about. Taggart felt dazed. It seemed increasingly improbable that he was really awake. All this was much more likely to be happening in some sort of bad dream.

'Do you have a warrant?'

'Certainly, sir.' The man's excessive politeness added to the dreamlike atmosphere. He produced his warrant. Taggart studied it. There didn't seem to be anything wrong with it.

Gloomily Taggart stomped upstairs and took his time about dressing. He was letting his beard grow again. It was at a singularly unattractive stage. No wonder Belinda hadn't wanted him to stay yesterday. As he fumbled about, he could hear the policemen digging around his premises. Better keep an eye on them. He watched, outraged and powerless, while they riffled through his files, turned out his drawers, poked impersonally around the mess in the kitchen, went through the piles of dirty clothes in his bedroom. It had to be admitted that the place didn't look noticeably different after they'd finished with it. Finally they seemed to grind to a halt.

'Found what you wanted?'

'That's not for me to say, Mr Taggart. Shall we go?'

'Let's,' said Taggart. At least, he thought, nothing can happen to me while I've got police protection.

CHAPTER 25

The police car was parked a couple of doors down. Mrs Jenks next door was peeping out from behind her yellow-grey net curtains. She was not one to miss an event such as the departure of her neighbour in a police car. Taggart waved to her and she immediately vanished. She must have been used enough to this sort of thing, he reflected; it had happened to her old man often enough. Not that he had anything to worry about. If they wanted him to answer a few questions, he'd answer them. Do his honest citizen bit. As for the search, he could only assume that Peter Fischer was trying in some way to pre-empt the piece he had just written. And sent off—so *that* was all right. But what had that got to do with answering questions about the bearded man's death? Perhaps Fischer was afraid that Taggart was going to point the finger at him. And perhaps Taggart was.

They drove to the police station—not Taggart's local station, which was Dalston, but the big, shiny modern one at Holborn. Here, waiting for him in a small interview room, he found Detective-Inspector Rogers from Leamingworth.

Rogers was studying some papers. When Taggart came into the room he went on studying them for a few minutes. Obviously they went in for very old tricks in Leamingworth. Not to be outdone, Taggart brought out his diary and began to check through it. He was supposed to be meeting someone on a key story today at ten. Well, if he was late he'd have to phone. Be a pity, though. It hadn't been an easy meeting to set up. He was aroused from these thoughts by Rogers's voice, sounding somewhat nettled. 'If you're quite finished, Mr Taggart, we'll begin.' Didn't like being played at his own game, silly bugger. In the corner Taggart could see his young policeman stifle a giggle. Better be careful. No need to alienate people unnecessarily. He smiled helpfully and put his diary away.

'Fire away.' As an afterthought he added, 'There wouldn't be a chance of a cup of tea, would there? There wasn't time for breakfast and my brain doesn't really function this early in the morning.'

Detective-Inspector Rogers looked at him gravely. Then he said, 'I don't see why not. Go and get him a cup of tea, Robertson.'

'Sugar, sir?' asked the young officer.

'Four, please,' said Taggart.

They sat in silence while the tea was brought. Taggart took it gratefully. Through the sugar it tasted pretty stewed, but he wasn't going to worry about niceties.

'Ready now?' said Rogers.

'Go ahead.'

'Now then, Mr Taggart, what exactly is it you do?'

'I'm a journalist. I write mostly for *New Politics*.'

'Not a magazine I ever read, I'm afraid. Pretty left-wing, isn't it?'

'Comparatively.'

'Compared to what?'

'Most of the rest of the press.'

'Well, we won't argue about that. What is it you write about?'

'I'm an investigative journalist. I dig up scandals.'

'I thought I recognized your name.' Rogers looked at him with a new interest, not altogether friendly. One of Taggart's biggest recent stories had concerned police corruption.

'I'm fairly well-known.'

'I'd like to know more about your friendship with Mrs Watson,' said Rogers.

'What about it?'

'What sort of friendship was it exactly, Mr Taggart?'

'I don't see what that's got to do with this case.'

'I'm afraid you'll have to leave that to me.'

'We had an affair. Is that what you wanted to know?'

'You comforted her in the absence of her husband?'

'You could put it like that if you wanted. I'd just say we had a nice time.'

'So you must have been rather annoyed when he reappeared in—in another guise, shall we say.'

'I should say I was more interested than annoyed.'

'But you didn't see her after that?'

'No. She wanted a bit of time to sort herself out. Understandably, really.'

'But you remained on good terms?'

'As far as I'm concerned. As you say, I hadn't seen her. She hasn't been easy to contact. Besieged by the press. I thought the kindest thing I could do would be to leave her in peace.'

'Until yesterday.'

'Yes, I'd arranged to go and see her and—Charles—yesterday.' Taggart wondered how Rogers could have known this. Well, maybe he hadn't. Maybe he'd just deduced that Taggart wasn't in the area simply by chance. And more than one person in the street must have known about him and Belinda. Rogers had presumably been around talking to people yesterday, and someone had passed on this helpful titbit.

'So you knew they'd be at the house.'

'That was where I'd arranged to meet them.'

'But you didn't go straight to the house when you arrived in Leamingworth.'

'No, I found I was able to get away earlier than I'd thought, so I decided to have lunch there and a bit of a walk first. As it was such a lovely day.'

'Where exactly did you walk?'

'Down by the river. There's a pub by the bridge, the Mill, well, I expect you know it. I had lunch there. There's a nice walk you can take from there.'

'Upsteam or downstream?'

'Either. Well, you know the place.'

'And which way did you go?'

'I believe I told you yesterday. I went up in the direction of Mrs Watson's house first, and noticed someone in the pavilion. I felt a bit of a fool, didn't want to be noticed staring, so I went back the other way down to where it opens out into the fields. That was where I heard the crack I suppose must have been the shot.'

'Was anybody with you when you went for this walk?'

'No.'

'Did anybody see you go? Or see you while you were out walking?'

'Not that I remember. It was very quiet. It always is, even at weekends.'

'We found the weapon, by the way,' Rogers said.

'Oh, did you?'

'Yes. Rifle, expensive one, all the latest stuff, impossible to miss at that distance, really. No skill involved.'

'Where was it?'

'In the river. Obvious place. Chap didn't care about it being found, just wanted to get rid of it.'

'Any fingerprints?'

'They're looking. You can never tell. People sometimes aren't as clever as they think they are.' He looked hard at Taggart. 'Ever done any shooting, Mr Taggart?'

'Never. I'm a pacific sort of person.'

There was a silence, each of them apparently lost in his own thoughts. In the corner the young officer, who had been writing busily during the interview, licked his pencil and studied the wall opposite.

'Well, Mr Taggart,' said Roberts. 'I'm going to caution

you. I'm charging you with the murder of the man known as Charles Watson. You don't have to say anything, but I'm warning you that anything you do say may be taken down and used as evidence against you.'

'What on earth d'you mean?' said Taggart. Of course he knew what Rogers meant—he wasn't deaf, and he was as well acquainted with this hallowed formula as anyone. It was simply that he couldn't believe his ears. Perhaps he was stupid; certainly it had been a pointed sort of interview; but still . . . 'This is ridiculous,' he said.

'If that's all you have to say—'

'No, it bloody well isn't all. I want to phone my lawyer, and I'm not saying another word until he's arrived.'

'Go ahead,' said Rogers. 'It's your right. Robertson, take him to a phone.'

Taggart telephoned *New Politics* and spoke to the editor. 'David,' he said, 'something bloody stupid's happened, and I need a lawyer quick. Can you call Phil Redvers and get him to come down to Holborn police station. I don't know his number offhand. It's urgent.' Redvers was the *New Politics* solicitor, a combative figure whom Taggart would have trusted with his life. Was, it seemed, trusting with his future. He still couldn't believe it.

After that Robertson took him down to the cells and locked him up.

CHAPTER 26

'But it's ridiculous,' said Taggart. 'They haven't got a thing against me. It's purely circumstantial.'

Phil Redvers sighed. He was a small, round man, with shiny black hair and round black spectacles. 'As far as that goes, are you sure you can't think of anyone who might have seen you while you were on that wretched walk?'

'I really don't think there was anybody. Not even a solitary dogwalker by the time I got to the cows. I remember thinking how amazing it was that there still are places where you can just not see anyone at all. You forget, living in London.'

'Well, we can advertise,' said Redvers, writing busily in his notepad. 'You never know. But in fact I believe it isn't entirely circumstantial. That's their line, anyway.'

'How could it not be? What could they possibly have? I didn't do it. And it isn't as if it happened in the house. I mean, I expect my fingerprints are all over the place there, not to say hairs in the bed and bits of wool from my sweater in the vacuum cleaner. If he'd been killed with the breadknife, then I expect they'd find my fingerprints on the handle if they looked hard enough. But he wasn't. Anyhow, I've never touched a gun in my life. Of any sort. Why don't they give me a shooting test? I couldn't hit the circus fat man at five yards.'

'Wouldn't prove anything. You could be pretending. Or that might have been a fluke.'

'Good God, don't you *believe* me?'

'Of course I believe you, but that's what they'd say. If we aren't realistic we shan't get anywhere. No, as far as I can make out they're going to try and prove there's a security angle. They're pressing for the hearings to be in camera, at least partly.'

'Security! They really have gone mad.'

'You don't have many friends in high places,' said Redvers. 'There's a lot of people that nothing would make happier than to see you done for murder. And preferably espionage as well.'

'Are you saying they're setting me up?'

'I'm not saying anything. I'm just indicating what we seem to be up against. I'm assuming that this is to do with that bizarre story you delivered to the office the other night—'

'When's that coming out, by the way?'

'It's not. I put my foot down. Time enough for all that when you get out, or if the worst comes to the worst when we're trying to get an appeal going. As it is, we don't want you any more prejudiced than you are already. Also, we'll do better if we leave them guessing and nobody knows quite how much you know. So the first thing you do is tell me everything. But everything. Don't leave anything out.'

Taggart told it, and Phil Redvers listened intently, making notes from time to time. At the end he shook his head. 'Either I'm crazy or we really are going to be invaded by little green men,' he said. 'Do you believe it?'

'Believe what? That Charles Watson really was transferred into the bearded chap?'

Redvers nodded.

'Well, of course he wasn't!' Taggart exclaimed. 'Honestly, Phil, sometimes I wonder about you! Do you believe in fairies? No, what happened was that Wesley Mitchell has been taking Peter Fischer for a ride, just like Fischer's trying to take you and me and everyone else for a ride, if your guess is right. No, I've been thinking about this. In fact, that was one of the things I was wanting to ask Lulu—did I tell you that she's in England? They came over for a weekend. Wesley had some work to do, and Essie brought Lulu for her birthday treat—they were going to some theatres or something. I know because Lulu called me while I was at Leamingworth and left a message on my answering machine.'

'And what was this thing you were going to ask her?'

'When Wesley met Peter Fischer for the first time. She might have some idea. Or Ellen might, his secretary, and Lulu could find out from her. Because if I'm right, all this memory transplant thing never had any base in science at all. It was all a figment of Peter Fischer's overheated brain. Wishful thinking. The kind of thing he'd *like* to be possible. Just like Wesley would like a Nobel prize, Peter would like to be known for having been associated with this great breakthrough, where you could just take over the other side's chaps, put your mind into their bodies sort of thing. Well, don't laugh, look where it's got me! Anyhow, my guess is that Wesley and Fischer met at some intelligence junket. Wesley's very right-wing, always was and got more and more so. I mean, it was a kind of joke between him and Essie and poor old Charles Watson, what a reactionary Wesley was. Belinda told me. Only in the end it wasn't a joke. I'm pretty sure he had contacts with the CIA—I could find out: there's a chap I know in Washington who can generally tell me that kind of thing.'

'Let me have his name,' said Redvers. 'I'm going to have to do all that sort of thing on your behalf just at the moment.'

Taggart gave him the name. 'Now, where was I? Yes, well, my guess is that Fischer met Wesley one day when he was over in Washington, somewhere where people were discussing possible advances in intelligence psychology or something of that sort. I was at a do like that in Washington myself just a few weeks ago, and so was Peter Fischer. And Fischer puts forward his notion of becoming a sort of psychological Frankenstein, and Wesley latches on to it and sees it as a possible source of funding for all sorts of things he'd like to be able to do. And not just funding. Discreet facilities and not too many questions asked about awkward things like ethics. Where did ethics ever get a spook? So they take over, or create, Prospect Psychodynamics. Or maybe they just rent a floor of it. And that's where it's all going on in the memory transplant scene, or so Peter Fischer thinks.'

'And isn't it? What about all those things you saw there?'

'I just saw an operation taking place on someone's brain. Happens all the time. And met a few post-operative patients. Now that's a clinic full of perfectly bona-fide patients. It's just the top floor that's—experimental. Subjects provided courtesy of the CIA, no questions asked, with full collaboration from our very own Special Projects.'

'We could send someone to check the place out.'

'Good idea, let's do that. Who's paying, by the way? I don't expect I qualify for legal aid, and I certainly can't afford to send agents here, there and everywhere.'

'Don't worry about that. We'll sort it out when the time comes.'

'All right, if you're happy to leave it like that. So anyhow, Wesley gets a fine supply of experimental subjects. I expect he really is interested in memory location, nothing he likes better than tickling people's brains and seeing what they come up with. Cutting a few connections just to see what happens. I don't know. He's mad, over the edge. How is a perfectly normal person like me supposed to guess what goes on inside the head of a loony like that?'

'And meanwhile Fischer's pressing for a real memory transplant.'

'Exactly. And Wesley knows exactly who he'd like to transplant. Charles Watson. He's known him for ever, knows all about him, his personal life *and* his professional life. And he knows something else about Charles Watson, which is that he's screwing Wesley's beloved only daughter Lulu. Lulu didn't think he knew, but I'm pretty sure she was wrong. Things like that aren't so easy to keep hidden, and Wesley Mitchell's got sharp eyes. He didn't say anything, he doesn't want to alienate Lulu, but that doesn't mean he doesn't hate Charles Watson's guts. So he figures things out, and mentions Watson's name to Fischer as someone he'd like to have working on this with him. And they work out a way of making sure Watson goes and does what's expected of him.'

'You think it was a double act?'

'I'm sure of it. It isn't very hard to predict how someone like Charles Watson will react to the kind of proposal Fischer put to him. He chose his moment. He knew Watson was dead keen on doing some other piece of work of his own. After that he made sure the financial screws were put on Watson's department, which is not something that's very difficult to arrange in the present climate. Intellectuals, scumbags one and all, let's starve them into submission. And bingo! over goes Charles Watson to Jones U. Won't you come into my garden, said the spider to the fly.'

'And what happens then? You seem to have all this very well worked out. Did you metamorphose into a fly on the wall or something?'

'For one thing that's what I do for a living, work things out. And for another, what the hell else d'you think I've been thinking about these last two days? What I'm telling you, it's the only way that fits.'

'So then Wesley takes Charles over to this place in Brooklyn.'

'Probably. I mean, maybe he didn't even get that far. But I should think they went there. Assuming Wesley wanted to get rid of Charles, which is what I'm assuming, he'd have all the facilities there, wouldn't he? And for disposal, especially if I'm right about what he was really doing there. Accidents happen, and the people on the top floor are specially chosen because they don't have friends and relatives who'll barge in asking awkward questions.'

'So you think Watson's dead?'

'I'm pretty sure he must be. I don't expect we'll ever know for certain. But I don't expect we'll hear of him again.'

'And meanwhile this other chap's waiting there.'

'Yes. That I do know, because I saw him. Well, that would be the place, wouldn't it? That's where memory transplants are going on. That's where Peter Fischer comes to visit to see how things are going, and, bingo! it's happened. And to someone Fischer knows, so he can appreciate the perfection of the technique.'

'But meanwhile this chap's been learning how to be Charles Watson.'

'That's right. For however long Wesley's been working on this thing. A year, two years. He'd have tapes, videos, probably met the man himself, may even have spent quite a long time with him. Now there's no way of finding out about that, either.'

'So who do you think killed him? Mitchell?'

Taggart shrugged. 'It's possible. He wouldn't have any qualms. And he was in England. You could find out what he was doing that afternoon. He knows the layout of the Watsons' place at Leamingworth—he's stayed there, often. And he's a good shot. Goes hunting a lot.'

'And the motive would be to stop the new Charles Watson from making some silly mistake and blowing the whole thing?'

'Well, he'd made his effect, hadn't he? It's certainly worth looking into, anyhow.'

'But it isn't what you'd been thinking?'

'What I've been wondering is, how on earth did they get on to me? I mean, I know I was there at the house. But how did they know what I'd been doing earlier? Somebody knew just where I'd been. Knew it'd be an easy set-up. They must have been following me. They knew I was going to see Belinda—I suppose they were tapping my phone.'

'That's hardly something new, is it?'

'No, they've been doing it for years. All part of my ongoing battle with—Well, of course that's who it is. I should have realized. Peter Fischer.'

'You think Fischer did it?'

'Well, it's possible, isn't it? As far as the new Charles Watson's concerned, he'd have the same motives as Mitchell. *And* a fall-guy. *And* the fall-guy's me. Fifteen birds with one stone. It must have seemed irresistible.'

'But wouldn't you have recognized him if he'd been hanging around?'

'Don't be silly, Phil, I'm not suggesting he did it *personally*. That's part of the beauty of it, from his point of view. I expect you'll find he was in a meeting all that day surrounded by twenty other people. The point is, he has all these chaps just hanging around specially trained to do this kind of thing. That's why I make him so cross—I keep writing articles about them.'

Phil Redvers sat back and looked around. The surroundings were gloomy enough: Taggart was still in the police cell at Holborn, waiting until room could be found in a remand prison. A bed with a blanket on which they were both sitting, a bucket in one corner. 'Trouble is, our job isn't to find out who did it, it's to prove you didn't. Or raise a reasonable doubt at least.'

'So what happens now?'

'We wait. You'll go before the magistrates for the preliminary hearing tomorrow. We'll reserve our defence. They'll request an adjournment, which the magistrates will grant.'

'How long will that go on for?'

'I don't want to depress you, but it can take months. Before the police have got their act together, and then they have to find a slot in the Assizes. Or you might even get the Old Bailey, with all this stuff about security.'

'That'll be Peter Fischer, the bastard. I can't think what he's on about. Any chance we'll get bail?'

'On a murder charge? It's unlikely, I'm afraid. Of course, we'll do our best.'

'And what happens if we lose?'

'We won't lose,' said Phil Redvers. 'Just keep telling yourself that.'

'But if we did?'

'I don't know. Fifteen, twenty years?'

'God.' Taggart stared at the ground, appalled. Why on earth had he chosen to visit Belinda and her new spouse on that day of all days? 'The bastards,' he said. 'The fucking bastards. Just let them wait till I get out.'

CHAPTER 27

Things turned out very much as Phil Redvers had predicted. The case was adjourned, and adjourned again. Finally the prosecution decided it was ready. 'This week,' Phil Redvers told Taggart one day in January.

Taggart had by now been moved to Pentonville. He had often seen the place from the outside, since it wasn't very far from where he lived, and more than once he had wondered what went on behind those huge spike-topped walls of grimy brick, those tiny barred windows, those enormous arched gates. Now he knew.

In fact, although the prospect of spending years of his life cooped up in such surroundings was appalling, Taggart did not find this experience as distressing as everyone expected him to. Partly this was on account of the normal physical conditions of his life. Of course, his house did not approach Pentonville when it came to squalor. It had a proper bathroom and toilet, for one thing, facilities which Pentonville absolutely lacked. But in general Taggart was heedless of the æsthetic niceties of life. Of course he didn't like the horrible smell, the constant noise of shouts echoing round the landings, the ugliness, the lack of privacy. How could he? How could anyone? But more than most he was able to disregard the material aspect of his surroundings. He didn't even mind the food: it was stodgy and tasteless, but then tasteless stodge was what he actually preferred, though not taken to quite such extremes. His cellmate was a Pakistani awaiting repatriation, and in Pentonville pending his appeal against this sentence (on the probably correct assumption that if he were let out on bail he would take the opportunity to disappear). The Pakistani spoke some English, and Taggart spent a lot of time talking to him about life in Pakistan, why he had left and why he wanted to come to England, of all godforsaken places. He also enjoyed talking to the other inmates, and kept notes of all that was said and everything that went on for possible later use. For the rest, like everyone else, he waited for time to pass. Every week he appeared before the magistrates, to be remanded for another week, and Phil Redvers would take the opportunity to let him know how his case was going.

'Our chap found that place you were talking about,' he said. It was then halfway through December. 'In Brooklyn.'

'The Prospect Psychodynamic Clinic.'

'That's the one. Was shown all over it.'

'Including the top floor?'

'Nothing on the top floor, he said. Disused. Quite empty. They said they didn't need the capacity. They were hoping to expand up there sometime.'

'Did he get a list of the directors?'

'Yes, I've got it here.' He fumbled through his briefcase and produced a xeroxed sheet. 'Tannenbaum, Dr Feinstein, Costakos, Mrs Costakos . . . No Mitchell. As far as the records show, he's nothing to do with it.'

'And of course they all denied ever having heard of him.'

'That's about it.'

Taggart tapped his teeth with a fingernail. 'Of course, as far as they're concerned, it's my word against theirs, and they're planning to discredit me pretty comprehensively.'

'I imagine so. We shall know what their case is as soon as we get this hearing.'

'Shall we?'

'Well, yes, of course—they have to disclose it. How can we answer a case if we don't know what it is?'

'There's British justice for you. And do we have to tell them everything we're going to do, too?'

'No, not unless we're planning to plead an alibi. We'd have to disclose that so the police could check it out. But unfortunately we don't have one.'

'Did your chap get in touch with Lulu? To ask when her dad first met Fischer?'

'Yes, but she didn't have any idea. I expect his visits were kept rather unofficial.'

'Not to say dark. I bet she was surprised to hear what had happened.'

'Seemed scared, apparently.'

'Poor kid. All this just because she had father-figure fantasies. Listen, I'm beginning to have an idea. Can we subpœna anyone we like?'

'Yes.'

'From anywhere?'

'Anywhere in this country. From anywhere else we might do better to send a polite request and an offer to pay their fares.'

'Right,' said Taggart. 'I'll make a list for you.'

'How're you making out?'

'It could be worse. I could be in solitary confinement, or dead.'

'I expect you're getting lots of letters.'

'Hundreds. I hadn't realized what a public I had!'

'Oh, you're quite a *cause célèbre*. Lefty journalist accused of murder, you can imagine.' Taggart could: at the first hearing, he had hardly been able to leave the court for photographers and television cameras. 'Of course, nobody can say too much because the case is *sub judice*,' Redvers went on. 'Though I think they've all been on poor Mrs Watson's tail. Neighbours couldn't resist making a bit of money and mischief slipping someone a hint, you can imagine. The general assumption is that this is a crime of passion. But all your fans insist that it's nothing but a set-up by hostile forces who are itching to get rid of you.'

'And aren't they right!'

Taggart had also had a number of visitors. One of these, to his surprise, was Belinda.

They sat staring at each other across a table in the interview room.

Taggart found that, for some reason, the sight of her did what nothing else had done, and made him want to cry.

'Andrew! Don't! What's up—don't you want to see me?'

'I wasn't expecting to,' he mumbled, then shook his head and regained control of himself. 'I'm sorry. Of course I'm glad to see you. It's wonderful. It's just—all too much.' He forced a smile. 'Does your daughter know you're here?'

'Caroline? She'd probably want me tried if she knew!'

'So you don't think I did it?'

'Of course I don't! You didn't, did you?'

'No. Though sometimes I begin to wonder. Can I really be going through all this if I didn't do anything at all?'

They looked at each other. Belinda looked dreadful, about ten years older, terribly thin, with all sorts of lines on her face Taggart had never seen before. Of course, Taggart reminded himself; she'd been widowed, in a sense, twice at one go. Her hair was noticeably greyer. 'Of course, I've had to go and live somewhere else,' she said.

'Where?'

'A friend lent me a house in Essex. It's a weekend cottage usually. Later on I'll put the house on the market, when things have died down a bit.'

'Do you see anyone? You oughtn't to be alone too much.'

'Well, there's the children, of course. They've been sweet. Even Caroline, I know she's severe, but she's very kind really. Poor things, they've lost their father, it isn't as though they were little, but it's never easy.'

'You're assuming Charles—the first Charles, I mean,' he qualified awkwardly, 'is dead, then?'

'Well, I think he must be, mustn't he?'

'I expect,' said Taggart gently, 'that as far as Stuart and Caroline were concerned, they realized they'd lost him when—the other chap appeared.'

'I expect so. I just sort of—lost my head. Well, I just wondered—is there anything I can do to help? I feel I got you into all this.'

'Heavens, whatever you do, don't feel that. Nobody's responsible for me except myself. As for helping, I'm not sure you can, much, in the way you mean. I mean, it helps me to know you don't think I'm guilty. But I'm afraid you saying that won't advance my case very much. Quite apart from anything else, no one would believe you're impartial. And it would be pretty awful for your children. I'd keep out of it as far as you can.'

'I shall have to appear, to say what happened.'

'Of course you will, but leave it at that.'

That was the only time he'd seen her. Of course there'd been other visitors. Not family—Taggart didn't have any family to speak of. His parents were both dead, and his only brother lived in Australia. His editor came several times, and so did various journalistic friends. But somehow these visits made scarcely any impression on the grey round of days.

Time went by. Taggart's editor came to see him and told him that the *New Politics* board of management had agreed to underwrite his legal fees because Phil Redvers had convinced them he was being framed—Phil wasn't saying who by—and because the paper felt that this was probably on account of work done in the course of professional duty. That was a relief. It meant that he could afford to hire an excellent barrister, which might be important.

The magistrates' court hearing finally took place half way through January, a cold, raw day. Taggart was driven out to Leamingworth, where the case was to be heard, in a police car, handcuffed to a constable in the back seat. As the familiar world rolled by Taggart could hardly believe that he wasn't free to be out in it, to drive himself (not be driven) down the nastiness of the M1, to stop for a pee at the service area if he felt like it. To call by and see **Belinda**.

Phil Redvers met him at the court, his round, beaming face slightly toned down by his sober suit. 'Dressed up for the occasion, I see,' said Taggart.

'Glad you can still joke. They've rolled in the big guns.'

'Oh? Who?'

'Michael Skillen, QC.'

Taggart digested this in silence. Skillen was a formidable prosecutor much used by the Crown in particularly delicate cases. 'What about us?'

'You're in my tender hands.'

'Well, that's all right, I suppose,' said Taggart doubtfully. It wasn't that he didn't have confidence in Redvers, who was exceptionally competent. 'But shouldn't we have someone to match, just for the look of the thing?'

Redvers shook his head. 'What's the point, at this stage? We shall be trying to show there's no case to answer.'

'Is there?'

'Not a strong one, I wouldn't think. They've taken all this time because they've been trying to dredge up some solid evidence that isn't circumstantial.'

'How can they do that? There isn't any. They just picked me up because I happened to be convenient. From every point of view,' Taggart said bitterly. 'The only thing connecting me to that shooting is that I happened to be near there at the time.'

'Ah, well, apparently not,' said Redvers.

'What d'you mean, not? What can they possibly have?'

'Apparently they found something when they searched your house.'

'Found something? What?'

'A glove. Apparently it matches a glove that was found in the river with the murder weapon.'

'And they've taken all this time to tell us? That's ridiculous. It's a plant. They've got a cheek, trying to pull that one on me.' Taggart, as Phil Redvers knew, was referring to his exposés of police corruption, which had included, among other things, planted evidence.

'That's what you say, of course.'

'Don't you believe me?'

'Of course I believe you. But that's not the point. You know the presumption's always that the police are telling the truth.'

'What are you trying to say? Don't you think we'll win?' Taggart sounded horrified. He was horrified. For the first time, he realized that this might not be a temporary interlude.

CHAPTER 28

The magistrates, a fat, elderly woman with a county suit and voice, a competent-looking middle-aged woman of the sort that is found running voluntary organizations, and a thin man with iron-grey hair and a rather mayoral air, sat on their bench and looked unimpressed while Michael Skillen ran through the prosecution case. Taggart had been in town. He had a motive for wanting this man out of the way—jealousy. He had been in the area on his own admission. He had no alibi. So far, so bad. Then Skillen said that he had an exhibit to show the court. At this, the clerk of the court picked up a plastic bag which had been lying on the desk in front of him and handed it over. It contained a glove. It was labelled A. Skillen held it up so that everyone could see it. 'This was found in the river near the rifle which was used in the crime,' he said. 'Can I have Exhibit B, please.'

An identical bag containing an apparently identical glove—the left hand of the pair—was handed over. 'This glove,' observed Skillen tonelessly, 'was found at the house of the accused. It has been established that they are two of a pair, bought at a Marks and Spencer store probably in the spring of last year. The assumption of the prosecution is that the right-hand glove was inadvertently thrown into the river with the rifle and that the accused didn't notice what he'd done.'

'Have you anything else to say, Mr Skillen?' asked the

chairman of the magistrates, the competent-looking woman.

'Yes, your worship,' replied Skillen. 'Might I request that the court be cleared.' He went over to the magistrates and held a murmured conference with them. The chairman nodded her head.

'Clear the court, please,' she called, in tones that might have terrorized many a Girl Guide jamboree.

There was a pause while public and press trooped out of the courtroom and the doors were shut. 'All right, Mr Skillen,' said the chairman. 'Go ahead.'

'Thank you, your worship,' said Skillen, looking down at his notes. He was a rather cadaverous figure, with a long face and hollow cheeks, thin silver hair, rather tall. He wore half-moon spectacles which made him look schoolmasterly and benign. Now he looked up at the magistrates. 'The prosecution will attempt to show,' he said, 'that the accused has for some time been acting in the interests of a foreign power. The murdered man was part of an extremely delicate and secret experiment being conducted on behalf of this country in association with its allies. The accused, under cover of his journalistic activities, found out about this experiment and then did everything in his power to disrupt it. Let me explain . . .'

Taggart listened in a detached sort of way to Skillen's voice presenting, in a sense, his own life. For many years engaged in subversive activities, trying to undermine the workings of the state through the magazine which employed him. Several times narrowly escaped prosecution. Found out, not known how, about the work Charles Watson engaged on. Seduced his wife. Followed him to America. Specialized in reporting intelligence activities—impossible he should not have known this was one such. Extraordinary new breakthroughs which might be of the greatest strategic importance. Seen in the laboratory where the experiment was taking place. Ran off when challenged. Known to be preparing report. Seen in the town. Then this death. Prosecution would if necessary bring evidence from the highest quarters. Suspected to have produced report containing matter in the highest degree deleterious to the interests of this country. Death of the greatest convenience to those who did not wish this country well, casting as it did a now unresolvable doubt about the genuineness of the experiment's results . . .

Skillen sat down. Redvers rose.

Taggart knew that, until the production of the glove, there had been no solid evidence to connect him with the murder, and that Redvers had been hoping that the magistrates would find that there was no case to answer. But that could not be the line now. It only needed a tiny piece of real evidence—such as that of the glove, if the glove had belonged to him—to send all the circumstantial stuff clanging into place. They would have to contest the evidence of the glove and hope to convince a jury that the police had planted it. It wouldn't be an easy case to make.

'As far as I can see,' said Phil Redvers gravely, 'the only thing connecting my client to this case is the glove produced by m'learned friend. All the rest is supposition and circumstance. As for the gloves, my client absolutely denies that he has ever seen them before. They do not belong to him and never have done. We shall be seeking to know why the police have taken all this time to produce them in evidence if, as they say, the left-hand glove was found during the search of my client's house. Other than that, I submit that there is no case to answer.'

There was another pause while the three retired and the press and public (a substantial number, for this was an interesting case and a number of national papers had sent representatives, as had a couple of radio news networks) filed back into the room. They waited. Finally the magistrates returned. They sat down. The chairman studied her notes, then looked up. 'We find there is a case to answer,' she said clearly. 'The case will be sent to the high court. Next, please.'

CHAPTER 29

By the time the case of Queen vs Taggart was finally heard, the accused's normally buoyant spirits were at a very low ebb. When I get out, he promised himself, I shall run a campaign about the rights and conditions of remand prisoners. Imprisoned although not convicted, contrary to the radiant judicial tradition of our sceptred isle, and in what lousy conditions only those who have experienced them can truly judge. Not a sexy subject—what were they doing to get themselves caught in the first place, eh? But one of which I shall have undeniable first-hand knowledge. No good trying to do it now. Prison governor probably wouldn't let the stuff out. I could give it to Phil, of course, lawyers' visits privileged and all that, but it would put him in an awkward position, *and* my life would be made even more of a misery than it is. But just let them wait till I'm out.

There was, of course, no question about that: it was when, not if. He hadn't done it, had he? Well, had he? Sometimes he wondered. Was it really possible for something like this to happen by mistake? Could he be sure he hadn't perhaps wandered down the river bank in the opposite direction to the one he thought he'd taken clutching a rifle he hadn't realized he possessed in his gloved hands, till, just as he'd expected, there were Belinda and her born-again husband silhouetted in the summer-house enjoying the unseasonable sunshine . . . But no; he mustn't even begin to entertain such fantasies. Because this wasn't a mistake, it was a frame-up. Someone wanted him sent down and was going to considerable lengths to make sure that would happen. Everywhere he looked he could see people with good reasons for wanting him out of the way. Peter Fischer. The police—who must be pretty pleased to have him where they wanted him, and might be prepared to take the risk of planting even more evidence in order to make sure of convicting him. By now there probably wasn't even much of a question of personal motivation in it. Things had taken on their own momentum. It was essential that he at least remain quite clear in his mind as to what *had* happened, what he had and had not done.

So here he was, week after dreary week, banged up in his sordid cell in this horrible place (because remand prisoners don't get to do any work), no privacy, and at the same time enough of his own thoughts to last him a lifetime. And because judges only work from ten until four, with a generous lunch-hour into the bargain, cases are not dealt with quickly. So January became February, February, March—and, finally, in April, his case was listed.

'At least they didn't decide to take it to the Old Bailey,' Phil Redvers said. 'That really would have taken forever.'

'I'll remember to be grateful.'

Redvers looked at him anxiously. 'Try not to be too bitter. We'll soon have you out of here now.'

'You try not to be bitter, in my shoes.'

'OK. It was a stupid thing to say. Anyhow, I think we're coming along quite nicely. John Stone's very good—we couldn't have anyone better. I'm seeing him tonight.' Stone was the QC who was going to represent Taggart in court. He had a reputation for taking up and winning cases unpopular with the Establishment. Like Taggart. 'Now,' continued Redvers, 'there were just one or two things I wanted to go over again . . .'

It's curious, thought Taggart, how detached one feels. Here I am, sitting in he dock, the centrepiece of this ludicrous theatrical occasion, and here are all these gents and ladies in gowns and wigs fussing about, all employed on my account one way or another, and all these jurors, God, do they look dim, all resenting this bloody waste of time, and I don't even feel involved. The accused sat there with an expressionless face. I don't have any feeling. None whatever. I expect it will come. When I see them standing up there lying their heads off.

It is amazing how many of life's big events consist, to a very large extent, of sitting around and waiting for activities to begin. Taggart had already had extensive experience of this while engaged on this story. Now there was more of it. Jurors were sworn in, wigged and gowned persons scuttled back and forth, the public gallery filled up. Finally, the accused was brought into the dock. Taggart looked to see if there was anyone there he knew. Yes: there was Caroline Watson. She looked characteristically severe, a plain grey sweater, no make-up. Poor kid, thought Taggart. Lost her father and probably feels she's lost her mother, too. Perhaps all this will shake them back together. No Stuart, he noticed. Too busy at university. Keeping his head down and pretending it had nothing to do with him, probably. The press benches were full. There had already been some preliminary legal argument during which the judge had refused the prosecution's request that part of the trial be held *in camera*. He had less qualms about that kind of thing, it appeared, than the Leamingworth magistrates. Meanwhile, the word had gone round Fleet Street, Wapping and points east to the effect that there were to be sensational revelations—quite apart from the fact that the trial of Andrew Taggart for murder was a sensation in itself. Taggart could picture the headlines. BOLSHIE JOURNALIST IN MURDER SENSATION. DEFENCE DENIES CRIME OF PASSION. Just wait till they hear what it's *really* about... A couple of his mates from *New Politics* were on the press bench. He smiled at them and they gave him thumbs-up signs. As at a football match. May the best man win. What a ludicrous system it is, Taggart reflected. No question of an inquiry designed to elicit the truth, but a contest all decked out like amateur theatricals. All those damned stupid wigs. Resisting change to the last. Is your life safe in their hands? You must be joking.

Michael Skillen stood up to make his opening speech. His delivery was the reverse of dramatic. Taggart could not help reflecting on the gap between the average courtroom and the average courtroom drama. In the drama, advocates deliver their lines snappily, with due regard for timing and effect. In real life, they speak in a dreary legal monotone, constantly referring to their notes, and often with long gaps when they lose their place and their train of thought.

Trance-like, Taggart viewed his life through Skillen's spectacles. The beginning of his friendship with Belinda Watson, apparently so casual, was really, he learnt, merely the first move in a deep-laid plot which was designed to bring him in contact with the work on which Belinda's husband was engaged. That work would be described when the time came. All his actions from that time on, as the prosecution would show, could be seen as an attempt to prevent that work succeeding and, when that failed, to destroy all evidence of it. In this his personal involvement with Belinda only strengthened his resolve. Taggart's life, as viewed and presented by Michael Skillen, was all one big plot: to deprive the state of its assets and security, to deprive the absent Charles Watson, who was only doing his patriotic duty, of his wife. No one should be surprised at this. Was not the whole history of Taggart's association with *New Politics* one of anti-patriotic subversion, masquerading as, but in reality grossly abusing, the freedom of the press? But all that, bad as some people might think it, was merely a mask for more genuinely subversive activities, of which the present case was one example. The shot which had destroyed Belinda's lunch companion on the banks of the Leam that November day was merely the culmination of a career which had, inexorably as it might be seen, been leading to that one inevitable conclusion. The court would be presented with evidence unequivocally linking Taggart with those sad events.

Skillen sat down. The occupants of the press benches scribbled as though their lives depended on it. That should raise circulation a bit, thought Taggart. MEMORY TRANSFER DON SHOT BY JOURNALIST IN PAY OF KGB, COUNSEL ALLEGES. There would be paragraphs in the *New Scientist* describing the technicalities of the affair, and assessing the chances of Wesley Mitchell having achieved what he said he had achieved. WAS MURDERED MAN REALLY CHARLES WATSON IN NEW BODY? IS MEMORY TRANSPLANT POSSIBLE? No and no. Next question, please.

John Stone rose. He was a stocky man of medium height,

and his delivery was a good deal more forceful than the languid Skillen's. The defence, he told the jury, would show that Andrew Taggart's involvement with Belinda Watson, and thence with all the rest of the affairs referred to by the prosecution, stemmed from his perfectly legitimate and often admirable work as a journalist for *New Politics*, an old-established and reputable publication. Taggart himself, when he took the stand, would describe how that acquaintance had first arisen. He and a number of other witnesses would show how Taggart had done his best to help Belinda when she became, perfectly justifiably, concerned about her absent husband. The powers that be might not like his activities, but that did not make him a murderer. The court would see that the prosecution had very little evidence linking Taggart to these events, and the defence would fiercely contest what little there was.

Things began undramatically. Various policemen were called to testify as to where and how they had found the body. Detective-Inspector Rogers described his various interviews with Taggart, more or less accurately, Taggart thought. In this case it was not so much a question of exactly what had been said, but of the weight you chose to give things. Taggart *had* been there. He *had* been having an affair with Belinda. He *had* been making Peter Fischer's life a misery, as far as he possibly could. All that was incontestable. Whether any of it was very sinister was another matter.

John Stone stood up. He said, 'Mr Rogers, two and a half months elapsed between the time when you first took my client into custody and the first production of the—' here he glanced at his notes—'*gloves*, which, I believe, are the only evidence you have in any way linking my client to this crime. Can you tell me when you first fished up the glove that was, as you say, discovered with the murder weapon?'

'It was found at the same time as the gun,' Rogers said firmly.

'And the other glove?'

'That was found when the defendant's house was searched.'

'On the day he was taken into custody.'

'Yes.'

'You knew about it then, on the day he was taken to Holborn police station?'

'Yes.'

'Yet it was never mentioned when you questioned him that day, nor indeed at all until its existence was disclosed to the defence just before the magistrates' court hearing in January, two and a half months later. Why was that?' Stone's tone was silky, but the drift of his questioning was obvious.

'I expect we didn't consider it necessary,' Rogers replied coolly.

'Necessary for whom? Necessary for Mr Taggart to know the nature of the evidence you intended to bring against him?'

'We did nothing that was in the slightest degree irregular,' Rogers said. 'The law requires us to disclose to the defence any evidence we intend to bring in prosecution. We did that.'

'All I'm saying is that you took a very long time doing it. As long as you possibly could.' Stone looked down at his notes again. Rogers said nothing. Then Stone said, 'I suggest to you, Mr Rogers, that the reason you didn't say anything about these gloves for such a long time is that you didn't have them. You'd arrested Mr Taggart, you'd decided that he was the person who had committed this crime, but you didn't have any real evidence against him. You realized that without some such evidence your case would simply be thrown out. So you conveniently found some.'

'That is quite untrue,' said Rogers firmly.

'I suggest that it is true,' said Stone. 'I suggest that that's exactly what happened.' He stared at Rogers for a moment, then said, 'No more questions, m'lud,' and sat down.

Skillen called Belinda. He established that she was married to Charles, that they had been married for nearly twenty-five years, that she was generally acquainted with his line of work. 'Of course,' she said. 'How could one not be?'

'Were you surprised by his sudden decision to leave for America?' asked Skillen.

'I was, really. He was just about to start on a piece of work I knew he was very interested in.'

'Did he say why he was going or what he was going to do?'
'In a way.'
'Either he did or he didn't, Mrs Watson.'
'Well, you know academic politics.'
'I'm afraid I don't. Can you describe them to us?'
'Oh well, academics always seem to be at one anothers' throats. There's an awful lot of rivalry. Always has been. But these days, with all the cuts, it seems to be getting even worse. At least, that's what I gather. I mean, Charles is—was—always going on about some frightful calamity that was just about to overtake his department or the university or something, and this time it had really happened. That's what I understood.'
'Didn't you ask?'
'Not really. I mean, it was more or less a constant theme, especially recently with all the cuts. Not very good pay and not even any job satisfaction any more. So he said he was going.'
'Did he say where, or didn't you ask him that, either?'
'Yes, he said he was going to work with Wesley Mitchell for a while. They'd often worked together before.'
'So you didn't worry.'
'No, why should I?'
'And you didn't go with him.'
'No, I preferred to stay home. I don't much enjoy visiting America. There didn't seem any particular reason for me to go.'
'Did you know what kind of work he was going to do?'
'No, not really. I mean, I knew what the general area must be. No more than that.'
'And that would be the biology of the brain, would it not?'
'That was it, yes.'
Skillen turned over a page. On to a new tack.
'And how long after your husband's departure did Andrew Taggart appear on the scene, Mrs Watson?'
'I don't really remember. A month, perhaps. A bit more. Charles went in April, the middle of April. Perhaps late May. I remember the garden was just about to come out, just a few things really flowering. It must have been about then.'

'You don't keep a note of such things?'
'No.'
'Did you know Mr Taggart before?'
'No. I knew his name, of course.'
'I see. Can you tell us what happened that day?'
'He phoned and said could he come round.'
'Did he give any reason for this sudden telephone call?'
'He just said could he come and see me.'
'Did he say what about?'
'He said, if I remember, that he'd rather not talk about it on the phone. Too complicated, or something like that.'

'Yes.' Skillen eyed the jury: he evidently found this significant. Then he continued, 'What did you talk about when he came?'

'He said he'd seen Charles with a man called Peter Fischer, and wanted to know if I knew him and if I knew why he'd been talking to Charles.'

'And did you?'

'Slightly. I used to be in the Civil Service with him years ago. I'd no idea what he'd been talking to Charles about. I remember telling Andrew—Mr Taggart—that Charles did tell me he'd met some civil servant who wanted him to do some work connected with the military, but he wasn't interested. We both assumed that must have been it, I think.'

'Did he pursue this line of inquiry?'

'Not with me. There wasn't anything more I could tell him.'

'But you did see him again?'

'Yes, quite often.'

'You became lovers, I believe,' Skillen stated, checking in his pile of papers, as though he didn't know.

'Yes,' said Belinda evenly.

In the public gallery, Caroline Watson let out her breath with an audible hiss. She hadn't been able to stay away—how could she just read about the circumstances of her father's life and probable death in the Sunday papers, like everyone else?—but she hadn't reckoned with the amount of public humiliation involved in a courtroom. Not that her mother

looked humiliated. That was almost the worst part of it.
'And your husband remained in America.'
'Yes.'
'Didn't you wonder what might be happening to him?'
'Yes, of course, from time to time. But he'd been away before.'
'So time passed.'
'Yes.'
'And then you suddenly got worried about your husband?'
'I realized how long it was since I'd heard from him.'
'And what happened then?'
'I phoned Wesley Mitchell, the friend he'd gone over to work with.'
'And what did he say?'
'He said he hadn't seen Charles since May.'
'And it was now?'
'September.'
'And what happened then?'
'I got very worried. Nobody seemed to know where Charles was. Then Andrew said he'd got to go over to America soon anyway and he'd see what he could find out.'
'And you were happy to trust him to do that?'
'Why not? He's used to finding things out.'
'You didn't feel he might have an ulterior motive of some kind?'
'No. I thought he'd try and help me.'
'And what form did this help take?'
'He went to Jones University. Where Wesley works. I gave him the names of some people Charles might have known.'
'And did he find anything?'
'He hadn't when he first came back. Then he suddenly went rushing off again.'
'And this time he found something?'
'He came back very excited and told me he thought a man was going to come to see me and try to pass himself off as Charles. Something about memory or personality transplants.'
'Did you believe him?'
'No.'

'And did this person come?'

'Yes.'

'And had there been—a personality transplant, as you put it?'

'It was Charles,' Belinda said simply. 'Just in a different body.'

A murmur rippled through the courtroom. The usher called severely, 'Silence in court!' Taggart reflected that if the pressmen went on scribbling at this rate, they'd soon run out of writing materials. Someone, he noticed, was making sketches. At least, if he was for once making the news instead of reporting it, what a story he was giving them! He felt almost sorry that he was going to puncture their fantasies when he entered the witness-box himself.

'And you resumed married life?'

'Yes.'

'And what happened then?'

'That was October. Early October. Then in November—' And here Belinda shook her head and was unable to continue.

'I'm very sorry to subject you to this ordeal, Mrs Watson,' said Skillen, who didn't sound sorry at all. 'This is the man who was shot?'

'While we were having coffee together.' She had collected herself again now.

'You were expecting the accused at the time?'

'Yes, he'd telephoned and made an appointment to interview—Charles.'

'He hadn't approached you earlier?'

'No, not after the evening he first came to warn me. We'd been besieged by the press.'

'And now he thought he'd see you when things had quietened down?'

'I suppose so. I didn't ask him. I didn't think I could really say no, considering.'

'Considering?'

'Considering everything that had happened.'

'What happened then?'

'Charles fell backwards. There was a hole in his head. I

ran and called 999. The police and the ambulance came—I don't know who was first exactly. Then Andrew arrived.'

'Did he seem surprised by what had happened?'

'Yes. Yes, I think so. He said he'd stay with me.'

'And did he?'

'For a while. Then I sent him away.'

'And that was the last you saw of him.'

'Before he was arrested, yes.'

Skillen did not take up this opening, but said, 'Thank you, Mrs Watson,' and sat down.

John Stone stood up. 'Mrs Watson, are we to understand that you've seen Mr Taggart since his arrest?'

'Yes, I've visited him.'

'Why?'

'He's a friend of mine.'

'In spite of what happened?'

'I don't think he had anything to do with that.'

'You don't think this was a crime of passion, then?'

'I can't imagine a more ridiculous idea.'

There was a pause while Stone flipped through his notes.

'Mrs Watson, there was one more point I wanted to take up. You said you gave Mr Taggart the names of "some people your husband might have known". Can you tell the court who those people were, exactly?'

Belinda swallowed nervously. 'I told him to get in touch with Lulu Mitchell,' she said. 'Wesley's daughter.'

'And why was that? Why did you think Miss Mitchell would know about your husband's whereabouts?'

'Because they were having an affair,' Belinda said, softly but clearly.

At the press table, pens scratched furiously on pads. In the public gallery, Caroline clenched her fists till her knuckles whitened. Lulu! Her friend! Or so she had thought.

'How long had this been going on?' asked John Stone, echoing her thoughts.

'I'm not sure. About two years, maybe. It wasn't anything I ever knew for certain. But I was pretty sure. They thought they were being terribly discreet, but it was pretty clear to me.'

'Did anybody else know about this?'

'The Mitchells might have. Lulu's parents. Of course I never discussed it with them. But she was particularly close to her father. I'd be surprised if he didn't suspect something.'

'How would you describe Wesley Mitchell's relations with your husband?'

'Uneasy. Wesley was never quite sure where he stood with Charles.'

'And your husband? How did he feel about Dr Mitchell?'

'I think he thought he was rather a joke, always rushing round the world. Not always a particularly good joke, though.'

'But they were friends?'

'Old friends,' said Belinda. It was impossible to tell from her voice what value, if any, she meant to impart to this phrase.

'Thank you, Mrs Watson.' Stone sat down.

CHAPTER 30

'We can't get Mitchell,' said Phil Redvers. He, John Stone and Taggart were conferring in a cramped little room tucked into a corner of the Victorian labyrinth of the courthouse. 'Says he's too busy. Much regrets, etcetera. He's in Hong Kong or somewhere.'

'Regrets my foot,' said Taggart. 'Isn't there anything we can do?'

''Fraid not. Not in our jurisdiction. You can't extradite someone just to be a witness. It's hard enough if they're a criminal.'

'How about Lulu?'

'Not sure. I'm trying hard to persuade her.'

'What are the chances?' Stone wanted to know. 'She's an important witness for us.'

Redvers shrugged. 'I wish I knew. One minute she says she will, and then she won't. She isn't even in the country yet. We've had at least three separate tickets booked for her. Keeps getting cold feet. Of course she's very young, and she knows it's going to be very unpleasant for her.'

'For a few minutes,' said Taggart. 'Perhaps you might try and point out . . .'

'I'm appealing to her better nature,' said Redvers. 'I haven't given up hope yet.'

'What about Fischer?'

'Oh, he can't escape. No way out for him. He's British like the rest of us.'

'Bully for him,' said Taggart.

Fischer, in the stand, looked as usual bland and slightly contemptuous. His round spectacles glistened below his domed forehead. The Cupid's bow mouth was slightly pursed between the round, pink cheeks. He agreed that he was Peter Arnold Fischer and that he worked for the Ministry of Defence and stood awaiting further questions with weary resignation, a tedious interruption in a busy life. He was appearing as a defence witness: presumably, since the judge had refused the request for a hearing *in camera*, he preferred not to go into too many details of his work on the prosecution's behalf. Far from being eager to implicate Taggart in a deep-laid plot to disrupt secret work of the highest importance, he seemed now more concerned to dissociate himself from the whole thing.

'How long had you known Charles Watson?' asked John Stone.

'Oh, for years . . . That's to say, we used to know each other about twenty-odd years ago. I hadn't seen him much since then, if at all.'

'What made you suddenly arrange a meeting with him after all those years?'

'What makes you think I did?'

'Answer the question,' said the judge.

Fischer shrugged. 'I didn't arrange anything. I ran into him. We had lunch together—one could hardly do less, after so many years. We discussed the educational situation— naturally, that was his field.'

'During this lunch, did you try and get him to drop the

work he was currently doing in order to do some work you were interested in?'

'I believe he worked in psychology. That is not my field of interest. I am a civil servant in the Ministry of Defence.'

'With professional interests in many different fields, I believe.'

'A number.'

'Did you threaten Dr Watson during that meeting that if he didn't undertake the work you were outlining, he would soon find the facilities for the work he was doing disappearing?'

'How could I possibly do that? My department has nothing to do with educational policy or allocations.'

'And isn't it a fact,' Stone went on, 'that not long after this meeting he did in fact find himself unable to go on with his research, and went to America to work with Dr Wesley Mitchell, who was interested in precisely the field you had been trying to persuade Charles Watson to work in?'

'Possibly. I really wouldn't know.' Fischer was so bored it seemed a miracle he was still awake.

'Do you know Wesley Mitchell?' Stone now inquired, consulting his notes.

'I know the name. We may have met at a conference.'

'Your acquaintance doesn't go any further than that?'

'We've met perhaps once or twice.'

'Was it on your department's behalf that Dr Mitchell was conducting experiments on memory transplants, if that's what he was doing?'

'No.'

(And that probably wasn't a lie, either, Taggart reflected. It would have been for the CIA, with Fischer's lot taking a polite interest.)

'All right. One last question, Mr Fischer. Are you acquainted with my client, Mr Andrew Taggart?'

'We've met, from time to time.'

'You wouldn't describe yourselves as friends?'

'Certainly not.'

'Have you anything against him personally?'

'I scarcely know him personally. I read his stories from

time to time, but I don't have much of a taste for fiction.'

'You don't feel he's ever conducted, let's say, a vendetta against yourself or your department?'

'He has certainly behaved extremely irresponsibly from time to time.'

'But you've never thought of prosecuting him? Trying to get him out of the way?'

'If he had done anything actually illegal, I have no doubt we would have charged him.'

'The possibility has been discussed?'

'Possibly. It wouldn't be my decision.'

'Thank you,' said Stone, and sat down.

Michael Skillen stood up. 'Illegal or not, your department was doubtless aware of the activities of Andrew Taggart?'

'Certainly.'

'How would you describe them?'

'He is rather more than a nuisance. From time to time, in my opinion, what he does has bordered upon treachery.'

'But you haven't prosecuted?'

'There's no point in mounting a prosecution if it's not going to succeed. I believe advice has been taken from time to time.'

'Would you say his career has shown a pattern?'

'There's been a consistent attempt to disrupt intelligence activities, yes.'

'With what motivation, would you say?'

'I don't quite take your meaning,' said Fischer. 'To disrupt them, of course.'

'In a private or a—more directed—capacity, would you have thought?' Skillen said imperturbably.

'It's impossible to say,' returned Fischer, after a moment's thought.

Skillen sat down. Stone got up again.

'Mr Fischer, if you suspect my client of being in the pay of the KGB or some such thing, am I right in assuming you keep an eye on him?'

'Probably.'

'I'll be more specific. Is he followed? Is his telephone tapped?'

'I can't possibly answer questions of that sort,' said Fischer.

'You're not prepared to give me a negative?'

'I'm not prepared to answer the question at all.'

Stone sat down.

As the trial wore on, Taggart became more depressed. The excitement that had carried him through until now was evaporating in the court's slow and solemn routine; and although he knew that much of what the prosecution was alleging was preposterous, and all of it untrue, or slanted—which was even further, in a way, from the truth than a straight lie—he couldn't believe that, having got so far, they would not be allowed to achieve their aim, get him convicted, and have him incarcerated for—how long? At the best, with remission and parole, eight, ten, years? He couldn't bear to think about it. Speaking to Stone and Redvers later that evening, he found it hard to share the lawyers' jubilation at the news that Lulu appeared finally to have succumbed to pressure and her better nature. 'I believe she's actually on the plane now,' said Redvers. 'Unless something very funny happened when she got to the departure lounge. Of course we're meeting her at Heathrow.'

'I can't imagine quite why you think she's so important,' said Taggart querulously. 'I mean, she can't exactly tell the court anything new, can she?'

'You'll see,' said Stone. He was a quiet, almost mousy man, unimpressive without his wig. Taggart wished he could have more faith.

'How d'you think it's going?' he asked.

Stone shrugged. 'Hard to say.'

'I'm very depressed.'

'Don't be. Not now we've got the lovely Miss Mitchell. Is she lovely, by the way?'

'I'd say she was striking rather than beautiful. Why, does it matter?'

'Not in the least. I just wondered.'

And now here she was, standing in the witness-box, her shock of yellow frizz held ineffectually back by two combs.

She avoided Taggart's eye, or seemed to do so—it was hard to tell, since half her face was covered by enormous shades. Poor girl, she must feel washed out, rushed into court after one of those unspeakable overnight transatlantic flights. Taggart hoped she wouldn't go to sleep on the stand. It seemed unrealistic to expect coherence under these conditions. Still, even a half-asleep Lulu was better than no Lulu at all. That was what John Stone seemed to think, anyhow.

Yes, her name was Louise Alexandra Mitchell. Yes, she lived in Southampton, Massachusetts, USA.

'It's most kind of you to come all this way to help the court, Miss Mitchell,' said John Stone, trying to put her at her ease.

'I just had to,' she replied.

'All right, Miss Mitchell. Now, could you tell the court about your relations with Charles Watson?'

'We loved each other,' Lulu said, looking Stone straight in the eye. 'I knew him all my life. Then, two summers ago, we just fell in love.'

'And the relationship continued?'

'When we could. We didn't meet that often.'

'And then he came over to Southampton to work?'

'Yeah, I couldn't believe it, there he was.'

'And you continued from where you'd left off the previous time?'

'Not really. You see, he was staying with my parents. And he—we—felt—that we, um, couldn't—He had to get his own place.'

'I can see that,' returned Stone gravely. 'And did he?'

'Yes, he did.'

'And were you able to resume your relationship there?'

'No, we weren't. Because the very day he got it, I met Charles and we were going to have lunch there together. And then when I got there he said my Dad wanted to take him off someplace to see some piece of work he wanted Charles to help with, and of course it was important Dad shouldn't know what was going on. Because—well, it would have been impossible. So we had lunch in a deli and fixed to meet up after he got back. And that was the last time I saw Charles.'

That was the moment, of course, thought Taggart. That was Wesley's bad luck. What else could possibly have connected him with Charles's disappearance? Nothing. After that, all he had to say was what he did say—that he had no idea what happened to him. You can't keep tags on grown men.

'Your father didn't know about this relationship?'

'I didn't think anyone knew. Seems like I was wrong. So maybe he did know, or guessed. But if he did I never realized.'

'Would he have minded?'

'Yeah—I think so. He's never much liked any of my boyfriends, and this, well—'

'What happened then?'

'Like, nothing. Charles didn't appear, and I was really busy, and I wondered about him from time to time, because of course I missed him, and it was kind of funny that he didn't get in touch, but what could I do? I could have asked Dad, in fact I did mention it a couple of times, but I didn't want to make a big deal of it all. And then the vacation came—'

'And then Andrew Taggart appeared.'

'That's right, and then we started to look for Charles.'

'Would you like to describe how you went about it?'

Lulu did so, from the hunt through Wesley's desk to the night in the high school opposite the Prospect Psychodynamics Clinic.

'You and Mr Taggart seem to have invested a considerable amount of effort and ingenuity in this hunt.'

'I was personally involved. And it's the kind of thing Andrew does professionally all the time.'

'You wouldn't say he was personally involved?'

'Not the way I was.'

Michael Skillen did his best to discredit Lulu as a witness.

'Wouldn't you agree that you've behaved in a rather underhand way vis-à-vis your family and friends, this past couple of years, Miss Mitchell?' he inquired loftily. 'You engage in a thoroughly disreputable love-affair, you carry it on under the noses of your family and your lover's wife and family, you go through your father's desk, you trick him, you tail him through the streets. It's hardly the kind of behaviour one would expect from one's daughter or one's family friend.'

'I guess that what Dad did to Charles is hardly the behaviour you'd expect from your friend either,' Lulu replied stoutly.

'You hardly have proof that he did anything at all to Charles, do you?'

Lulu said nothing.

'They went off together, that's all you know.'

'Until this other person appeared.'

'Well, if his wife was happy enough to accept him, you could hardly grumble, could you?' observed Skillen insolently. Taggart, physically restraining himself, could see Lulu struggling to keep her temper. 'Anyhow,' Skillen added, 'you never saw this person with your father. The only thing you have to connect the two is what Mr Taggart here told you, isn't that so?'

'I guess that's true.'

'Did it never cross your mind to wonder if he had his own *parti pris?*'

Clearly it never had. Lulu said nothing. Skillen sat down, and Stone got up again.

'Just a couple more questions, Miss Mitchell. Am I right in thinking your family was in fact over here when the murder of which my client is accused took place?'

'That's right, Dad had some conference to go to, and it was my birthday, so Mom said she'd take me to a couple of shows in London for a treat.'

'Am I right in thinking your father is an excellent shot?'

'Objection, m'lud,' said Skillen, leaping to his feet. 'This court is not here to listen to insinuations about third parties that can have nothing whatever to do with the course of events we are considering here.'

'What is your line of questioning, Mr Stone?' asked the judge. 'It hardly seems very relevant to this case.'

'I believe it is, m'lud.'

'Very well, you may go on. But please be careful.'

'Thank you, m'lud. I hope to show that this line of questioning is thoroughly relevant to my client's case.'

'Please answer the question, Miss Mitchell,' said the judge.

'Yes, he's a very good shot.'

'How do you know that?'

'We go hunting together. Have done for years.'

'Are you a good shot yourself?'

'Not bad.'

'Objection, m'lud,' interposed Skillen, leaping to his feet at the same time as Lulu gave her reply.

'I really fail to see what possible relevance this can have, Mr Stone,' said the judge.

'You will, m'lud. Miss Mitchell,' Stone went on, turning back to his witness, 'can you tell us what you were doing on the afternoon in question, the afternoon my client was in Leamingworth?'

'Why, I—I think I was out shopping.'

'Were you with anyone?'

'No, Mom felt tired—the jet-lag. She stayed in the hotel while I went out.'

'Did you buy anything?'

'I don't really remember.'

'So you could have been anywhere. In Oxford Street or, for that matter, in Leamingworth. Did you go to the theatre that night?'

'Yeah.' Lulu now sounded thoroughly alarmed. 'We did. I wasn't in Leamingworth!'

'Thank you, m'lud.' And Stone sat down.

CHAPTER 31

Taggart was surprised to see how calm he felt when Detective-Inspector Rogers took the box. Here, after all, was the man who was trying to frame him. It would be on Rogers's evidence that he was or was not convicted. And he probably would be. He was enough of a realist to know that.

Skillen took Rogers through what he had to say. Meeting Taggart in Leamingworth. Deciding it was worth looking further. Searching his house. Finding the glove.

Finding the glove.

Undeniably the pair of the one found with the rifle in the river?

Yes.

Found where?

In Taggart's bedroom.

So that, taking one thing with another, it seemed pretty plain that here we had the man who had killed the man masquerading—or not masquerading—as Charles Watson?

That was what we concluded, yes.

Skillen sat down. There wasn't much Stone could do with Rogers. He agreed that Taggart had consistently denied having shot 'Dr Watson', that he had denied ever having handled a gun, had denied ever having seen the gloves before. Stone didn't bother to ask him what he thought of these denials. He sat down. Skillen had no more to ask.

'Any more witnesses, Mr Stone?'

'I should like to call Mr Andrew Taggart, m'lud.'

Taggart felt dry-mouthed as he mounted the stand. Stage-fright. His starring role. The court was buzzing with interest. Gently, breaking him in, getting him used to it, John Stone took him minutely through his story, from the beginning, when he happened to be walking down Pall Mall and glimpsed Fischer and Charles Watson together on the steps of the Reform Club, to the end, when he found Belinda standing, appalled, over the body of the dead man who seemed to have taken over so much of what had belonged to her husband.

'Do you have any reason, apart from having seen them together that first day, to connect Peter Fischer with what happened to Charles Watson?' Stone asked.

'He kept appearing. We met at a conference in Washington. That was why I was going to be in America, when I told Belinda I'd try and find out what had happened to Charles. Then, when I went to Jones, there he was again, with Wesley Mitchell, going into Mitchell's lab. And then there he was again at the clinic, with Mitchell and the new version of Charles Watson. That was what made me quite sure it was an intelligence thing, the two of them being in it together. With Watson at the centre, somehow.'

'Have you any idea what happened to Charles Watson?'

'I'm afraid I haven't. I'd be surprised if he were still alive.'

'And now we come to the question of the gloves, Mr Taggart.'

Stone paused. Taggart said nothing.

'Are they your gloves, Mr Taggart?'

'The first time I ever saw them was in the magistrates' court.'

'Have you some gloves like them?'

'No.'

'Have you ever had gloves like them?'

'No.'

'Can you be sure? Several million people in this country probably have gloves of this sort.'

'Not me. I never wear gloves.'

'Never?'

'Never. I hate them. I have excellent circulation, and my hands don't get cold.'

'So whoever threw that glove into the river with the rifle, it was not you?'

'No.'

Stone sat down. Skillen stood up. They were like weathermen in their little house: they could only come out one at a time. 'If this was not your glove, Mr Taggart, how do you explain the undoubted fact that it was found in your house?'

Taggart looked him in the eye. 'I can only think that someone has made a mistake.'

'Can you explain just what you mean by that?' Skillen sounded indignant.

'I mean that I don't think it was found in my house.'

'Do you realize what you are implying?'

'Yes.'

'You are accusing the police of perjuring themselves.'

'I'm afraid so.'

'That is a very serious accusation, Mr Taggart.'

'Yes, but it isn't unknown.'

'I put it to you that it is much more probable that you would like to save yourself than that the police would lie to put you in prison. What possible motive could they have for such a thing?'

'I have no idea.'

Skillen, with a significant look at the jury, sat down. Stone rose again. 'Mr Taggart, would this be the first encounter you had made with what I believe is known as the planting of evidence?'

'No.'

'Would you like to tell the jury about your previous encounters in this field?'

Taggart gave a brief description of the campaign he had conducted against police corruption and its role in securing the quashing on appeal of two convictions, in both of which evidence had, it turned out, been planted by the police.

'Am I right in thinking that the Court of Appeal was extremely unhappy about these cases?' Stone went on.

'They didn't want to hear them, no. They accused me of bringing the judicial system into disrepute. But things got to such a pitch that they couldn't ignore what we had to say any longer.'

'And did you kill the—second Charles Watson, Mr Taggart?'

'Well, of course I didn't!' said Taggart.

Michael Skillen rose. 'Why should the court believe a word you say, Mr Taggart?'

'Because I'm on oath, and I'm telling the truth.'

'You are asserting that the unfortunate Dr Charles Watson has been somehow spirited away, that his personality was transferred, by unspecified means, into this second gentleman, and that you happened to be present at the moment of his death simply in the pursuit of a good story?'

'That's not what I'm asserting at all. I think Charles Watson is probably dead, and I don't think his personality was transferred to anybody. I do think that that's what some people wanted to make everyone believe.'

'I submit, Mr Taggart, that you've been engaged, throughout your professional life, in an unremitting campaign to undermine the authority of government in this country.'

'I wouldn't put it like that.'

'How would you put it?'

'I've been engaged in a campaign to stop government overstepping the bounds of its authority. Governments are inclined to do that. The job of a journalist like myself is to point out when it happens. Naturally we're not very popular with people in government.'

'I put it to you that you thought you'd stumbled over a top-secret intelligence project, and that you decided to wreck it on your masters' behalf.'

'Objection,' shouted Stone, leaping to his feet.

'Please phrase your question differently, Mr Skillen,' said the judge. 'Members of the jury, you are to disregard the implications of that question.'

'I put it to you that you thought you'd stumbled over a top-secret intelligence project, and you decided to wreck it for your own reasons.'

'I certainly thought the project was funded by intelligence,' said Taggart. 'I hadn't the slightest interest in wrecking it. What I was going to do was report it. That was why I was in Leamingworth that day—to get the interview which would have put the finishing touch to my report.'

'It may interest you to know that according to an agent's report I have here—' Skillen handed a copy of the report to the judge and another to Stone—'the Prospect Psychodynamics Clinic in Brooklyn is a sort of convalescent home for those recovering from nervous disability. It does indeed exist, but it has no operating theatres and the management denies any knowledge of Dr Wesley Mitchell or of Mr Peter Fischer.'

'Yes, I heard they'd stripped out their top floor.'

'I put it to you that in the course of your investigations you became very attached to Mrs Watson, and that the sight of her so obviously engaged with another man was most hurtful to you.'

'Even if that was true, I should scarcely have plotted to kill him. It's happened to me before. One gets over these things.'

'But I put it to you that this time your personal inclinations coincided with certain professional instructions you had received.'

'Objection, m'lud!' cried Stone.

'Really, Mr Skillen, please restrain yourself.'

'No more questions, m'lud.'

Michael Skillen's closing speech for the Crown very much reiterated his opening one. Who but Taggart would have killed the second Charles Watson? Taggart had every motivation. He was in love with Belinda, he had had some success with her, and now he saw himself supplanted. Moreover, the man supplanting him was living proof of the success of an operation he was trying, for his own reasons, to discredit—'just as he had tried to discredit so many of the successes of this government, members of the jury, in the course of the past few years. Indeed, you may feel that the career of this man is an example of the harm that may be done with impunity within the bounds of the law, at a time when so many people are making such a fuss about the supposed severity of that law.' But this time things had gone wrong. Personal inclination and political opportunism had coincided; he had come prepared—perhaps hidden the murder weapon among some trees on the river bank near the point opposite the Watsons' garden, in readiness to make the most of any opportunity, should it present itself. 'And knowing Mrs Watson and her habits as he did, he must have known it was almost inevitable that, on a day like that, she and—Dr Watson—would come out into the garden, and would spend some time sitting in the summerhouse, thus presenting the easiest of targets.' The existence of the weapon showed that the murder was premeditated. 'This was not the kind of weapon you could pick up at the corner shop, to coin a phrase,' Skillen informed them. It was deadly accurate and extremely expensive. And whoever had used it had worn gloves. One of these gloves had, for what reason no one could know, been thrown into the river with it. The other had been found in Andrew Taggart's house. No doubt, if the circumstances had been different—the weather had not been so good, for example—another venue would have been chosen: the unfortunate man might have been picked off as he left the house, or in some other way. But things had been as they were, and he had died in the way he had. And then Taggart, supremely confident—'over-confident, you may think, members of the jury'—had had the cheek to present himself at the house as if he had known nothing about what had happened, and had actually stayed to comfort Mrs Watson in her distress. It was a most unpleasant crime, the apex, as it might be said, of a most unpleasant career, and it should be justly punished. With which Mr Skillen sat down.

John Stone stood up. 'Members of the jury,' he said, 'it may be that you have never heard a more extraordinary story than the tale which has emerged of the goings-on which led to the disappearance of the first Dr Charles Watson, the appearance of his alter ego, and the involvement of my client in all this. That is very possible. But what is certain is that you will never have heard a more unsatisfactory farrago of insinuation and circumstance deployed to bring a man to trial on a charge as severe as this one. In all my years at the bar, I certainly have not. What are the facts of the case? My client has been investigating a story, which is what he does for a living. This is a story in which he himself has a certain involvement, but that is hardly illegal or unknown, and it doesn't affect the facts of the case. By a mixture of luck, perseverance, and the ability to draw connections between apparently disparate persons and events—that is to say, by being a good journalist—he gets his story. Then, at the very last, just as he is about to lay his hands on the final piece in the jigsaw, a man is shot and he finds himself accused of the shooting.

'Now what evidence is there to connect him with this shooting? If we clear away all the layers of insinuation and innuendo, only three facts remain. He was in Leamingworth at the time the crime was committed; he was near where it was committed; and he could have done it. That much is fact, and, far from disputing it, or trying to conceal the fact of his presence in the town, as he so easily might have done, he presents himself at the Watsons' house and is perfectly happy to tell the police what he's been doing. You may feel that this, far from being insolent over-confidence, is simply the act of a man who hasn't the slightest idea what has been going on. His appointment is for two-thirty, and that, or a little before it, is when he turns up—to find, as we all know, that his interviewee has just been shot.

'He could have done it; but, for that matter, so could a number of the other parties involved in this strange story. You have heard Miss Louise Mitchell testify that she was in this country on that day, that she went out by herself and met her mother to go to the theatre in the evening. What was to stop her taking the train to Leamingworth and firing the fatal shot? You have heard her say she was an excellent shot. I'm not saying she did do it. All I'm saying is that, just like my client, she could have done it. That's all. And she had just as much, or as little, motivation. She may have hated the deceased because he supplanted her lover. She may have intended the shot for Mrs Watson, whom she presumably resented, but her hand slipped at the last. All this, of course, is the purest speculation—just like most of the case against my client. Or what about Dr Wesley Mitchell? It may interest you to know that he was not addressing his conference until the day after this crime took place. On the day in question he was, presumably, in the audience. He was, we have ascertained, certainly seen there when it opened, at nine o'clock, but no one has any particular memory of seeing him after that. He may have been there, but he may not. And he, too, was an excellent shot. Or let us suppose that someone somewhere in the Ministry of Defence had become tired of the perpetual nuisance my client represents. You have heard Mr Peter Fischer attest to his unpopularity in those circles. You heard him refuse to deny that my client is closely watched—probably that his telephone is tapped. What could be easier than to hear him make an appointment to see someone, be somewhere, at a certain time, and then prepare to make the most of any opportunities thus offered? If you fail, no matter. If you don't, you stand a good chance of extracting a nasty thorn from your side. Again, this is pure speculation. Just like the case against my client.

'There remains the question of the glove. The famous glove. You have heard my client deny that it was anything to do with him, any more than the gun was. He has never fired a gun in his life, and he never wears gloves. What, then, was it doing in his house—if it ever was in his house? That, members of the jury, we cannot tell. But I must ask you to bear in mind my client's previous investigations of cases where evidence has been planted before you dismiss out of hand what he has told the court on this subject.

'Members of the jury, you have a duty not to convict if there is any reasonable doubt. In this case, as far as I can see, there can only be doubt. There is no certainty about anything.'

CHAPTER 32

It was mid-afternoon when John Stone sat down and the judge began his summing-up. By the time the court went into recess at four o'clock he had not finished, and did not do so until midday next day. By the end of that afternoon, the jury had still not been able to reach a conclusion, and were sent to a hotel for the night.

'In with a chance,' said Stone.

'He wasn't exactly on our side, was he?'

'He could have been worse. All in all, it's not the kind of tale you could expect a judge to be enthusiastic about. Or your career for that matter.'

'Perhaps the jury realizes that.'

'Perhaps they do. Nothing more we can do, anyway, for the moment.'

By midday next day the jury was still unable to agree. The judge sent word that he would accept a majority verdict. At three o'clock they indicated that they had reached a verdict, though it was not unanimous. Taggart, who had been waiting in the cells below, was brought back into the dock. His mouth was dry and his hands soaking with sweat. The foreman of the jury came into the court.

'Foreman of the jury, do you find the accused guilty or not guilty?'

'Not guilty, my lord.'

Taggart felt the room revolve around him. Then John Stone was shaking him by the hand, and Phil Redvers was saying, 'Let's get the hell out of here before they think up something else.'

Later, in a pub near the *New Politics* office, Redvers said, 'I can tell you now, I never for a moment thought you'd done it, but I certainly didn't think you'd get off.'

'It's my winning personality . . .'

'No, I think they just weren't sure . . .'

'You sure gave me some bad moments, though,' said Lulu, who had tagged along with the party. 'I really thought your lawyer was going to turn around and say I'd done it.'

'That wasn't his drift, was it? I mean, he pointed out that you might have done. So might about fifty thousand other people. That was what he mostly had in mind with regard to you. I thought. Of course, I may be wrong.'

'OK, who do you think it was?'

'Oh.' Taggart shrugged listlessly. 'Somehow that aspect of it almost doesn't interest me any more . . .' He looked across at her. 'Who do you?'

Lulu met his gaze, then dropped her eyes. 'I don't want to think about it.' She shook her head. All around them, happy drinkers roared. They moved to a corner, as private, amid the racket, as if they had been alone.

'I don't blame you. But it seems a distinct possibility.'

They sat for a while in silence, the same picture going through both their heads. Wesley Mitchell slipping out of his conference. Driving down to Leamingworth, which he knew so well from so many previous visits. Taking expert aim. Driving back. Giving his paper. Leaving the country. And not coming back, even though he knew an innocent man was being tried for the killing of Charles Watson the Second . . .

'No, I don't think it was him,' said Lulu after a while. 'He could have, physically. I agree about that. But why would he? Why should he shoot the guy? I mean, this was his experiment. As far as he was concerned, the more the guy was around, the more credit he got. I mean, he knew it wasn't a memory transplant, or whatever the hell that weird story was. But everyone else really believed it, and that includes the guys with the moneybags who commissioned the whole thing in the first place. The CIA or whoever. They'll believe anything. Everyone knows that. Look at Gordon Liddy.'

'That's true, but I tell you who never would believe it, and that's anyone remotely in the same field. Anyone who knows anything at all about it. That's why it was so important your Dad should never be connected with the business. He's a respectable scientist who runs a respectable lab. No one would ever take him seriously again. That was the beauty of all this, from his point of view. The military would provide the secrecy *and* the facilities. Money, subjects . . .'

'I can't believe it.' Lulu was nearly in tears.

'Oh, I could believe it. I think your father's a pretty ruthless guy. But I don't think it was him, as a matter of fact.'

'Why not?'

'Because where would he have got that gun? This isn't America, you know. You can't walk into a shop and buy a gun, just like that. You have to have a licence or else know someone who knows someone . . . Not that it's very hard to get a licence, but not for someone like your father, just over for the weekend. So where would he have got it? He's probably got fifteen at home, but you can't just pack one in your suitcase and hope no one'll notice at the airport. Not these days.'

'No, that's right,' said Lulu, brightening.

'That doesn't mean to say I don't think he's a murderer. I mean, who else disposed of Charles Watson? The real Charles Watson? Your father, no one else. But of course, there he had more of a personal motive.' He looked across at her bleakly, and she flinched. 'Don't get me wrong. I'm not suggesting he was in any way justified, or any rubbish like that. But I don't expect it made things harder.' He went on quickly, 'I'm sorry if I seem brutal. The last few months haven't improved me. I should leave me to stew if I were you. I haven't exactly brought sweetness and light to your life, have I? But I really am terribly grateful to you for coming over. I know it was awful for you. I hope somebody paid your fare at least. If they didn't, let me. It's the least I can do to thank you.'

'No, don't worry, your paper paid. Will you go on working for them?'

'Why not? If they'll have me.'

'Are you going to write the story of your experiences?'

'Maybe. Not just yet. First of all I want to get some things sorted out.'

'Like what?'

'Like I'd like to find out just what did happen,' said Taggart. 'Like it shouldn't be beyond the bounds of human ingenuity, if people really set their minds to it. Which nobody has done yet, believe me. I feel like setting myself up as a fairground exhibit. Andrew Taggart, public convenience.'

'You must try not to be bitter.'

'Somebody said that to me before. Well, I'll find out what happened, and then I'll write it down, and perhaps somebody will pay me lots of money for it. Meanwhile, I'm off. I really am grateful, Lulu, and I think you're a terrific girl, and one day I hope we'll meet again, though I doubt it, somehow. But I won't forget you. And don't let this stupid business hurt you too much.'

Lulu put down her glass and said, 'Give me a call when you feel better.'

'Maybe,' said Taggart.

CHAPTER 33

Taggart dialled Peter Fischer's number and braced himself for a fight.

At the other end someone picked up the phone. 'Yes?' Don't give anything away, whatever you do.

'Is that Peter Fischer?'

'Who is this?'

'Andrew Taggart speaking.'

'Oh, hello. I wondered when you'd call.'

Well, that was a surprise and no mistake. He'd assumed Fischer would go to any lengths to avoid him. That's what *he'd* have done, in his place. Wouldn't have the nerve to face him. Instead of which . . .

'I'd like to see you sometime.'

'Yes, I expect you would. What would suit you? Lunch?'

'No, I don't think so.' The thought of sitting watching that round, gleaming face engulfing quantities of rich food was more than flesh and blood could bear. Taggart thought he'd probably throw up if he were subjected to such a spectacle.

'All right then, what would you prefer?'

'I'll come to your office.'

'Just a moment, I'll get my diary.' Couldn't do enough for him, now. 'All right, when did you have in mind?'

'Now.'

'What—now?' The voice at the other end sounded a bit weak. Caught him on the hop there.

'Are you busy?'

'Well—no, not particularly.'

'Then I'll be with you in half an hour.' And Taggart put the phone down firmly.

He wondered what Fischer would be doing in the meantime. Positioning his heavies ready to intervene if things got out of hand? Did it cross his mind that Taggart might try to kill him, assault him at the very least? After all, that was the kind of chap Taggart was supposed to be—wasn't it? And where Peter Fischer was concerned, it might well be the kind of chap he actually *was*. Rarely had he felt so murderous—in fact, he now realized, never in his life before. So this was what it felt like. It wasn't pleasant. He didn't like this new version of himself. He hoped he wouldn't encounter it again.

At the MOD building he was checked in, confirmed as acceptable and expected, given a little badge and conducted to Peter Fischer's office. Just as if nothing had happened and this was a normal call. Not even frisked. He felt like saying to them, Aren't you worried I might be carrying a neat little revolver tucked away somewhere? After all, I've just been tried for murder. Acquitted, but that's a mere afterthought. And only just.

He padded along the corridors behind the lame attendant, who knocked respectfully on Fischer's door. 'Come!' said a voice. And there they were, facing each other.

'Taggart, my dear fellow, do sit down,' said Peter Fischer. He was sitting behind a large desk with almost no papers on it. Not risking exposing anything to the prying eyes of journalists. Or maybe the kind of thing he did didn't get written down. On the other side of the desk was an armchair. Taggart didn't sit in it, but wandered over to the window. He preferred to remain in a position of superiority. 'May I congratulate you,' added Fischer.

'What on?'

'Why, the successful verdict . . .'

'On not being convicted of a murder I didn't commit? You didn't think I did commit it, surely? You of all people.'

'Not for a moment,' said Fischer serenely. He was leaning on his desk playing with a pen, looking up at Taggart almost roguishly, his eyes blank behind the round black spectacles whose lenses reflected the light.

'I can believe that,' said Taggart. 'Since it was a set-up and you set it up.'

'Did I?'

'Of course you did. You heard me make that appointment. My phone's been tapped for years, that's nothing new. It was just a question of someone listening actively instead of making tape-recordings for future reference. You set someone on to me. They made sure the job was done when I could have done it. Perhaps you did it yourself. I don't know. One of the many things I don't know about you.'

'Then let me tell you one thing for certain, and that is that I was at a meeting all afternoon of that particular day.'

'I'm sure you were. Why do your own dirty work when you can get someone else to do it for you? What did you want to kill the poor chap for, anyway? Hadn't he learnt his part thoroughly enough? Were you afraid he'd give himself away?'

'What are you talking about?' said Fischer.

'I'm talking about that man that got himself killed somehow last November in Leamingworth. Remember? The one I heard talking to you and Wesley Mitchell in Brooklyn in October. Unless you didn't see me there? I've often wondered.'

'I saw you all right. But he wasn't an impostor.'

'You mean you believe it?'

'Of course I believe it.' Fischer drummed on the desk with his pen. 'You may say what you like about Wesley Mitchell, and I can assure you I don't hold any illusions about his personal character, but he's a great scientist, and some of the work he's doing has the most shattering implications for us all.'

'God, you really do believe it.' Taggart shook his head, like a dog trying to dislodge drops of water, or maybe he was merely trying to shake his brain into accommodating this new and astonishing fact. 'So maybe it was Mitchell after all. How can you be so naïve? Didn't you take advice from anyone else in the field? It can't be done, what Mitchell's trying to do. What he *says* he's trying to do. That's not the way the brain works, or memory.'

Fischer didn't say anything.

Taggart said, 'Oh, why waste time bothering about it. It's an irrelevance, isn't it? Facts are a complete irrelevance. You manufacture your own world. You, Wesley Mitchell—all you're concerned with is your audiences. Other scientists, other spies. The only people the facts matter to are the fall-guys. People like Charles Watson, poor devil, and that other man, whoever he was, and me. We're the ones that get killed or put in prison. Do you realize, you bastard, that I could have been locked up for fifteen years? Have you ever been in a prison? Do you know what it's like in there?'

'I do absolutely realize that. But fortunately it didn't happen.'

'Is that all you've got to say?'

Fischer leaned back in his chair, balancing it on its hind legs. 'Oh, by no means.' He had put down his pen now, and was studying the wall opposite him, his arms hooked around the chair back. 'You say the facts are an irrelevance. Well, as far as I can see, they are and they aren't. Some facts are and some facts aren't. It depends where you're looking from, doesn't it? Let's think of an irrelevant fact,' he went on dreamily. 'All right, here's one. Who killed the chap that was having lunch with Mrs Watson that day? It might have been you, it might have been Wesley Mitchell, it might have been a member of my department, though I can assure you it absolutely wasn't me. In fact, you're clearly not going to believe this, but I've absolutely not the faintest idea who it was. I mean, it wasn't anything to do with us. I'm not pretending that that sort of thing is beyond the bounds of possibility. But it wasn't what happened this time. I'd just like to get that straight. Anyhow, the question of who actually did what is perfectly irrelevant to me, and to you, I should think, provided nobody thinks it was you. It's just about as irrelevant as whether the fellow and Dr Mitchell were shamming, as you say, or whether they weren't, as I'm inclined to believe. Irrelevances. Now here's a relevant fact. It was quite within the bounds of possibility to make perfectly sensible people think you had actually shot the chap. That's a fact: they arrested you for it, and tried you, though there wasn't quite enough there to convict you. Fortunately. And here's another fact. A surprising number of people would have been very happy if you had been convicted, whether you'd actually done the deed or not. That's a fact.'

'I'd already deduced that for myself.'

'Quite. Nobody ever said you weren't intelligent. Now, wouldn't you like to change that state of affairs?'

'What?'

'I said, wouldn't you like to change that? I mean, as a way of life it has its inconveniences. You feel morally superior, and occasionally you chalk up a small victory over this or that, but in the end you really can't win. It's no good spending your life kicking against the pricks, not when the pricks are as large and powerful as—the ones that seem to obsess you. It's such a waste of energy. They'll get you in the end, and people won't even know you're a martyr. Think if you'd been convicted. How many prisoners spend their entire time inside telling anyone who'll listen that they didn't do it? Endless numbers, I can tell you, and nobody takes a blind bit of notice of any of them, even if they're telling the truth. Especially if they're telling the truth. Because as that eminent fellow Lord Denning said, that would cast doubt on the whole system, and we can't have that, can we? So why don't you opt for something more peaceful and productive?'

'Such as?'

'Such as, such as. Well, how about this? You presumably are hoping to go on working for *New Politics*.'

'I suppose so.'

'And I expect the zest for scandal-gathering has rather atrophied just at the moment?'

'My zest has atrophied. Full stop. Except for murder. I'm getting quite keen on that.'

'I can imagine how you must feel. But always bear in mind that there are such things as tape-recorders, and remember what the inside of a prison is like. Now, here's a thought. I might be able to put you in the way of some really excellent stories from time to time. If you were able to use those in *New Politics*, let us say, then I think you might find you were advancing rather more rapidly in the world than you'd ever thought possible.' He let his chair fall forward with a thud. 'Why don't you go away and think about that? We'll be in touch. Don't forget.' He got up and went to the door. 'Oh, and Mr Taggart. Just one more thing. These things are never as difficult as you think they're going to be. Once you've got started, it all seems perfectly normal. In fact, you'll wonder what you ever did before.' He opened the door, and held it while Taggart walked through. 'Goodbye, Mr Taggart. And as I said before, congratulations.'

CHAPTER 34

By the time Taggart came out of the Ministry of Defence it was lunch-time: he had rung Fischer first thing. He felt suddenly hungry, and made his way to a pub he knew behind St Martin's-in-the-Fields where one could generally be sure of a large lunch and a quiet corner. There he sat, chewing and thinking, for a long time. Then he suddenly banged the table, jumped up, and left the pub with an access of energy such as he hadn't felt since—well, since he had been carted off to Holborn police station all those months ago.

Hoxton is not actually all that far from Holborn as the crow flies, but buses are not crows. In his hurry to get to Peter Fischer's office Taggart had taken a taxi, an extravagance he was not about to repeat. So it was more than an hour later before he was finally seated at his desk in front of his telephone. He punched in Belinda's number and sat waiting. As usual, the phone at the other end rang and rang, and as usual he let it ring. Finally it was answered.

'Hello?' She sounded suspicious and defensive, which was hardly a surprise.

'Belinda, it's me. Andrew. I want to take you out to dinner.'

'Andrew?' She sounded surprised now. Astonished.

'I'm feeling like a celebration. Come on, let's cheer ourselves up. Where were you, in the garden? At this time of year?'

'No, no. I just didn't feel like talking to anyone. I only answered the bloody thing to shut it up.'

'Time you got out of there. Is it on the market yet?'

'Yes, but things are rather slow at the moment.'

'Never mind. Have a nice long bath, get into something glamorous, and I'll meet your train. I'll even have a bath myself. I'd tell you to shove some things into a bag and come over here to change, but this place isn't exactly likely to lift a person's spirits. It's even started to get me down a bit.'

'But I don't feel like celebrating. I don't feel like coming out.'

'You don't feel like anything, right? Nevertheless, you're doing it. Get the timetable and tell me what train you'll be on.'

Persuading Belinda was not easy. Nevertheless, Taggart managed it, partly by bullying, partly because, if one has no engagements whatever, it seems really rather stupid to turn down dinner at the Escargot. 'But what shall I do afterwards? I shan't want to take the train back at that time of night, and—well—'

'You don't want to sleep with me, and even if you did, you wouldn't want to sleep with me here, right? OK. I'll drive you back. Now I really can't say fairer than that, can I? I'll see you at seven-fifteen, then, right?' And he rang off before she could object, and then left the house and went to the office so that she could not phone him back to tell him she'd changed her mind. He returned to take the promised bath and put on clean clothes only after she must be safely on the train—he even polished his shoes—and was waiting, unnaturally spruce, by the ticket barrier at Euston to meet the 7.15 from Leamingworth. He wouldn't have been surprised if she hadn't been on it, even after all that: but no, there she was, a familiar figure, wearing, he was glad to see, a scarlet coat, not that eternal black. Black didn't suit her: it made her look dingy and dragged down. Or maybe it was that when he'd seen her wearing black she was feeling dingy and dragged down. He kissed her warmly.

'So what's this all in aid of?'

'I'll tell you later. Let's get settled first.'

It wasn't until half an hour later, when they were sitting with a drink at their table, that he would talk about anything but future plans, hers and his, if any. 'I'm assuming you don't want to marry me,' he said then.

'You're assuming rightly. You didn't get me here to ask me that, did you? I was afraid it might be something like that.'

'No, it wasn't that, though I thought I would ask. While I happened to have you here.'

She shook her head. 'What was it, then?'

'Ah, well. I've suddenly realized who did it. Who actually shot him.'

Belinda looked suddenly grey, as she had when she came to visit him in prison that time. 'And that makes you this cheerful?'

'It's nice to have something cleared up. Part of what's been depressing me is all the dreadful uncertainty. I mean, I know I didn't do it, but it's sometimes seemed to me that that's all I do know. The whole of the rest of life sometimes seems sort of enveloped in grey mist. It was a great relief, clearing that up.'

They were interrupted at this point by the waiter bringing their starters, delicious-looking little quenelles in pink crayfish sauce. Taggart lifted a fork and dug into his with unusual gusto, but Belinda didn't even glance at her plate. 'Try one, they're good,' he said.

'So who was it?'

'It was Caroline, wasn't it?'

He held her eyes for what seemed a very long time. Then she nodded her head and began to cry, the tears dripping unchecked into the pink sauce.

'Don't. Don't cry. Please.' He reached over and took her hand, which lay limply under his own on the table. After a while she shook her head and raised a tear-stained head to face him.

'How did you know?'

'Well, you can imagine, I was thinking and thinking. I mean, what else did I have to think about all that time? Anyhow, it seemed to me it had to be one of two people. Either Wesley Mitchell or else Peter Fischer, through some sort of surrogate, of course. Mitchell needed to save his scientific reputation from being connected with an obvious fraud—that's to say, it would have been obvious to anyone who knew anything about the subject, not because the chap wasn't perfectly convincing—I mean, he convinced you, didn't he?—but because the physiology's impossible, whatever people like Peter Fischer might wish. But when it really came down to it, I couldn't make myself believe it really was him. Not because I don't think he's capable of it—I'm quite sure he killed your husband—but because the motive wasn't strong enough. I mean, why should he think he would be blown? The chap himself wasn't saying anything, and he didn't know I was on to him. Hell, he didn't know me at all, so even if he had seen me that time in Brooklyn he wouldn't have worried. Whereas with Charles there was that business with Lulu. You could see that as an unbalanced father's just revenge. Someone else enacting his own barely repressed incestuous fantasies or some such thing. It was just too near home and too threatening.'

'That still leaves Peter Fischer.'

'That's what I thought. I was really sure that was who it was. I mean, that all made so much sense. He's hated me for a long time, and I'd really got him worried this time. Not just about this, there was all that business about Juliette Correa, I don't know if you remember—that girl who seemed to have slept with just about every politician and journalist in London, got them all telling her their little secrets—and it turned out Fischer was one of her conquests, though she conveniently moved on to Madrid just when that emerged. He thought it might have been me that blew that—'

'Was it?'

'Yes, as it happens, though the thing that convinced him was nothing to do with me. She turned up again at that conference in Washington, she's got her hooks into some congressman now—couldn't stand being sidelined in Madrid. And then along I come, just on cue, and he not only gets his job done, gets his chap safely out of harm's way before anyone can try and blow his cover—while he's still got the opposition worried, whoever the hell *they* are, though

I think that's almost immaterial, there's always some enemy somewhere and the game's the thing—but he gets me into the bargain. Two for the price of one. Motive and all. In fact I'm quite sure part of that is right. I'm sure it was him that framed me up so beautifully. He more or less admitted it himself. He hasn't got where he has without knowing how to make the most of an opportunity if it presents itself.'

Taggart paused. Across the table, Belinda wasn't looking at him. She was staring down at her untouched plate, her head in her hands.

'But you see, it didn't really add up there, either. Because why should he kill the chap? The fact is, he really believed in him. Just like you. You both *wanted* to believe in him, that was the point. You because you fell in love with him, and believing the story made life easier for you. Him because this was the ultimate rabbit which he'd really pulled out of the hat. Why should he organize the assassination of his own rabbit? He was amazed when I put it to him. As I say, he admitted the frame-up, but not the rest.'

'And you believe him.'

'Well, as it happens I do. So then I started to think again. And then I realized there was one person who really fitted the bill. It was easy to imagine her wanting to do it. You told me yourself how close she was to her father, and you don't need to tell me what she thought of anyone she saw as usurping his place. I've experienced that for myself more than once. And I wasn't even a real threat . . . And she was having troubles of her own. This new chap turning up must have been the last straw, the thing that pushed her over the edge. And she could have done it. She wasn't at her flat when when we phoned that afternoon, and we didn't try her office. And that was just after she'd actually met him, when she might have been at her most furious and appalled . . . It's very easy to picture. As for the gun, maybe she belongs to a rifle club—lots of people do. Maybe she used to go with her boyfriend. It'd be easy enough to check up . . .'

'You haven't checked?' It was almost pathetic, Belinda's eagerness.

'No. I only just thought of it today.' He ate another quenelle. 'But you'd thought of it, hadn't you? You knew.'

She nodded. 'I was afraid it might be something like that.'

'What would you have done? If I'd been convicted?'

She shrugged miserably. 'I don't know. I just kept telling myself you wouldn't be.'

'What faith.'

Belinda said, 'What are you going to do?'

'Do?' Now it was Taggart's turn to be surprised.

'Well—' She made a hopeless little movement of her hands. 'The case is still open, isn't it?'

He shook his head. 'Darling Belinda, I'm not the police. It isn't my business to see that Justice is Done. On the contrary. What d'you expect me to do? Go and denounce her?'

'I don't know.'

'Do me a favour. What good would it do? Would it enhance anybody's life? She isn't going to do it again. She probably feels terrible about it. I'm not going to do anything. But she should probably know someone knows. Or suspects. I'll leave that to you. She's your daughter.'

The waiter came to take their plates. 'Has madame finished?' he asked.

'I don't feel hungry. In fact, I don't feel like staying here at all.'

'I'm not surprised. Let's go. We'll have the bill now, please,' Taggart told the astonished waiter.

They walked up Greek Street in the direction of Tottenham Court Road and started, by tacit consent, in the direction of Euston. Belinda said, 'When the house is sold I'm going for a long holiday. A world tour.'

'Sounds like a good idea.'

When they arrived at Euston Taggart said, 'When you get back, get in touch. If you need any help or anything.'

'Maybe,' said Belinda.

THE END

Twelve Quakers and Faith

by
Quaker Quest

Quaker Quest Pamphlet 8

Also available in this series:

Twelve Quakers and God (2004)
Twelve Quakers and Worship (2004)
Twelve Quakers and Pacifism (2005)
Twelve Quakers and Evil (2006)
Twelve Quakers and Simplicity (2006)
Twelve Quakers and Jesus (2007)
Twelve Quakers and Equality (2007)

Published in 2009 in the United Kingdom by Quaker Quest Network, an independent outreach project and recognised informal group within Britain Yearly Meeting, of the Religious Society of Friends (Quakers).

Copyright © Quaker Quest Network, 2009
All rights reserved. Requests for permission to reproduce in any form whatsoever any part of this text, other than brief quotations in articles or reviews, should be made to: Quaker Quest Network,
71 Aberdeen Park, Highbury, London, N5 2AZ

ISBN: 978-0-9558983-1-0

Preface

Quaker Quest is a series of open meetings for people interested in the Quaker way as a spiritual path for our time which is simple, radical and contemporary. The project began in London in 2002 and now Quaker Quest events are held throughout Britain and increasingly in other parts of the world

Twelve Quakers and Faith is a collection of reflections on faith, all written by Quakers. All contributions are anonymous. It is hoped that they reflect the diversity of Quaker belief, but also the shared understanding that faith, however it is defined, has an extraordinary effect on our lives, both in terms of belief and in terms of faith in action.

We hope that this may be of help to those who are beginning to explore the Quaker way.

Introduction

From earliest times, Quakers have been wary of the use of formulaic creeds to define their faith. George Fox, who is regarded as the founder of the Quakers, said, 'You will say, Christ saith this, and the apostles say this; but what canst thou say?' Still today Quakers believe that words may form a barrier that prevents us from living out our faith.

This faith is closely related to beliefs that may have been shaped by upbringing or informed by reading the Bible and other sources. Faith is also seen as being linked to the trust that arises from an inward knowledge of God's love.

The twelve Quakers who write about their faith in this book are from widely varied backgrounds and their experiences in life differ. However, they all value the freedom and 'secret power' of the Quaker meeting for worship as a place to work out and establish their own particular expressions of faith.

Common to all is the need to put faith into action, to 'live adventurously'. This may impel one to a choice of career or a change of lifestyle, or to try to live faithfully in the detail of everyday life. What emerges is that, far from claiming to be a religion of certainty, Quakerism should be a religion of uncertainty in which each of us can shape our own life, inspired by the inward promptings of God's love, into an expression of individual faith within the community of the Quaker meeting.

1

I used to be an expert. I would run courses in my chosen subject and people used to believe what I said. If they did disagree, I felt sufficiently clear of my ground to argue back. The interesting question is how I came to be so certain. Much of the advice I delivered came from received wisdom, taken from books and supplemented by my own thinking and experience. However, from time to time I was aware that my thinking had moved on. I had read some new research; I had talked to another expert. I had found something out myself. My own process of change was slow and uncomfortable, because it is always humiliating to admit that you were wrong before. Nevertheless, I had no alternative. I could not go on saying something I knew to be untrue.

My faith is no different to that. When you are a child you believe what you're told. It is a painful part of growing up to question that and decide what you believe for yourself. I was brought up in the Church of England and so much of my belief was cultural as much as theological; implicit in it was church architecture, music and literature. However, it became increasingly clear that, whatever I believed, it didn't fit in with the Church of England and there came a time when I had to leave. It was a great relief to become a Quaker and not to have to say things like 'he descended into hell. On the third day he rose again…' and all sorts of other things I didn't understand or believe anymore. Nevertheless, being a Quaker actually imposes a far greater responsibility. I couldn't use a ready-made theology; I actually had to make up my own mind about what I did believe. This certainly didn't come easily. I would read a book and consciously reject it because it ran counter to my existing beliefs. Somehow though, the ideas would lodge like grit in an oyster shell. Finally, the idea would rise unbidden to the surface and I would recognise it as the truth. Equally, on other occasions, I would hear an argument that seemed on the surface to be very convincing, only for time to make me realise that it didn't hold water.

I actually find 'the truth' as good a word for what I mean by God as anything. It seems to describe some sort of bedrock beneath a shifting world, something which acts as a foundation upon which everything else can be built. To continue the analogy, you have to shift an awful lot of rubbish away before you find this foundation. Much of what appears to be solid belief doesn't seem to have much in the way of foundation, and as soon as you investigate it, it collapses. Yet eventually you find what appears to be essential, the bedrock. The Quaker concept that 'there is that of God in everyone' seems to me to be part of this bedrock, together with Jesus' words that we should love our neighbours as ourselves.

Once you have made a decision about what you believe, this has implications for the way you live. You can't – or at least you shouldn't – continue talking about something unless you put it into practice. You actually have to live what you believe. This is frequently painful. It certainly isn't easy to do the right thing. If one helps one person it is often at the expense of someone else. What is right in the long term often seems wrong in the short term. Nevertheless, I believe there is a kind of essential touchstone – that what you do has to be actuated by love.

It is easy to see the Quaker way as simply a kind of lobby group – a kind of offshoot of CND or the Green party. Actually, though, while we might be called to protest about nuclear armament or lobby for green issues, we do not become Quakers because we believe in these things; we do these things because we are Quakers. Our vision informs the way we behave and we have continually to test these things against our vision. It is this continual testing that I see as integral to my faith – to take nothing for granted, but continually to use my experience of the world so that my understanding evolves. I know what I believe now, but it is, at best, an interim statement of belief.

2

'Take heed, dear Friends, to the promptings of love and truth in your hearts. Trust them as the leadings of God…'

This is the first piece of advice which we Quakers give ourselves; and there, in a nutshell, is my faith. For me, the starting point of faith is not about 'believing' a set of words. Words come later. First there is experience of 'heeding' and 'trusting' which lead to action. But how do I know that these promptings are indeed the leadings of God? Is it not more likely that I will convince myself that whatever I want to do is a leading? Think how many terrible acts have been committed by people claiming to be led by God!

So how do I learn what to heed and where to place my trust?

I can look to the past, learning from the stories of others, of all faiths and none – not least the Bible. I am culturally steeped in Judaeo-Christian images and constantly find new inspiration from its pages. I grew up with this extraordinary record of thousands of years of people's search for God. Their search enriches mine. Their failures speak as powerfully to me as the depth of their insights.

For me, the life and teaching of Jesus open the clearest window into the nature of God. Because of Jesus, I find I can never give up my conviction that faith is alive when we work to bring into being a peaceful world where all are equally valued and loved – and I can never give up hope that this is possible. If my life is to be part of that, then the 'leadings' I can trust have to reflect the values he lived by.

Then I find that the more I try to live out those values in all aspects of my life, social and political, the more I meet that same hope and spirit in other people. Their lives strengthen my own faltering attempts to be loving and just, to eschew all violence and to try to respond to that of God in all people. So by my actions, I am taken full circle back to trusting that there is a power of love and truth in which I can have faith.

Embracing the experience of past and present, there is prayer, especially when it is a wordless waiting, slowly loosening the bonds of self-aggrandisement, self-centredness, self-protection and self-delusion until what is left has a sense of true life within it. The more I make this a daily discipline the more I am able to discern when there is a difference between what I want to do and what I must do, and the more they become the same.

Above all I do not seek to live this life of faith alone. I have chosen to travel with Quakers. In the joint search for stillness in the silence of a Quaker meeting for worship, the 'promptings of love and truth' in our hearts become more distinct. When they arise from those promptings, spoken words can enrich and deepen the stillness. We strengthen one another's will to goodness. We are helped to move forward.

'Take heed, dear Friends, to the promptings of love and truth in your hearts. Trust them as the leadings of God whose Light shows us our darkness and leads us to new Life.'

3

Central to my position is the difference between faith and belief. Belief, according to the dictionary, is accepting something as true, whereas faith is placing trust in something. My own journey has been from the rejection of beliefs which seem to me untenable to the development of trust in something beyond the everyday.

Aged eleven I went to a very Christian school. The war was ending, and the horrors of the holocaust started to emerge. Such evil and suffering seemed to me then, and now, incompatible with belief in a loving God who created the universe, still less in one who continues to intervene in it. The Christian answer given to me was twofold. God gave us free will, so if we do evil it is not his fault; and suffering is good for us because it leads to growth. But if there were a creator, our propensity to evil is surely a result of how we were created, whether in a day or through aeons of evolution. And whilst suffering can indeed lead to growth, it can also send people mad, kill, destroy. So I became the school atheist.

There remained with me, however, a sense, a faith, that there is a dimension to life which goes beyond the everyday. There are those timeless moments of being a part of everything. There are the beauty and power of mathematics, the awesome nature of the cosmos which science is unfolding, the weirdness of the connection between physical events in the brain and conscious experience, a quite different sort of stuff.

There are the courage, dignity and love which people can show in dreadful circumstances. Einstein wrote of a third stage in religious experience, based not on fear or morality, producing no notion of God and no theology, but awakened by wonder at the sublime order in both nature and the world of thought. He called it 'cosmic religious feeling'. I think that is the faith I am groping for. Thinking of my cat eating his tinned tuna, I wonder whether we know as little of what is out there in the world of spirit as he did of the processes, from the Big Bang onwards, that put the food on his plate.

After school came a life crowded with marriage, children, friends and work, and little time for things spiritual. But when it quietened down, I went looking for a non-Christian community where I could explore and share this aspect of life. I joined a Buddhist group, where I discovered a set of ideas which I warmed to, and the quiet of meditation. Yet something was still missing: a link between all this and practical involvement in the problems of the day, especially after 9/11. Someone had told me that you had to be a Christian to be a Quaker, but I discovered that this was not so, and walked in through the door of my local meeting house. That first meeting for worship felt like coming home.

In terms of inner experience, maybe I had always been a Quaker. But the powerful, almost palpable, shared stillness of meeting for worship – to me another mystery – consolidated my faith that there is some unknowable 'other'. I also found the link I was seeking between this faith and action. Indeed, Quakers prefer to talk about faith in action, regarding our testimonies to peace, equality, simplicity and truth as something we show in action, rather than written ideas.

This faith in action has taught me a lot since I joined Quakers. I don't do any difficult frontline job, but some in our meeting do. As treasurer I run the system which enables us to give the financial support essential to Quaker work at all levels, from helping improve the lives of sex workers in the East End to running offices which assist conflict resolution behind the scenes at the United Nations. Quaker values also affect how we do business. Whereas I used to go to meetings to win my corner, in Quaker business meetings people listen to each other and seek to work together to find the best way forward. Meetings begin and end with silent worship; some would regard this as seeking divine guidance, but to me as an agnostic it is rather a matter of opening up to the better side of ourselves. Such an approach can be carried through into all aspects of everyday life. So faith for me is not just that there is some unknowable 'other' but also that if we give ourselves time, we can experience a stillness where our perceptions of the world and the way in which we act are changed.

4

My early experience proved that I could trust life; it was dependable. In looking at a world where half its people are starving or war victims, sufferers from natural disasters or unwanted from broken homes, I see tragedy, despair and no evidence of fairness. Yet deep within my bones, at the centre of my consciousness, I have confidence that my way of being is as it should be: the rest is aberration. I am one of the inordinately fortunate ones: I have no alternative but to repay life by being fully committed to it and to live with profound gratitude. This is my understanding of loving God. It is my faith.

In the reflection of old age, I see how extraordinarily privileged I was to grow up embraced by love. My security and trust, and so my faith, come from a happy family, both as a child and later as a father. During the war, my sister and I were evacuated separately, yet surviving its fear and horror led to a further family strengthening. This came without possessiveness; my sister and I were always given generous freedom to make up our own minds about things.

Neither parent went to church, but to curb some of my growing naughtiness I was sent to a local church cub pack, moving on to scouts and senior scouts, and eventually I began attending evening service with other young people. Community, more than church beliefs, spoke to me. My deepest early spiritual experiences were through nature – bird-watching, climbing mountains, going down pot-holes, over waterways, or through creativity – song-writing and intensive theatre projects.

The rationing and deprivations of being a war baby, with its spirit of mucking-in together to face a common threat, and the dedication to service of the scout movement and its outdoor bonding, are deeply etched into my way of being. They are my foundations. Our current lifestyle of consumer growth and waste, with the social inequality of celebrity and the bonus culture, cuts totally against the grain. My faith has always been rooted in people working together in group-created projects, in creativity and imagination, in caring and sharing. When I discovered Quakers I knew immediately that this was right for me. It was then that the spiritual in worship came to mean something more.

Here were a band of disciples of the human Jesus, sage and healer. The Quaker testimonies of simplicity, peace, integrity, community and equality are based on his teachings. Quakers follow his way, but Quakers today have not made Jesus into a God. The nativity, resurrection and nature of Christ were symbolic, poetic, trying to express the highest values and deepest feelings about how life may be lived.

For me, faith is not about creeds and doctrines and beliefs that have to be believed, but about values in action. No one lives without understandings and assumptions – our everyday structures of making meaning – but such beliefs are best held lightly, so that they can be readily changed when we have to accommodate fresh insights. Faith becomes what you do, how you live your life, how you follow the path of love and peace. Action cannot be separated from faith; it is faith-in-action all the way.

I was greatly influenced by reading about George Fox,

whose life, in and out of prison, witnessing for his faith, was instrumental in laying the foundations for the Quaker way. Troubled by the lack of integrity amongst the clergy of the established church, he went, an earnest nineteen year old, to the annual Atherton Fair with two companions. There, his cousin challenged him to a drinking match with the loser paying all. An incensed George threw down his groat and stormed off, indignant that those who professed Christianity could encourage drunkenness. It precipitated a spiritual breakdown and breakthrough. He left home and took to the road for many years, seeking a way of integrity, where the life lived celebrated the faith proclaimed. The Society of Friends was founded on that rock of integrity.

If we claim a label, like Christian or Quaker, and do not live up to it, our faith is hollow; or we may call ourselves humanist or atheist and our lifestyle can express more of the Spirit and compassion than many a self-proclaimed believer. Labels of belief are inevitable dividers, while only dialogue can bridge the way to common ground. Within the Society of Friends we must speak more confidently of our spiritual way with those searching for an authentic faith. In the world at large, a listening dialogue is crucial between those of clashing beliefs, whether political terrorist or religious fanatic, if we are to find peace and security. Is dialogue the lodestar of Quaker faith today for us all?

5

It seems to me that we live in almost complete uncertainty. We are nearly always acting on what we now believe is or will be true, since what we can be certain of is so limited.

To act, we must act on our beliefs, and in doing so we express our faith in them. Faith is belief enacted.

Belief is different from knowledge, and to act in faith is to step into the unknown, to walk on uncertain foundations, to take a risk, to trust. The measure of our faith is the extent to which we risk ourselves, and what we value, against those beliefs.

We develop our beliefs on the basis of experience modified, more or less, by reason. Some can change rapidly, for example if we are alerted to danger or discover something new about our close family, whereas others are hardly ever modified. If we allow our beliefs to be questioned I suggest that no belief can be held with one hundred per cent conviction, and that we will trust each one with varying degrees of confidence.

Living in faith – acting on belief – is the natural state, against which we struggle to develop understanding, certainty and security. It may start off blind and unquestioned, but from early childhood we start to interpret and evaluate our experience. This takes time, and in between we must borrow the faith of those closest to us. So, on this basis, I would get into the dangerous car with the others, because my elders put their faith in the driver, and beyond him, his mechanic.

Gradually, as we place confidence in our experience, we decide to trust this belief but not that one, or perhaps not in that circumstance, and so on. In this way we build the foundations of a reasoned faith, including a faith in our own judgement. This has enabled me, for example, to risk my life and others' lives, and to trust the new restaurant's kitchen staff, the pension fund managers, the hospital doctors and so on. Each of us may have blind, borrowed and reasoned faiths in different areas of life.

In the religious context, the term 'faith' can be used to describe a system of beliefs, yet it is not our beliefs that comprise our faith, but rather the trusting and testing of those beliefs – the same as with other aspects of our lives. What seems different though is that in this area my beliefs use a higher level of intuition than reason. I 'feel' my way to a position more than think it, guided by the spiritual teaching I have adopted.

In my early teens I attended Boys' Brigade Bible classes. There I was invited to borrow from my elders the Christian code of beliefs and to live according to the precepts and example of Jesus. Gradually I came to love his teaching with all my heart and, although I lacked commitment to the code of beliefs, this led to a peak experience, a point of personal enlightenment.

From the time when I united with the spirit of Jesus, this has been what I worship, what I have given greatest worth to – it is the spirit that is holy to me. I believe that the human Jesus saw that by being true to his vision of the Jewish Messiah, he could bring about a saving change for humanity, and that he continued with it even when he realised it would lead to his death. This, to me, is the highest expression of humanity. The light that the life and teaching of Jesus has shed will have saved so many from lower aspirations and a life of darkness.

In my own case, I decided to trust that if my life were guided by the spirit, I would always have what I needed to live. This led to my leaving work in commerce, which seemed to offer little opportunity for expressing this spirit, in favour of becoming a youth worker.

My faith in living in the spirit is expressed in many small ways, supported by the still attention given in a Quaker meeting. For example, in my work, I have found that when I am threatened, I can trust the non-violent response. Giving opposition while offering respect for others and for myself, but no reciprocal physical threat, has so far been an effective defence and a route to equitable treatment.

Intellectually, my views have continued to distance themselves from formal Christianity, a de-mystification that has had no bearing on the values guiding my actions. I have moved away from a belief in an omnipresent, omnipotent being with human traits, who dispenses reward and final judgement according to our deeds. I see us as called to a life driven by the eternal positive qualities and the desire for us all to reach our fullest potential.

6

A faith is generally seen as a system of belief, almost always expressed in a creed, a form of words, at least in our culture. That is not what faith is to me.

'Quakers don't believe in creeds.' Is that a contradiction, thus impossible, or a paradox pointing to real truths?

I write 'truths' in the plural, because I see many truths, in the world and among Quakers. Each of us has to do hard spiritual work to understand truth, to find words true to our own experience, and also because our truths grow as we and the world shift and develop. That work leads to a very different relationship with truth (which for me is godly): rather than conform to truth, we can discover truth and live truthfully. As the Quaker Isaac Penington said, 'All Truth is a shadow except the last, except the utmost; yet every Truth is true in its kind. ... The shadow is a true shadow, as the substance is a true substance.'

We don't put our faith in a formal expression of faith (although Quakers do behave characteristically), we don't live by particular words (although Quakers do read, contemplate and quote familiar phrases and stories). Our shared faith is not a set of concepts to accept (though we do think and discuss). It is an experimental faith: we live an idea, we observe and examine, we test our insights. Together we seek clearness; together we find the way forward. Thus a creed, in the sense of a form of words that has to stand for all our faiths, all our truths, for all time, is irrelevant to the Quaker way. A faith is much, much more than belief.

Our truths are not weapons. I stopped saying 'I believe ...' or 'Quakers believe...' three years ago. It's not that I, and Quakers generally, have no beliefs at all – I can't imagine a mind empty of insight – but I realised that words like 'belief', and, even more, 'religious' or 'Christian', could mislead. People I met often assumed that any belief in a religious context involves some fictional being, or wishful fantasies about creation or immortality, instead of provable scientific fact. Such assumptions often stopped any discussion. I don't see faith as something I construct or a lifestyle choice. It is more like the lifelong, ever-changing yet constant relationship of love that I have found in my marriage.

Thus sometimes I read religious texts as a record of human understanding of the world, still developing and growing: I take delight in the discoveries of science and art. At other times, I see strong truth in myth: I imagine myself in the place of the Creator, grieve for this damaged world, and work to save this beautiful, unique planet from environmental destruction. Yet other times, the account of a prophet, a suffering servant like Jesus, gives me a framework in which I too can respond to the challenge of love. Just a few ways of doing faith in an infinite richness: what other ways are possible?

How do we know what our faith calls us to do? If we are each responsible for listening to that of God within, isn't that just selfish individualism? Why do we need a Society? Is there a Quaker community, and what is it for? I am comfortable living with reasonable uncertainty, as the broadcaster Gerald Priestland put it. However, the Quaker practice of discernment provides a solid basis for faithful living.

First, last, and always most importantly, we meet for worship. It is possible to be open to the Spirit on one's own, but when we meet together for worship, there is a power for good, a mystical movement that is more than the sum of our individual experiences. Not at every meeting, but there have been times when my life has changed, when I have encountered the divine and known transformation.

I have grown to know and love my fellow worshippers, and so I turn to them in need. Several times I have faced decisions and not known which path to follow. I have asked a small group of Friends to help me discern the way forward. In worship, in trust, they have put aside their own curiosity and preferences, to ask the best questions they could. Not, for example, 'What do you want?', but rather 'What is the Light showing you?', which was a more productive question, because it made me search for a different, better vision. It is our experience that when we give enough time to discernment, we can feel a unity indicating that, probably, we have found 'the will of God for us at this time', in traditional language. We look at past experience, and build on the wisdom of earlier Friends: for example, our sense that slavery is plain wrong continues, though the form may have changed.

If you want to know what the faith of Quakers is, look at how we live. Consider the questions we ask ourselves, and whether we grow in understanding. Our lives will speak, without a creed.

7

I used to think that faith meant accepting a set of propositions about religion: 'I believe in one God, the Father Almighty, maker of heaven and earth …' When I began to doubt and question traditional Christian belief, I felt I had to make great efforts to overcome my lack of faith. I really tried to understand and accept what the church taught, but to no avail. In the end, with a mixture of guilt and relief, I gave up the struggle. My interest in religious matters was still high – I taught Religious Studies in a high school – but for a while, I concluded that a personal, living faith was not for me.

My problem was that faith would not leave me alone! I found I could not get away from the idea that somewhere there was a spiritual path that was right for me. I found it by responding to a small advert in a national newspaper offering an information pack about Quakers. What I read about Quakers appealed to me immensely, but it took some while before I felt able to attend a Quaker meeting. Once I did, I discovered that the Quaker way was the approach to faith I had been yearning for.

Following the Quaker way, I have come to see that ideas or beliefs about religious matters – what Quakers, traditionally, call 'notions' – are much less important than responding to the promptings of love and truth within, promptings which we trust to be the leadings of God.

The Quaker Beth Allen describes my own experience perfectly, 'A common Quaker experience is that of an inner nudge or leading. We feel this as a thought or a prompting that will not go away: 'Ring up Susan'.'

James Naylor, an early Quaker, meditating on the things of God while ploughing, experienced such a nudge. He heard words addressed to Abraham in the Old Testament addressed directly to him: 'Get thee out from thy kindred, and thy father's house.' He felt commanded to travel west, not knowing where he should go or what he should do there, but he acted in faith and found that his trust was vindicated.

When I retired early from teaching, I wondered how I should usefully fill my time. In our local paper, there was an advertisement that encouraged people to volunteer to work with the local Youth Offending Team. This spoke clearly and directly to me: I was given an unmistakeable inner nudge to volunteer. I wondered whether I would be able to communicate with offenders and whether I would have the ability to handle the painful emotions that are associated with offending. The trust in my leadings has been rewarded over and over again.

Working with other volunteers in the Youth Offending Team has shown me that those with no faith in divine guidance also experience these inner nudges to do good things. When we identify such inner promptings as the leadings of God, are we using religious language to describe something that is essentially a human experience?

I have come to accept that the divine works in and through the ordinary activities and experiences of daily lives, and that because there is 'that of God in everyone', as we Quakers say, then people have the capacity, the predisposition to co-operate with the divine whether they realise it or not. We are not programmed to behave in particular ways, but the creative spirit that is in us all invites us to work together for good.

Where and when are these nudges, these promptings or leadings of God, received? It would be tidy to be able to say that they always came to people engaged in a religious activity, such as meeting for worship, or quiet reflection when on their own. They do come in this way, but in my experience, they come in all kinds of secular situations, too.

Very recently, my wife and I were in a bank, and while the person dealing with us went away to photocopy a document, it came to us clearly that we should move our account to a bank with ethical principles. This had been in the back of our minds for some time, but on that day, the challenge came to us quite insistently and clearly: it had to be done now!

James Naylor was moved by words addressed to Abraham. Abraham is remembered as a great man of faith, not because he could accept certain prescribed doctrines, but because he was willing to trust that the inner promptings he experienced were of God and that to act on them was the right, the necessary thing to do. That trust in divine leading is, for me, the essence of faith.

8

When I first encountered Quakerism, little did I realise how much it would come to influence my thinking and my practice. In retrospect, I think that previously I had understood that there were certain fixed teachings that were fundamental to a faith. From young adulthood this had bothered me, because some of the teachings I had encountered in my then church were hard for me to believe, let alone to practise. Eventually I was so uncomfortable that I was unable to practise conscientiously the faith I had been taught.

After some years I had such a powerful intimation of the 'something beyond', of what is often called God, that I knew I needed to be with others who were on a similar path and to worship with them. For some time I went to different

Christian churches, but although I was able to respect them and the people I met there, I still had hesitations. Finding Quakerism was enlightening and reassuring. Here were people who seemingly did not lay down their faith in church teachings, in words. Their meeting for worship did not require me to repeat any words at all, nor did the Bible – or its interpretation – seem to be the only voice of authority. Before my first Quaker meeting for worship, I wondered how I would get through the silence of an hour. I asked myself what I would do and was somewhat uneasy. In the event, I found, as have so many others, that the only words that could get in the way were my own. After many, many years they still can!

Very soon I knew deep within me that this was the path for me. I quickly lost my unease about the silence, for there I became comfortable and so it has remained the place where I am stilled and quiet, sustained by a limitless power. For me, this is having faith. I am following something I cannot leave alone. Something unseen, yet for which Quakers often use the metaphor of the Light: sometimes blinding in its intensity, whilst at others an almost infinitesimal glimmer. The compunction to try to find it is always there.

So it was from the Quaker way of worship that I recognised that this was my way. For me, it is the discipline of my Quaker faith that upholds me. In times past, Quakers used the word discipline much more freely than is done today. No doubt in general usage its meaning began to imply something imposed from the outside and hence it has fallen into disuse. However, I find no other word satisfies me when I think of what my practice is. Not that I could ever suggest that I manage faithfully to follow this discipline, but I try.

On the surface it may appear that Quakerism is not very demanding: however, if you really follow the guidance given, then the real demands are revealed. What are the leadings that I try to follow? I see myself as a follower of Jesus, the man, and his teaching that we should love God and our neighbour. From this stem my faith and my practice. For me, these two words, faith and practice, lie at the heart of Quakerism and are inextricably interwoven.

Our beloved collection of writings, *Quaker Faith and Practice*, reflects this. No creedal statements define the Quaker faith, for words restrict and bind as well as blind. Nevertheless, from the beginning I have found this book so valuable. The title of the first chapter, *Advices and Queries*, offers a fascinating insight into the manner in which Quakerism is communicated. We are advised, and we are given questions to consider, and after that it is our responsibility. The introduction begins, 'As Friends we commit ourselves to a way of worship which allows God to teach and transform us.' In quiet worship with others, and at other times, I am led to find my own truth, to find my faith in my own personal experience. For me, it is in the practice of my faith that I find the truth. It is there I find wholeness.

9

I have only just come to an awareness of how faith has been within me throughout the years of my life. This is a surprising discovery for me as I had thought of faith as a troublesome, perturbing thing. Perturbing because I am, and have always been, a creature of the enlightenment, of rational thought of the existence of evidence, facts, discovery and scientific endeavour. Not someone who accepts magic, superstition, mantras, chants and creedal statements of belief. And yet, whilst accepting all this, I also know that my experience of being alive cannot, and could not, be adequately defined solely through enlightenment thinking.

I was born into a Quaker family. Although valuing the fellowship and values I experienced during these early years with Quakers, I resigned my membership at the age of twenty-one. At that time, I could not articulate my faith, but nevertheless felt I should be able to. I thought that the Quakers I met must somehow have access to a deep and unshakeable well of faith that I was not experiencing. So I left; I wanted clarity and convincement for myself and not merely to drift into cosy belonging. What use is faith? Is it a delusion? These were intractable questions.

However, I came to understand that my faith doesn't exist on a piece of paper in words – it exists through my experience and actions. The biggest challenge to my faith was and continues to be, death and cruelty. I first encountered what I now realise was a faith reaction within myself when I was about seven. A pale, silent little boy had recently arrived at my primary school. One morning the head teacher told the whole school that a very naughty boy had been found stealing. Later that day I saw a policeman walking across the fields with the little boy to the place where he had hidden whatever he had stolen. He was never seen in school again. To this day I can still feel my horror at the absence of love in that little boy's life, and the cruelty with which he was being treated and talked about.

I felt at that time the stirrings of a faith which I now see was a bedrock which I couldn't ever gainsay, and which has propelled and become the basis for my actions in the world. It was simply the experience that everyone is precious, unique, that there are invisible webs of connection that feed and nourish us, that if these are broken through cruelty, fear, mistrust, thoughtlessness we are all diminished, and that the business of being alive is to cherish all of this.

I have since worked in schools, mental hospitals and prisons. That early experience has been strengthened and grown stronger; I am starting to use the word trust in conjunction with faith, as I now realise that faith is the enabler of trust which is the antidote to fear.

When I am wrestling with people who wish to kill themselves, when they feel so hopeless and useless – the opposite of precious – I draw on that invisible web of connectedness, that trust, that faith that life is worth living.

Life is worth living. This really works – I return to my meeting to dip into that fountain of goodness that we are all nourishing together, knowing that this will always be there. It's not a well I can just take from; it needs my active involvement – I both replenish and take.

Twenty-five years after I resigned from the Society of Friends, I returned. I realised that faith was not a substitute for thought but an enhancement of my thinking. Faith – or trust – which I am increasingly calling my experience – provides the lever with which I can throw open the windows and let the light in. For it is a glorious world and we are all part of making it so. I ask myself what my life would be like without this faith – it would be a life rinsed of colour and meaning.

As my father lay dying I took immense comfort from the knowledge that there would be a meeting for worship to give thanks, in the traditional words, 'for the Grace of God as shown in his life', to share with Friends the loss and value of a precious life. A phrase from the poet Virgil has haunted me all my life, 'There are tears for things and human woes touch the heart.' This has been my experience, but my experience has also been one of joy when faith, trust and love burst through.

10

Faith – so hard to define, perhaps easier to recognise as something others possess – or are possessed by! For me, faith has been infectious, something caught, like a good germ. As a young person I recognised what I took to be faith in others: members of my family, people I looked up to, Friends in meeting. It was what made them the people they were. It gave them character, strength, power, enabled them to witness for peace and justice, to stand out from the crowd, to be their true selves. Faith gave them the energy to work for change; it was a life force shining through and directing their actions and lives. They had a God-given vision of a better, fairer world and their faith gave them the drive to pursue their vision in whatever way was right for them.

Gradually some of their faith rubbed off on me, but of

course it eventually had to become firsthand, for I doubt whether secondhand faith can ever survive testing. Seeing faith give others the passion and energy to live good lives, I knew it was something I wanted too. And it came not with a bang but as a series of stepping stones. My developing faith was nurtured by reading, by the fellowship of several Quaker meetings, by joining the Student Christian Movement at college and entering a whole new world of ecumenical dialogue and sharing. Acquiring faith has been a process, a growing recognition that deep down in my spiritual centre are convictions, priorities and standards that both consciously and unconsciously govern my life. They lead me to behave and respond in certain ways. When confronted quite unexpectedly with words of blind prejudice at a business lunch, I had a split second in which to decide whether to challenge what had been said or let it pass. The voice of faith inside me nudged me, 'You know what Jesus would do!', so I did challenge and knew it was right to do so. In however modest a way my faith had been tested and gave me the strength to do the right thing.

When we speak of 'a leap of faith' we surely mean something different from a carefully calculated risk assessment! Jesus, Elizabeth Fry, Gandhi, Martin Luther King, Nelson Mandela and so many others each made a leap of faith. They were impelled to actions whose full consequences they could not know. Faith empowers us to venture into the unknown, the unplanned, the unexpected and provides the resources to cope with the outcome. My own faith is not of that world-changing order, but nevertheless when I heard those words of the women at Greenham Common, 'We were taking charge of our lives for the first time,' I started to take stock of my life priorities. And when, as a consequence, I decided to retire early to be available for service, both amongst Quakers and in the wider world, I knew it was the voice of faith, not reason, prompting me from within. Faith is the engine that turns principles into practice; it is one of those rare commodities that grows with use, or, as the Quaker Caroline Fox wrote, 'Live up to the light thou hast and more will be granted thee.'

Faith helps me make decisions, influences my choices and my lifestyle when I heed the inner voice, when I respond to those 'promptings of love and truth in our hearts'. For others, and maybe one day for me, faith is tested in much more dramatic, even life-threatening ways, and the example of others continues to inspire me, taking me a bit further along those stepping stones. True faith empowers us to take risks, to 'live adventurously', to choose the unpopular path, to be radical. But it requires us to trust, to discern that the calling is 'in right ordering', from God. And when we discern rightly, faith feeds us, reassures us that the power of God is within us, and will somehow see us through, whatever happens en route. It is a source of energy that mobilises us to pursue ideals of peace, justice, equality, respect for creation. Above all, faith gives us grounds for hope that, in the visionary words of Julian of Norwich, 'All shall be well, and all shall be well, and all manner of things shall be well.'

11

Faith is for me the foundation (or discipline) of my Quaker life. Without always understanding the detail, I trust in the power of God's goodness; thus faith is the point of reference for my Quakerism in action.

However, I believe it not possible to be(come) a Quaker from a standing start. Inevitably, we are influenced by the tradition in which we are brought up (including atheism), and either we reject it and turn away or else we adapt it and build upon it. In my case, the tradition was Judaeo-Christian, strongly influenced by the pacifism of my parents in response to the second world war.

My faith has been further informed and nourished by the experiences of my life and the people I have met, both Quakers and other Christians, and it continues to change and develop. Since the Religious Society of Friends has, so far, resisted the temptation to express its beliefs by means of dogma and creedal statements, it is almost certain that fellow-worshippers in my local Quaker meeting differ from me in terms of belief, but this does not prove an impediment in sharing worship.

In addition, my faith draws on the narrative given in the Bible of the development of religious understanding in the early Hebrews, who thought of themselves as the 'chosen people': granted God's favour and protection, they were obliged by their covenant with him to live life responsibly and considerately, as we are today. I am not overly concerned with the historical accuracy of those accounts, but with the truth that emerges through myth and metaphor. The descriptions of the faith of Job and Samuel in the Old Testament, for example, are a constant source of inspiration to me. The lives of early Quakers are similarly inspiring.

Similarly, for me the authenticity of the Gospels is of secondary interest when compared with the force of the message of Jesus, which he delivered through his words and by example. This message continues to be accessible and relevant to the struggle that we face in the twenty-first century to live responsible and righteous lives. While the facts of Jesus' birth and death are of little importance to my own faith, I recognise that the stories attached to these events are important in the faith of others in the relationship between God and his creation.

In order for faith to be a valuable basis for life, it needs to be made manifest in some way. My own faith impels me to action, and in my life I have found opportunities to express this through my professional employment and my voluntary work, and it has shaped the life of my family.

However, before putting faith into action comes the exercise of waiting for the direction of the Holy Spirit (which for me is the indwelling God or inward Light, as it has been variously described). This waiting is a form of payer, although at times it can seem long and frustrating. In such arid moments, it is comforting to be upheld within the silent worship of a Quaker meeting, where sometimes shape can be given to one's unformed thoughts, and sometimes they are subsumed into the wordless power of its corporate strength. Part of the process of turning faith into action is the willingness to be used in ways which have not been imagined and which may be alarming or dangerous. In a Quaker meeting for worship, we lay aside what the early Quaker John Woolman called 'worldly cumber' in order to open ourselves to the leading of the Holy Spirit, and to seek the means to express the faith not only of the individual but of the group though action. Such faith can move mountains.

12

What follows is not easy, nor perhaps is it simple, but it is true. For me, faith concerns itself with matters eternal, but I have learned that faith can change as part of the journey. I am totally convinced that I may be mistaken. Even if I am not mistaken today, I may well be mistaken on the same subject tomorrow. I was yesterday. So I live in the moment. The eternal modified in the ephemeral sounds like paradox. Yet wherever I meet paradox, I find I am close to truth.

So what is faith to me? The definition that sits best with me is 'Knowledge of the unknown.' I am unable to explain that further – it simply has the right flavour about it. As with most – if not all Quakers – mine is an experience-based faith. My experience is that I have no formal (or normal) faith; I am not Christian, although I was brought up in the Judeo-Christian tradition. I admire the beauty and wisdom I find in the Bible. I admire the same beauty and wisdom in the Bhagavad Gita and the Upanishads – the Sanskrit scriptures and texts sacred to the Hindu faiths. I have not read the Koran but have listened to those who have, and I have admired the wisdom and beauty I heard, as well as that found in Buddhist writings. For me, my God is a shy

God, hidden in the misting rain or quiet by the rushing beck behind the hill.

St Julian of Norwich was optimistic in her faith, 'All will be well and all manner of things will be well and thou shalt see for thine own self that all is well.' I note that she does not say that it will be as we want it to be, but that it will be well. Similarly, Max Ehrmann in Desiderata says, 'And whether or not it is clear to you, no doubt the universe is unfolding as it should.'

Faith is wise but may not be logical.

First, last and always people matter – all of them. People are contrary, infuriating and very, very silly but every single one matters – including me. For me, like most Quakers, there is that of God in everyone, therefore there is that of God in me. If that is so, in the same way as I am responsible for my words and actions, I am responsible both to God and for God – alarmingly, I am God, so are you, so are we.

Faith is priceless but exacts a cost. Sometimes that cost may appear insignificant, sometimes that cost may be life itself. In John Bunyan's allegory *The Pilgrim's Progress*, the character Faithful was martyred by the citizens of Vanity Fair simply because he was impelled to speak out against what he saw as injustice – even when he understood that his words would cost him his life. Central to the story of Jesus of Nazareth is the period of reflection in the Garden of Gethsemane. Jesus could simply have got up and walked away. Who would have blamed him, who would have known? Certainly not us – we simply would have not heard the story. Yet Jesus said, 'Let this cup pass from me, but not as I will...' That is faith.

More recently, and much better documented, the faith of Ghandi and of Martin Luther King cost each his life. Faith demands commitment, and yet tomorrow that faith may be proved wrong, misplaced, superfluous. Intrepid, resolute – is that faithful? Not quite. Something of mystery, something taken on faith is needed. And so it all starts again.

Recommended reading:

Quaker faith & practice: the book of Christian discipline of the Yearly Meeting of the Religious Society of Friends (Quakers) in Britain. London: Britain Yearly Meeting, 3rd edition, 2005

Advices & Queries. London: Britain Yearly Meeting, 1994

Allen, Beth: *Ground and spring: foundations of Quaker discipleship*. London: Quaker Books, 2007

Dale, Jonathan, and others: *Faith in action: Quaker social testimony*. London: Quaker Books, reprint 2008

Fisher, Simon: *Spirited living: waging conflict, building peace*. London: Quaker Books, 2004

Gillman, Harvey: *A light that is shining: an introduction to the Quakers*. London: Quaker Books, 2005

Kelly, Thomas: *A testament of devotion*. NY: Harper Collins, 1996

Stoller, Tony: *Wrestling with the angel: Quaker engagement in commercial and public affairs*. London: Quaker Books, 2001

Wildwood, Alex: *A faith to call our own: Quaker tradition in the light of contemporary movements of the spirit*. London: Quaker Books, 1999

This pamphlet and the books listed above are available from:

The Quaker Bookshop
Friends House
173-177 Euston Road
London NW1 2BJ
020 7663 1030/31